MIDNIGHT MIAMI

A GRITS & GRAVY PARANORMAL MYSTERY

THE GRITS & GRAVY MYSTERIES
BOOK 1

S. M. CHASE

S. M. CHASE PUBLISHING

Paperback ISBN: 979-8-9947637-0-4
Ebook ISBN: 979-8-9947637-1-1
Hardcover ISBN : 979-8-9947637-2-8

CONTENTS

PROLOGUE

MIAMI, FLORIDA—SUMMER 1981

Tuesday, 10:07 PM
Midnight Miami
1555 Collins Avenue, South Beach

DEWAYNE SHELBY PACED the alley behind Midnight Miami, orbiting the service door that opened into the kitchen. The big guy had told him to be there at ten sharp; Dewayne had been waiting since 9:45. Every few seconds, he checked himself in the greasy reflection of a barred window over the garbage cans.

He paused, took a breath, and reminded himself of the only fact that mattered.

He was the Employee of the Month.

Dewayne had been a dishwasher at Midnight Miami for six weeks. As a two-time loser fresh out of the state pen, job options weren't exactly plentiful, but he'd climbed the ladder faster than most—helped by the fact that at least four dishwashers had been fired since he started.

Last night, when the big man called him out to the alley, Dewayne figured he was about to join that parade. The others had made the same walk and were never seen again.

Instead, the big man told him he was doing great. *Employee of the Month.*

The reward: an all-expenses-paid celebration at Midnight Miami the following night. No cover. Open bar.

Dewayne couldn't believe it. The club had only been open a few months and already sat atop the Miami food chain—beautiful, decadent people with money, time, and drugs to burn.

Before he could say thanks, the big man shoved a dry-cleaned sport coat—still on its hanger, plastic rustling—into his chest.

"You wear this coat. Come at ten tomorrow night. Meet me here, behind kitchen. Don't tell anyone. They get jealous. Wear the coat or you get thrown out. Try not to look like bum," the big guy said in clipped, accented English.

His name was Golyam—Bulgarian for "big," Dewayne had been told. It fit.

Dewayne wasn't small—just under six feet, a shade over two hundred—but next to the 6'5" slab of man, he felt like a kid. Golyam's thick black mop looked like a horse's mane; his skin was an indeterminate brown, the kind you couldn't place on a map. But the eyes—flat, hungry, bottomless—those were what stuck. They reminded Dewayne of a starving dog that haunted his childhood trailer park.

He tried to say something. Golyam repeated, "Wear the coat," and vanished back into the kitchen.

Dewayne lived at the Miami Paradise Apartments, a husk of an Art Deco relic at 2nd Street and Collins, smack in the squalor of South Beach. When he woke late the next morning, he finally unwrapped the coat. Light gray with a purple windowpane. It was the finest piece of clothing he'd ever laid hands on.

No label. He pinched the lapel and felt the weight, the drape—then compared it in his head to the jacket from his polyester "going to court" suit. Same species, different universe. Secretariat standing next to a donkey.

A small pin rode the left lapel, gray on gray. When the bulb's light hit it right, a design appeared: a jackal or wolf dressed like a pharaoh. Maybe that's how the bartenders would tag him for the free drinks.

He'd need something to wear with it. He "shopped" the neighborhood—up Ocean Drive, zagging down side streets, scanning laundry lines fat with retirees' linen. In an hour, he had a white linen shirt and a pair of tan polyester trousers he convinced himself didn't look like polyester. (They did.)

Shoes were a problem. On the walk back down the beach, the sun beating his scalp, he remembered how movie crews worked South Beach: fresh paint on a condemned façade, get your shots, split before the paint dries.

Inspired, he ducked to Ocean, snagged a forgotten bucket of white, and hustled back to the Paradise. His plastic penny loafers — "going to court" issue—got the Miami makeover.

He set them in a sunbeam to bake. Faced with the prospect of literally watching paint dry, he cracked some toilet wine he'd been nursing and caught a nap that lasted till 8:30. Then he shit, showered, shaved, combed, and dressed.

At 9:45 he was back in the alley, checking himself in the window again and again.

At 10:08 the door opened. The big guy filled the frame.

"Good," Golyam said. "You don't look like bum. Let's go."

He frog-marched Dewayne through the kitchen and a door he'd never noticed.

Then Dewayne stepped into another universe.

Midnight Miami.

Neon everywhere—flashing, pulsing, breathing with the beat. The music wasn't the disco Dewayne remembered (and hated). This was new and synthetic, futuristic and filthy. It throbbed. It humped. It pumped. Dewayne felt it right in his pants.

The entire first floor was thr dance floor, and for a Tuesday it was packed. The people looked unreal—thin and young and beautiful, white and black and everything in between, gay and straight, decadent all the way down.

Golyam guided him by the elbow like a bouncer escorting out a drunk. Dewayne was too hypnotized to care. He didn't even mind the wet squelch his freshly painted loafers made on the floor.

Off to one side sat a row of semi-cloistered, elevated tables with a view of the writhing kaleidoscope below. Those faces, at least, made sense to Dewayne: pudgy dagos straight out of *Godfather* casting, Colombians in outfits that screamed "cocaine cowboy," businessmen in tasteful overpriced suits, on-the-take cops in tacky overpriced suits, undercover cops who looked like undercover cops.

They reached a corner roped off with velvet. A bouncer unhooked it.

Inside, at a table, sat three of the most beautiful women Dewayne had ever leered at. A knockout blonde. An even finer dark-skinned girl. And an Asian, maybe Japanese.

Dewayne's gasp disappeared into the bassline. Not that it mattered; the fix was in.

"Girls, this Employee of the Month," Golyam announced. "Bring to me at two. White Room. I need him awake."

The blonde stood, walked straight to Dewayne, and stared into him. Her right hand touched his lips; she pushed a pill onto his tongue and followed it with hers, a deep, greedy French kiss that left him wobbling.

She stepped back, flanked by the other two.

"Nice shoes," the black girl said, smiling.

The Asian just stared.

"Employee of the Month," the blonde purred, "your life will never be the same."

She wasn't lying.

Over the next four hours, Dewayne lived a carnal lifetime. He drank, snorted, and popped. He poked, prodded, and penetrated—and got the same. He barely noticed when the dark girl slid a syringe of something into his right cheek. He overcame his hatred of Asians. Twice.

He acted out *Penthouse* letters that would've been rejected as implausible—then drank and snorted some more.

At 2:04 AM, nursing a Jim Beam to take the edge off his last bump, he wondered why this private room on the second floor was called the White Room.

It looked like the others—one door, small bar, a couch big enough to sleep a football team, black curtains on the walls.

He felt the big man before he saw him. The door opened; music gusted in, then died as it shut. Only then did Dewayne realize the White Room was soundproof.

The three girls rose as if on a signal and glided past him without a glance. Dewayne stepped, confused, and Golyam's palm pressed him back.

"Employee of the Month, have seat," the big man said. "I have big surprise for you. Best one of tonight."

After the largesse he'd been swimming in, what could Dewayne say? He tried to thank him, which came out as gibberish. Lust beat back the trepidation. He sank into the couch and pictured all the things three women could get up to behind closed doors.

A synthesizer tone bloomed from nowhere, joined by a steady

beat. The curtains shivered in time. The lights died for a heartbeat.

Then they came back in pulses that matched the music.

Red.

Yellow.

Pink.

Blue.

Red.

Yellow.

Pink.

Blue.

Red.

Yellow.

Pink.

Blue.

White.

Red.

White.

Yellow.

Pink.

Blue.

White.

Red.

White.

Yellow.

White.

Pink.

White.

Blue.

White.

White.

White.

White.

White.

White.

White.

White.

White.

White.

WHITE.

WHITE.

WHITE.

WHHHHHHHHHHHHIIIIIIIIIITTTTTTTTTTTEEEEEEEE.

Dewayne dove off the couch and tried to bury his face in the carpet. Even with his eyes clamped shut, he could see it—the whitest white he'd ever imagined. It wasn't light; it was presence. It enveloped him, soaked him, swallowed him whole.

He stood up without meaning to and opened his mouth. A sound he'd never heard—never known a man could make—came out, a perfect soundtrack to pain. He felt every vein, every hair, every cell. All of it shredding from the inside out.

He didn't fall so much as wilt into a horizontal line.

He didn't notice Golyam at his side until the big man spoke.

"Find and feast," the big guy said, pressing a cloth under Dewayne's nose.

Dewayne sprang to his feet. The pain was already a memory. The cloth held a scent he'd never known. Layers and depths and angles his brain wouldn't have understood ten minutes ago. It was a new color, a new number, a new reason to live, a new reason to kill.

He wanted the source more than he'd ever wanted anything. Nothing would stop him. He would find it. He would consume it. All of it.

Dewayne Shelby felt himself slipping backward, something

feral and ravenous and unholy stepping into the space where he'd been. He caught a glimpse of himself in the bar mirror.

A giant wolf stared back.

The last human thing he remembered was the eyes—black and empty and hungry. Like that starving dog from the trailer park.

Whatever happened to that dog?

1

DEVOURED

Wednesday, 6:13 AM
Lum's
461 West 41st Street, Miami Beach

DETECTIVE RAFAEL PÉREZ thought he'd seen it all—until he saw the body behind Lum's.

Dead bodies weren't unusual to Pérez. He was a homicide man in his twenty-second year, and his adopted home was on pace to set a new record for murders in a calendar year. When the call came in from the restaurant famous for its *World Famous Hot Dogs Steamed in Beer,* the jaded part of him even found the location funny.

But that was before he saw what was left of the girl.

After the alley behind Lum's, Rafael Pérez never looked at the world quite the same way again.

At a quarter past six, Pérez parked his red '72 Chevy Impala convertible on Royal Palm Avenue and walked toward the alley.

The yellow tape was the beacon. A uniform handed him a steaming Styrofoam cup—Pérez liked his coffee hot, no matter how thick the humidity.

He nodded thanks and missed the quiet warning the officer tried to give him: FBI Agent Ronald Wilson was already on the scene.

The drug war had brought a new plague to Miami—federal badges.

DEA, FBI, IRS, Secret Service. Pérez couldn't blow his nose without a fed getting in his way.

Wilson moved to intercept. Pérez put up a hand.

"Dammit, Wilson, I haven't even seen the body yet. Go bother somebody else for five minutes and let me look at my crime scene."

He left the fuming man and ducked under the tape toward a large tarp guarded by a sheepish rookie.

"All right. What've we got?" Pérez asked. His daily ration of patience was already evaporating.

The kid opened his mouth, faltered, then managed, "Just—just see for yourself," and whisked back the tarp.

Pérez's eyes went to the face first. The victim lay on her back: white female, twenties; handsome more than pretty. Brown eyes open, more surprised than scared. A single claw mark ran from the center of her face down to where her throat should've been. He was struck by how clean the cut was; the jaw remained, the bone sliced instead of torn.

His gaze tracked down. From just below the ribs to the kneecaps there was nothing but absence. Flesh gone. Everything gone.

One word slid into his head.

Devoured.

Pérez turned, braced a hand against the alley wall, and emptied his stomach.

"Cover her up," he said over his shoulder, and walked back toward his Impala.

Over the last two months, there had been four unsolved murders of extraordinary brutality—wounds no ordinary man could make. The others had been ugly, but this one looked like something from the conclusion of last week's *Mutual of Omaha's Wild Kingdom*.

The working theory was a freak on PCP or some new poison they didn't have a name for yet. The only other explanation belonged in a zoo. Pérez wanted to stamp it *lunatic* and be done, but his mind wouldn't let him. This was different. This was a new category entirely—one that wasn't supposed to exist.

There was another connection to the earlier four. Given Ronald Wilson's presence, Pérez was pretty sure this one had it too.

He sat on his bumper. A veteran uniform slid in beside him and passed over a Thermos. Pérez took a pull—bourbon—and muttered a thanks.

"How'd the body get found? Garbage men?"

The cop shook his head. "Tip came in. Guy with a weird accent. German or Austrian."

Pérez stopped delaying. "Well?"

"Just like the others." The cop held up an evidence bag with a single matchbook inside—the same kind found on every victim. Embossed in foil.

Midnight Miami.

Pérez sighed and looked at his friend. "You know where I can find a pay phone?"

A few minutes later he stood at the booth on West 46th, gathering his thoughts.

For the past year, a handful of Metro cops had used a small agency for off-the-books consults. The Stone Detective Agency had been around since the war, but new ownership had raised eyebrows: two retired pros—one from NASCAR, one from the NFL.

Unorthodox, sure. Effective, annoyingly so. With their help, a "suicide" turned murder. Even his uncle, Arturo Santos—a pillar in Little Havana—had hired them when he thought his house was haunted.

The strangest thing wasn't their fame. It was the cases they took. The "suicide" involved a voodoo priestess. Vice told bar-stool stories about monsters. Witches. Vampires.

Pérez saw again, in his mind's eye, the impossible claw mark on the girl's face.

Miami had weathered a year of hell—cocaine cowboys, race riots, and Castro's gift of murderers, rapists, and lunatics hidden among the Mariel refugees. Whatever was behind these five killings felt like the spark that could burn away what was left of civilization. He meant to stop it if he could.

He finished the coffee, dropped a coin, and dialed his uncle.

After quick pleasantries, he got to it. "Tío, can you put me in touch with the Stone Detective Agency?"

He could hear Arturo's surprise. "Do you mean—"

Detective Rafael Pérez cleared his throat. He wanted the ridiculous words to come out clean.

"It's time for Grits and Gravy."

2

THE SHERIFF AND THE DEPUTY

Wednesday, 6:19 AM
South Dixie Highway, Homestead

"Uncle Cody, you think that's really him?" the new deputy asked, jittering in his seat like an eight-year-old on Pixy Stix.

"Boy, we're at work. It's Sheriff Hinton to you. And stop bouncing. Of course it's him. Who else would be driving that car?"

The sheriff couldn't believe his luck. He'd pulled the graveyard shift to show the ropes to his newest deputy—his sister's kid—figuring they'd snag a sleepy salesman or a drunk punching it through the sticks outside Homestead. Then a mustard-yellow '74 Dodge Charger blew past their speed trap. Now the sheriff was chasing a NASCAR Winston Cup legend.

Francis "Grits" McCoy had succeeded in poking the House of Krenn into a fight. The Krenns had odd rules about engagement—

the so-called Laws of the Shadows. Grits started the dance by chucking a brick through their Homestead window. Taped to the brick: a note not only challenging them to meet but listing the time and an exact location. By their rules the time had to be set by Vienna clocks, so this morning's 6:40 AM in Miami was written as 12:40 PM UTC. The location had to include latitude and longitude.

He'd baited his prey—and accidentally hooked a county sheriff running a speed trap.

The deputy, riding shotgun, couldn't stop bouncing. Not only were they in a chase; they were chasing Grits McCoy.

You didn't have to watch stock cars to know the name. For a stretch in the last decade he'd been the phenom, the bad-boy darling of Winston Cup. Women wanted him; men wanted to be him. That ended after the series' worst pileup ever—a fireball crash that killed four drivers. Legend said Grits himself was dead when they pulled him from his car. He got made the scapegoat and was banned.

The Charger they were chasing was one of his last stockers. No numbers, no sponsors—just mustard yellow with a black stripe, a tribute to the sponsor that stuck by him: Duke's Mayo.

The sheriff was proud he was keeping up with a pro, but one thought itched: Why was Grits McCoy doing a hundred in the middle of nowhere before sunrise on a Wednesday?

South Florida had turned mean the past few years. Cocaine did most of the work. To the sheriff the day the world changed was July 11, 1979—Dadeland Mall, broad daylight. Three men walked into Crown Liquors and cut down a Colombian trafficker and his bodyguard. After the Dadeland Massacre, the war wasn't a late-night, bad-neighborhood thing anymore. The tap of coke never shut off. Neither did the killing.

His train of thought derailed with his nephew's chirp. "Sheriff, I can't believe it's really him. Maybe somebody stole his car?"

Maybe that was the missing piece—some coked-up lunatic in Grits's wheels.

"You know what, Danny—Deputy—that's a good question. Let's ask the man himself."

He snatched the CB mic. "Breaker, breaker. This is Sheriff Hinton. Will the yellow Charger with a smokey on his rear confirm who's driving?"

Grits heard the call and groaned. If there was one thing he hated worse than CB radios, it was CB lingo.

He checked his watch, then his speedometer. Still on schedule. He thumbed the mic. "Sheriff, this is Grits McCoy. I don't have time to explain, but I'm not running from you."

"Then who you running from, boy?"

"You wouldn't believe me if I told you. Now back off and let me handle my business."

The sheriff felt his cheeks heat. He didn't take well to being sassed—especially not in front of his sister's kid. This pretty-boy racer needed a lesson.

He drew a breath, building his retort—cursing that damned *Smokey and the Bandit* for making him hear Buford T. Justice in his own voice—when a black Cadillac Eldorado materialized in his mirror and howled like a jet. Whatever lived under that hood wasn't from the factory.

The Caddy shoved the Gran Fury's rear bumper. The sheriff punched it to keep from getting spun, but the Cadillac slithered left and nudged the cruiser hard, forcing it off the road.

Grits used his rearview mirror for glimpses of the car now tailgating him. The windows were tinted an impossible midnight black. The roof was an armored hardtop that looked like an armadillo.

The House of Krenn.

Auto racing is dangerous work, but Grits had found a way to make life after racing worse. He'd crossed an Austrian nobleman named Prince Wym, who'd made ruining Grits's life his main focus. Grits was sure Wym had sent the Krenn to do his dirty work, but he wasn't about to sit around and wait for them.

A mile marker flashed. His exit was coming. He checked his watch—still good.

Behind him, the sheriff wrangled the cruiser back from the weeds. No trees, thank goodness; otherwise they might've flipped. He stomped back on the highway. The Charger and Caddy were nearly ghosts, but he could still track them.

He glanced at his nephew. The kid had stopped bouncing. Having your life flash by will do that. The sheriff almost told him to work the CB, then saw the kid's look and let him be. He tried the mic himself.

Instead of the usual click and hiss, a metallic whine stabbed his eardrums.

The deputy snatched the mic, twisting dials. Every channel gave the same shriek. He shut it off. "Something's jamming the CB."

The sheriff would normally bark at an underling for folding his hand, but his gut said the same. "Forget it. Eyes up. We're about to see how well that police academy training prepared you for the real thing."

As Grits crossed into Miami city limits, South Dixie turned into Brickell Avenue. He hung a hard right onto the Rickenbacker Causeway. This stretch worried him most. Any traffic—or worse, a raised drawbridge—and the plan was dead. But the lanes were clean and the bridge down. He blew past the tolls, snapping the gate, knowing more cops wouldn't be far.

The Caddy stayed glued to him yet didn't try to pass. Good. They were taking the bait. Next stop: Virginia Key Beach.

Once the "colored beach," now abandoned by the city, it was perfect: no sunbathers, no tourists.

He downshifted off the causeway onto Virginia Beach Drive, tore through the empty lot, hopped the curb, bumped over the little concrete walk, and hit the sand by the water. He angled the Charger slightly crooked to make it look like he'd been forced to stop.

The Eldorado plowed over the curb and slid to a block-off position. No easy exits for Grits.

The sheriff rolled up slow. The deputy clicked the CB on one last time and clicked it right back off as the whine squealed. No backup. Just the two of them.

They watched from thirty yards back. The Charger sat sideways with the driver's door to the ocean. Grits got out, walked around the nose, and squared to the Caddy.

Seeing someone from television in the flesh does a trick to your brain. The deputy knew without doubt he was looking at Grits McCoy. He first noticed Grits's blond hair, feathered and blow-dried, and how it highlighted the blue of his eyes—a thought the deputy quickly tried to push away. Grits looked like he'd just walked off a movie set instead of driving Florida back roads in the last vestiges of the night.

He wore a real fireproof jumpsuit in mustard Duke's Mayo yellow, number 13 stitched under the logo.

No weapons visible. Just fists.

The sheriff noticed Grits stood closer to the surf than the boardwalk. The Caddy had the better ground. If Grits bolted, he'd pay for it.

The two doors of the Cadillac opened and out stepped, or

rather slinked, six figures, three out of each door. The sheriff and deputy viewed the group from behind. Dressed in black, they appeared to be wearing scuba suits, except that they had large, brimmed hats, similar to sombreros, but definitely not sombreros.

The deputy recalled a black and white movie he saw on the late show a few months ago. The movie was called *Nosferatu*, about a spindly vampire that looked more like a rodent than a man. The deputy reminded himself vampires weren't real, and if they were real, vampires wouldn't be hanging out on a beach at sunrise.

The sun kicked a glint off silver in every hand. One carried a large, ornate ring of knives.

They fanned into a line along the concrete walk, twenty yards from Grits. The leader stepped forward. The sheriff parked behind the Caddy and motioned for silence, tapping his holstered pistol. They eased their doors open and drew down. If Grits or the black-clad figures saw, they didn't show it.

The leader began to speak, stabbing fingers at Grits. The others twitched behind him, moving like their joints were full of spiders. Whatever he said sounded like that same CB screech— wet metal. Judging by his body, it wasn't friendly.

Grits heard him fine. His response wasn't what the sheriff expected from a man outnumbered six to one.

Grits rolled his eyes and shook his head no, like a mother who'd heard a request for candy from her fat kid one time too many.

He put up an index finger. "No, no, no. That's bullshit. He's not late. I just got here early. He'll be here any second. And by the way —that's pretty racist."

He kept the finger up and checked his watch.

The black figures shifted, confused. The two cops felt the same.

The leader went still, then bristled. He shook out his arms like a fighter loosening up. Daggers flashed in both hands.

For two seconds Virginia Key fell quiet.

Then a man came belting the chorus to Petey Maymoore's "Freak for the Cheeks."

All eyes snapped to the boardwalk. The creatures looked right. Grits looked left.

A black man on roller skates glided along, singing to himself.

Close-cropped Afro, mustache, red suspenders, dark blue jeans. He had muscles on his muscles—oak-tree legs, granite torso.

As usual, he wasn't wearing a shirt. He didn't need a shirt. It would've been a shame to cover the body that the Good Lord had given Ernest "Gravy" Watkins.

In the excitement the deputy had forgotten Grits's more famous partner. Gravy had been a college legend and then the best rookie running back the league had ever seen. After several years and his best season yet, he stunned everyone and quit.

He and Grits now owned the Stone Detective Agency. Every cop in South Florida knew Cliff Stone and his daughter Eleanor; the only thing more shocking than Cliff's sudden passing was his daughter approving the sale of the family company to two retired pro athletes.

Still wearing skates, Gravy somehow handled the sand and rolled up beside Grits. They traded a ridiculous series of hand slaps and finished with wildly inappropriate pelvic thrust apiece.

They turned to the black-clad line, honestly surprised the party was still there.

"Gravy," Grits said, "this guy was winding up his speech, but I got him to wait till you got here. He started strong—said he accepted the challenge, then something about removing our guts and stuffing them through our faces. But then..."

Grits wagged a finger at the leader.

"...this guy insinuated you were late because you're black."

"What?" Gravy said, mock-offended.

The leader screeched something neither cop could parse. Grits cut him off.

"Nope. Not true. You said, 'Where is the Black One? Will he join you now, or is he on black-people time?'"

"What? That's some bullshit," Gravy said. "I'm always on time. I'm a chocolate Swiss watch. We said 6:40. What time is it?"

Grits checked. "Still 6:40. I got here at 6:38. You're right on time. I was early."

"Punctuality is a pillar of our friendship," Gravy said, glaring at the leader. "We focus on what we share—including pride in being on time. We don't let race get in the way. I don't have any problem with white folks—except Eye-Talians. *Rocky II* got the Eye-Talians looking at the world all wrong."

"That's right," Grits said. "I don't care that Gravy's black; he doesn't care that I'm white. And while I don't agree with his Italian thing"—which, truthfully, Grits meant to discuss; it was getting in the way of work—"I do need to admit something. I think I might be bigoted against Eskimos."

"Eskimos?" Gravy blinked. "We're in Miami. Why you even thinking about Eskimos?"

The sheriff and deputy both jumped when the leader screeched, but Grits again put up his index finger to stop him.

"You hold on a minute," Grits said, before turning back to Gravy. "I don't think about them a lot, but when I do, I can't get past the blubber eating. It's weird. Kinda freaks me out."

"I get that," Gravy said. "But 'bigoted' is harsh. You wouldn't make 'em sit in the back of the bus, right?"

"If some guy sat down next to me, then started eating a blubber sandwich ..." Grits started.

The leader shrieked louder. The rest joined him.

Annoyance bled into anger on Grits and Gravy's faces.

"Okay," Gravy said, voice rising. "If that's how you wanna be. Fine. I wasn't even gonna say anything about your hats—put flowers on 'em and you could sit with my aunties at church. You'd fit right in. But 'black-people time'? There's no need to bring race into this, you honky bitches."

Grits added, "We'll give you one chance. Get back in your car with your leather vests and go spank each other or whatever. Otherwise we're gonna light you up like the Fourth of July."

As if waiting for this cue, more figures poured from the Eldorado—another dozen—until eighteen in all formed a closing arc.

Grits and Gravy didn't blink. The sheriff and deputy traded a look—now they were really lost.

The leader stepped forward, voice like wet metal but words clear. "Enough of this foolish talk! The House of Krenn will take its vengeance and feast on your flesh!"

They charged—and ran headlong into the trap.

Crossing the concrete walk, they hit the tripwire Gravy had planted earlier this morning. A hidden *cheval-de-frise* of wooden spikes snapped upright out of the sand. Several vampires impaled themselves and shrieked as their bodies combusted.

At the same instant, two enormous shotguns sprang from the sand beside Grits and Gravy. Each man grabbed one of the cartoon-big double-barrels and started firing.

"Freak for the Cheeks" by Petey Maymoore blasted from the Charger's speakers at full volume.

Oh, smack smack

Yeah, clap clap

No need for you to speak

I don't think I'm unique

But you gots to know, baby,

I-i-i-i am a freak

A freak for the cheeks

At the first boom the two officers dove behind their open doors.

Looking up through the safety of his car window, the deputy saw a figure in black take a shotgun blast to the chest. The blast knocked the figure back ten feet and spun him so the deputy could get a good look.

The thing opened its mouth to scream—too wide, with too many teeth and long canine fangs. Skin white as paste, eyes lit up red.

It clawed at its chest like its clothes were on fire. They weren't, but the wounds were. T-shaped, little wooden crosses smoking in the flesh. As more fabric tore, the low sun kissed its skin and finished the job. The whole thing lit up.

The deputy noticed a handful of tiny wooden T's stuck in the cruiser's glass. Holy-loaded guns.

"Holy crap," the sheriff muttered. "These guys are vampires."

Amazement beat fear. The deputy slid out from cover, ignoring the sheriff's bark, and moved closer. The sheriff followed.

The traps and scatterguns had chewed through two-thirds of the brigade. Six remained, and they were in close with Grits and Gravy.

The pair weren't YMCA black belts. Their style was pure business—every strike setting up a stake to the heart, every stake ending in flame. With stakes cached in the sand at their feet, they carved the pack down while Petey Maymoore kept time.

Soon only three figures stood: Grits and Gravy facing the Krenn leader, everyone waiting for the break.

Up close the cops saw the leader's outfit was designed to cheat the sun—hat, cloak, gloves. It hadn't helped against crucifixes and wood.

The vampire twitched, as if to bolt for the Caddy. Then he screeched and charged.

Grits and Gravy looked like they'd rehearsed it. As the leader closed, Grits dropped and spun, sweeping the legs. The vampire face-planted. In the same motion Grits popped a stake into the air. Gravy—still in skates—leapt, caught it two-handed at the peak, and drove it down through the back into the heart.

Whoomph. Fire.

Silence took the beach. Small fires guttered in the sand. The spike fence burned itself out—conveniently. Everything they'd built was meant to disappear.

Gravy skated over to the sheriff with that movie-star grin. The sheriff opened his mouth and nothing came out; he was standing in front of the best back he'd ever seen.

"Sorry about the mess on your windshield, officer," Gravy said. "Pour a Coke on it. You'll be amazed what it takes off."

The sheriff turned toward his car and saw a smoldering clump of rags on his windshield—the remains of a creature he wouldn't have believed was real ten minutes ago.

Grits jogged back from the Eldorado with a canvas duffel. "Car's clear," he said. Sirens wailed in the distance. He nodded to the sheriff. "No hard feelings."

Warm kinship flared, but faded slightly when Grits gave him a friendly swat on the backside *en route* to the Charger.

"Gravy, we gotta go."

Gravy slid into the passenger seat. Grits scooped a final silver trinket from the sand—the knife ring—and stuffed it in the bag. He fired the Charger and, with a rooster tail of sand, blew out of the lot.

Thirty seconds later four county units screamed into the parking lot and braked behind the abandoned Eldorado.

The sheriff looked around. The little fires were mostly smoke now. The Caddy sat open. Their cruiser's windshield looked like it had collided with the world's biggest, greasiest crow.

The deputy eyed the approaching units. "Uncle Cody, what are we gonna say happened?"

The sheriff set a hand on his nephew's shoulder, gazed into the middle distance, and smiled.

"Grits McCoy touched my butt."

3

THE STONE DETECTIVE AGENCY

Wednesday, 10:04 AM
Stone Detective Agency
80 West Flagler Street, Miami

AFTER THE WAR—INCLUDING a Bronze Star at the Bulge—Clifford "Cliff" Stone came home to Miami, his wife, and their three daughters. He didn't go back to the Public Safety detective's desk. In 1949 he and his wife opened the Stone Detective Agency. Soon after, they welcomed a fourth daughter, Eleanor.

If you worked South Florida law enforcement, you crossed paths with Cliff Stone. The agency grew in respect and reach.

When Eleanor's mother died, Eleanor stepped in as Cliff's partner. It wasn't the plan—she'd been midway through the FBI Academy at Quantico after a criminology degree from Florida State—but it was the right thing, and Eleanor did the right thing.

Cliff wasn't built for retirement. Stopping meant dying. So when the time came, father and daughter agreed: the agency would live on with new owners. Eleanor would help the transition, then take her freedom—whatever that meant for a woman on the wrong side of thirty who still looked like she lived in a pool. Long legs—"gams," Cliff would've said—sun-kissed skin and hair from years of laps.

When Cliff passed, the plan rolled. The agency sold; Eleanor stayed on a few months to steady the new bosses, then take the payout.

That was the plan.

Instead, Eleanor had just passed her first anniversary with her new employers: a retired race-car driver and a retired football star. And while Cliff occasionally wandered into cases more *Twilight Zone* than *Columbo*, the new owners sprinted the other way— sometimes straight into *Scooby-Doo*. Same names kept popping up: Prince Wym. The Maiden. Laws of the Shadows. "Vampire" got tossed around more than Eleanor liked to admit. She'd told herself those were code words.

At 10:00 Wednesday morning, setting up the daily briefing, Eleanor thought some problems never changed (bills, calls), and some definitely had.

"Guys, I haven't heard back from Aaron Spelling's people about *The Love Boat*," she said. "It's not even eight in L.A., so don't hold your breath. Coffee, conference room—move."

Through the agency's work over the years—including assisting movie studios that used Miami as a location—Eleanor had made connections in Hollywood. She was quietly exploring the only thing Grits and Gravy loved as much as weird cases: a guest shot on their Saturday-night church. Her mistake had been telling them.

They watched *The Love Boat* at nine and maybe *Fantasy Island* at ten—two rich bachelors in eternal summer, locked indoors like altar boys.

In the conference room—same 1950s bland as the lobby and two small offices—Eleanor sat across from her bosses.

Grits had swapped the fire suit for his standard kit: cowboy boots, jeans, white button-up, three buttons undone, tucked in, chest out. Somehow the coiffure had survived a karate fight at the beach and a power nap.

Gravy wore his office uniform: dark jeans, black steel-toe boots, red suspenders. No shirt, as usual. Eleanor no longer noticed.

"New business," she said. "Detective Bill Jones from Homicide called. He needs to see you—urgent. Wouldn't say more on the phone. He's sending a car at eleven. He doesn't spook easy. He sounded spooked."

The men traded a look. Before they asked, Eleanor headed them off.

"This has nothing to do with your beach adventure," she said. "Dispatch says the official story is punk kids took a black Cadillac for a joyride and set a few fires. No Dodge Charger chase, no rumble. Case closed."

They relaxed. Gravy raised a hand.

"What time you think *The Love Boat* calls back?"

The unmarked slid to the curb at 11:00. Detective Bill Jones drove. Grits and Gravy convinced Eleanor to join them. Grits said he didn't want her stressed out waiting for Aaron Spelling to call back. Eleanor wasn't sure if he was joking, but she enjoyed the chance to play detective again.

On the way, Detective Jones kept it tight: they'd be meeting lead homicide, Rafael Pérez—Arturo Santos's nephew. Jones didn't mention Arturo had made the call (Pérez wanted plausible deniability if the meeting went sideways), or that he was trying to keep a certain FBI agent out of the room.

By 11:17 Jones parked in back of the Dade County Medical

Examiner's, near the delivery dock for cadavers. Not a detail Eleanor wanted to dwell on.

Jones led them down to a windowless conference room, opened the door, and left.

Two men waited. The first stepped forward. "Detective Rafael Pérez." Short black hair salted at the edges; yellow short-sleeve dress shirt straining over a late-night paunch; brown paisley tie that should've stayed in the store; matching polyester slacks. He said Jones spoke highly of them. More importantly, so did his uncle.

His eyes flicked to Eleanor. "Miss Stone. Good to see you here. Your father was a legend. And I know what you gave up to keep the agency running."

Eleanor gave a small nod. "Thank you, Detective. My dad always respected you."

The second man didn't get introduced. After an awkward beat, he did it himself. "FBI Agent Ronald Wilson." White, mid-thirties —or younger under a losing comb-over. Navy suit, white shirt, black tie. A catalog model for "federal agent."

Pérez motioned them to sit. Then he got right to business.

"In the last two months, leading to this morning," Pérez said, "we've had four unsolved murders in Miami. No connections between victims. All savaged—bites, tearing you'd chalk up to an animal attack—"

Wilson cut in. "We believe the perpetrator was under the influence—"

"We don't know that," Pérez said, slicing him off. "No proof. We just know it's unusual."

He let *unusual* hang.

"We kept it out of the papers as long as we could—no reason to start a panic. To be blunt, the victims were the kind you expect to end up dead." He grimaced. "Sunday, the *Herald* ran with it—"

"The Magic City Maniac," Gravy said.

Pérez had tried to manage the leak by working a friendly reporter—nearly full access, one condition: leave out the single detail linking every scene.

"This morning was number five," Pérez went on. "Different profile. Young Caucasian woman. Overnight cleaning crew at Publix on Dade Boulevard. No known vices. Based on her wounds, the perpetrator escalated."

"How do you know it's connected?" Grits asked.

Pérez slid a small evidence bag onto the table. Inside sat a gold-embossed matchbook.

Midnight Miami.

"On every victim, one of these," he said. "Forensics found nothing—no prints, no hairs, not even the victim's. So far, the only common thread."

Wilson asked, "You know what Midnight Miami is?"

"Biggest club in town," Grits said. "Might be bigger than the Mutiny at Sailboat Bay. Local and international celebs. Heard Chevy Chase and Warren Zevon were there last weekend."

"Petey Maymoore left the Mutiny for it," Gravy added. "Brought some DeBarges—Bunny, El, and Stan."

"Stan DeBarge?" Grits said. "After Bunny and El there's a Stan?"

"Of course," Gravy said. "DeBarges multiply like rabbits. They've probably claimed every name in the book."

Eleanor successfully held back a laugh, a feat made more difficult by the visible frustration on Wilson's round face. Grits ended the DeBarge talk by asking, "What do the owners say about their logo showing up on mutilated bodies?"

Pérez looked to FBI Agent Wilson. His turn.

"The Bureau suspects the club's tied to organized crime—old-school Italians, Colombians, maybe both. Maybe someone new. We're not sure."

"And you don't want to show your hand," Grits said. "So you haven't asked them about five dead bodies."

Wilson didn't answer. He set a manila folder down and opened to a black-and-white surveillance shot of a well-dressed, bearded man in his late fifties. Even without color, Grits and Gravy placed him as from that nether region between Europe and Mother Russia. The place where every story about vampires and werewolves seems to start.

"Victor Karanovo," Wilson said. "Owner of Midnight Miami. Twenty years in CIA files—murder, arms, terror, drugs. Operates mostly in Bulgaria. Showed up in the States late last year with a clean visa. Paperwork's so spotless it leaves no paper. An immaculate conception. Should've set off every alarm in Washington. Didn't."

He glanced at Grits. "We're not slow-playing this for a bigger drug bust. Drugs are the least of it. If he's moving something, we need to find it and pin him with charges that stick."

Grits and Gravy shared a look. Both sensed Agent Wilson was keeping something back.

"Who's the big guy?" Gravy asked.

In the background stood a mountain from the same neighborhood as Karanovo.

"Golyam," Wilson said. "Family bodyguard. You won't see Victor without him. Other than a name, he doesn't exist on paper."

Instead of dwelling on that, Wilson laid out a new photo. A cartoon of a thug—1930s gangster crossed with pro wrestler.

"Little Angelo Frusciante. Of the Frusciante crime family up in Tampa. Old Man Sal is a *Mustache Pete*. He kept his family off the drug train, but we think Karanovo pitched them a way in through Sal's nephew."

Wilson continued. "Little Angelo here is a small player with a big last name. Hungry, ambitious. He wants into drugs but knows the old man wants nothing to do with it, so we think Karanovo is working him. Did I mention Little Angelo's nuts? Al Capone reincarnated in his own mind. Wool suits in summer. Drives a '29 Cadillac. Also travels with two sidekicks."

New photo: two scrawny Cuban "teenagers" glaring in a mugshot. Eyes vacant, angry, hollow.

"Kids?" Grits said.

"Look like kids," Wilson said. "Twins, late twenties. Mariel 'gifts.' Institutionalized since toddlers. Malnutrition stunted their growth. They go by Doctor Fun and Cheryl."

Grits and Gravy looked at Pérez. He nodded. They'd heard right.

"Forget their real names," Wilson said. "Know this: Little Angelo brings them everywhere. The psychiatrist who processed them said she'd never seen psychopathic sadists like it. Absolutely hopeless."

"Bit harsh, isn't it?" Grits said. He didn't like writing anyone off.

Wilson slid a final photo across. "That's the psychiatrist—day after her evaluation."

Grits adjusted his thinking. He also had two new top candidates for the Magic City Maniac.

"How do the Colombians fit?" Gravy asked.

Pérez took it. "The bridge between Karanovo and the Frusciantes is this man. Real name José Gonzaga. Everyone calls him the Brazilian. Enforcer, hit man, cleaner for the Colombian cartels. Number two on the FBI's Most Wanted for torturing and murdering a Broward sheriff. He doesn't just kill—he carves. Rumor is he photographs his work and hangs it like art. He could be our Maniac for kicks. He's spending more time at Midnight Miami. We've clocked him and Little Angelo there at the same time—that's all we've got."

Eleanor had planned to keep her mouth shut. Her job was to help her new bosses get their feet wet. But she was still a detective. She said, "So, a guy with ties to Russia and a clean visa owns a nightclub where the local Italians and some Colombian to hang out. You have is guilt by association and barely that. You could make the same case against every restaurant owner in town."

Pérez smirked. Her new bosses did too. Wilson went from office white to beet red. Before he exploded, Grits stepped in.

"But you did give us four solid candidates for a killer who mutilates his victims. Before we go any further, I believe you've got bodies to show us."

4

THE DEAD SPEAK

Wednesday, 11:27 AM
Dade County Medical Examiner
1050 NW 19th Street, Miami

With Eleanor remaining behind, the four men crossed the hall to the morgue. The heavy silver doors swung open to a wizened, gray-haired medical examiner who'd been too busy for too many years. He stood beside a table under a white sheet.

Grits McCoy and Gravy Watkins had worked with the M.E. on other cases with Detective Jones. They knew him to be a decent man, but one who had become calloused to the harshest of the world by the nature of his job. Which is why what he said surprised them.

"Okay, fellas. This one's... this one's bad."

He lifted the sheet without flourish.

Detective Rafael Pérez and Agent Ronald Wilson watched

Grits and Gravy for their reaction. The private eyes stayed steady, eyes narrowing, adjusting to what lay there.

The examiner began, clinical: "Her name is—was—Jennifer Catherine Barrett. Twenty-two. Unmarried. Boyfriend, nothing serious. Overnight crew, Dade Boulevard Publix. Cause of death: massive blood loss. Right carotid severed with the neck wound. She was already dead when... all of this happened."

Pérez took in the body again. A turkey carcass at the end of Thanksgiving dinner. With effort, he kept everything inside his stomach inside his stomach.

Grits said, "What cut her throat? With the marks on her face, looks like a claw."

"Couldn't be," the coroner said. "An animal claw would've dragged the jaw and half the face. Look at the clean bone. Maybe a scalpel."

"Four scalpels at once?" Gravy asked.

"I'm telling you what I see," the coroner said. "Unless we're talking werewolves or some other imaginary monster, it wasn't a beast."

Pérez felt grim relief that someone besides Grits or Gravy said the word. In his periphery, Wilson tightened.

Pérez had sold Wilson on using the duo because of their celebrity—useful for slipping into Midnight Miami. Wilson wasn't sold on their supernatural reputation.

Since the werewolf was out of the bag, Grits ran with it. "Any murders line up with full moons?"

"How would I know?" the examiner snapped.

"Your wall calendar," Gravy said, pointing.

"Look for the date with the full moon," added Grits.

They watched the examiner compare notebook dates to the calendar.

"Interesting," he said at last. "First two murders were during the full-moon period two months ago. Third was last month's full moon. But the last two—both this month—neither under a full moon."

Pérez jumped in. "When's the next one?"

The examiner checked. "Saturday."

Wilson finally had enough. "What are we doing? I'm talking arms dealers, Mafia, hit men—and now the moon? Are you putting werewolves on the table?"

Gravy beat Pérez to the answer. "No. But if a crazy thinks he's the Wolf Man, the next full moon could set him off again." He conveniently ignored the two off-moon killings.

At that moment, Wilson realized Gravy Watkins had not been wearing a shirt this entire time.

Grits got the discussion back on course. "Where are the other bodies?"

"In long-term refrigeration," the coroner said.

Grits and Gravy exchanged a look. Then Gravy said, "We'd like a few minutes alone to examine them."

Everyone knew it wasn't by the book. These were not by-the-book circumstances. Pérez and Wilson looked to the coroner, who shrugged. Why not.

"Meet us back in the conference room when you're done," Pérez said, handing Grits the victims' folder.

Eleanor Stone wasn't about to sit on her hands while Grits and Gravy examined the remains of Jennifer Barrett. She took a slow lap of the halls to watch and listen—see what might shake loose. One perk of being an attractive woman in proper office wear was you could drift just about anywhere without catching grief. In a white chambray button-up and a knee-length navy wrap skirt—foam cup of water in hand—she could go wherever she pleased.

A lab tech in a paper cap hustled past and muttered to the

receptionist, "Same matchbook again. But what happened to this girl is unreal. Something ate her up."

Eleanor met the receptionist's gaze; recognition flickered in both faces.

The receptionist—a stout black woman north of fifty—stood. "Miss Eleanor, is that you?" She came around the desk and took Eleanor's hands. "We heard about your daddy passing. We're all real sorry. He was always good to us."

Eleanor flipped her mental Rolodex. "Thank you, Miss Patty. I appreciate it."

"What brings you down here?" Miss Patty asked.

Eleanor weighed what she'd overheard. "Can't say much. Let's just say... matchbooks."

Miss Patty's eyes widened. Staff always knew more than their bosses guessed. Eleanor was lining up a lure when the receptionist made it easy.

"Ooh—you're working with Gravy Watkins now, aren't you?"

"That's right. He's my new boss, for a few more months at least. Want to meet him?"

"Not right now," Miss Patty said quickly. "Not if he's tied up in this... matchbook business. Besides, I'm pretty sure he's always at the Burger King by my house."

"How about an autograph then? And I can bring it by along with some donuts." Eleanor remembered how her father always took care of the M.E.'s office and the cops—little visits when he didn't need a thing. Little things that added up.

Miss Patty nodded. Eleanor struck while the iron was hot. "Anything I can pass along to Gravy about the... matchbooks?"

Miss Patty glanced left and right. "Here's something strange that didn't make the papers. Two of these bodies were found from phoned-in tips. Each time, the caller had a weird accent. Not

German—what is it… Austrian. My friend said an Austrian fella told the police where to look."

Eleanor swallowed. Austrian. Like Prince Wym. Vampire.

When the morgue door clicked shut, only the remains of Jennifer Barrett lay under the lights.

Now alone, Grits and Gravy let their masks slip.

They belonged to a small club. They both knew what dead felt like.

Because of their experience, they could sense that Jennifer sat in a strange in-between. Undead. Which meant vampire or werewolf. Confirming which would narrow the hunt.

Before stepping toward the body, both men palmed a wooden stake in case the situation escalated.

Gravy leaned close, voice soft.

"Jennifer, I know you can hear me. My name's Gravy. This is Grits. You don't know us, but we're your friends. I know you're scared. I know you hurt, and it's hard to explain. We're going to get you home.'

Jennifer's eyes opened—scared young-woman eyes—flicking between the men.

The scalpel-clean "claws" pointed one way, but wounds could lie. Her response told the truth. Vampire contact brings a fight. This was fear and confusion, not hunger.

Werewolf.

"Jennifer, we're going to help you," Grits said. "For now, rest. You'll be home soon."

Recognition crossed her face. A blink, a glint of hope. Her eyes closed.

Gravy met Grits's look. She wasn't at rest yet—but she'd left them.

"Werewolves?" Grits said.

"Looks like it," Gravy said.

"Details will help. Should we hit the fridge?"

Gravy grimaced. "You know it's going to be nasty."

"It's the job," Grits said. "The faster we finish, the faster we get Detective Pérez to drive us to Burger King."

Gravy's face lit like a kid on Christmas morning.

Eleanor had been pushing back on Grits and Gravy about having lunch (and dinner and breakfast and dessert) at Burger King. She had nothing against the Home of the Whopper, but that was the only place they ever wanted to eat. Now, with a goal in mind, the pair took to the refrigerator.

Four bodies on gurneys, blankets knee to neck.

"Two hookers, a wino, and a junkie," Gravy said. "Worst *Merv Griffin* panel ever."

"Process of elimination," Grits said. "Junkie—no. Winos ramble. The hookers might have some good stories."

"Go with the most recent hooker," Gravy said. "Less jaded."

Grits found the file. "This is... Deborah Dawn Teats."

"Deborah Dawn Teats? Double-D Teats? Damn. Her folks set her up to be on the corner with that name."

Short, buxom, permed black hair. Face mostly intact, head barely attached. Aside from being a dead hooker, she otherwise appeared to be doing well.

They reached out the quiet way. Nothing. Grits flicked her nose.

Her eyes flew open. "Daffodil Phil? That you?" rasped out.

Grits and Gravy traded a look. Definitely a pimp name.

"Nah, baby," Gravy said. "Daffodil Phil's not here. We need some information. Tell us what happened."

"Who are you?" she asked.

They didn't give names to working girls, living or dead.

"Listen, Deborah—" Grits started.

"It's Deborah-Dawn," she cut in. "With a hyphen. Daffodil Phil said alliteration makes me exotic."

"I don't know how much advice I'd take from a guy named Daffodil Phil," Grits said. "But—"

"Give me twenty dollars and I'll tell you anything."

"You're dead," Gravy said, patience draining into hunger. "Twenty won't help you."

"Daffodil Phil won't let me talk if you don't pay me," she said. "Daffodil Phil says..."

Grits and Gravy looked at each other. This was just a waste of time. They had made a mistake in choosing Deborah-Dawn, but they made a bigger mistake by bringing up Burger King to each other. Now all they could think about was lunch.

"How do we turn her off?" Grits said. The Maiden had taught him, but it slipped. He snapped his fingers at her. Nothing.

Then Gravy spotted an empty metal organ pan.

Thirty seconds after one firm bonk, Grits and Gravy rejoined Detective Rafael Pérez and Agent Ronald Wilson in the conference room. Eleanor had already hitched a ride from Detective Jones back to the office.

"Learn anything interesting?" Wilson said, sour.

"Yeah," Grits said. "Don't take advice from a guy named Daffodil Phil."

Wilson heard a smart-assed *non sequitur*. Pérez's mouth fell open. No file mentioned the pimp's name; he only knew it from a vice friend.

Before Pérez could follow up, Wilson said, brisk and impatient, "If you've got nothing, let's move. Here's where you can actually help."

He laid out photos. A surveillance shot of a beautiful young woman exiting a restaurant, Golyam looming at her shoulder.

"Two leads," Wilson said. "First, Victor Karanovo's daughter—

Nina. See the resemblance. Mother unknown. Like Victor, her paperwork… appeared. And like Victor, she's never in public without the bodyguard. No record, no ties, besides being his blood. Intercepts suggest she thinks Daddy's a straight business-man. She wouldn't like arms and drugs."

He held up a color glossy: a young black woman with a micro-phone, coffee-colored skin, braided cornrows. "Second: Dee Wheatley. Lead singer for DeeLeon, house band at Midnight Miami. Tomorrow night Nina's hosting a showcase—a fundraiser for Mariel refugees. Record execs, bigwigs. Dee's older brother is doing fifteen in a federal pen in New York. We think we can get her to help if it trims his sentence."

The casual manipulation rubbed both men wrong. Pérez saw their posture harden.

"Agent Wilson and I want you ingrained with Nina and Dee," Pérez said. "Find out what's really happening inside Midnight Miami."

"Nina eats at Christy's every Wednesday," Wilson said. "I've got you a table next to her at seven."

Grits and Gravy tried to hide their joy. Christy's Restaurant was their favorite steakhouse.

"Dee's band has a warm-up set at the club tonight. We've got tickets."

Temperature in the room dropped. A clean way into Midnight Miami helped.

Wilson pulled an envelope fat with cash. Pérez watched, curi-ous. Detective Jones had said the pair had a habit of working free. He wasn't disappointed: revulsion crossed their faces.

"Listen, man," Gravy said, pushing the envelope back. "We'll do this as a favor to Detective Pérez. On our terms."

"If some nut thinks he's the Wolf Man, we've got three days before he kills again," Grits said.

"And one more thing," Gravy added. "This town is lousy with Feds trying to blend in. Stay out of our way. We don't need extra bodies because you watched too many episodes of *The Untouchables* as a kid."

Pérez stepped in before it turned into a brawl. "We're on the same team. We have a deal. I'll run these gentlemen back to their office."

Wilson stood, glaring. Pérez returned to the table, collected two manila folders, and handed them to Grits and Gravy.

"Everything we covered is in here," he said. "And—one detail from this morning's scene. Something the killer left."

Pérez fetched a clear evidence bag.

Inside sat one penny loafer.

Painted white.

5

THE TALK

Wednesday, 12:42 PM
Burger King
1309 NW 20th Street, Miami

DETECTIVE RAFAEL PÉREZ sat across from Grits McCoy and Gravy Watkins. In front of him: the remains of a Whopper and fries, and a chocolate milkshake he hadn't wanted but was starting to enjoy. His hosts had insisted on the shake.

They all had the same meal—except Gravy, who had three Whoppers.

Grits and Gravy were pleased about the milkshake. They brought clients here for a conversation they called The Talk. Milkshakes made The Talk go down easier.

There's a point, they'd learned, where a client must choose to accept how the world really works or stay in the warm bath of ignorance. Better to handle it on their terms, in a comfy booth under a paper crown.

Pérez stared out at the playground. Noon heat shimmered off the metal. A husky boy was wedged in a tube slide, watching Pérez like Pérez was the one stuck. The detective looked away first.

"How's that milkshake?" Gravy asked, unintentionally paternal. Pérez remembered bringing his daughters here for shakes when he needed to give them bad news.

He finally asked what he'd wanted to ask since they sat down. "How'd you know about Daffodil Phil? He wasn't in the file. I only heard the name from a friend in vice."

Grits and Gravy traded a look. They were about to start Phase One and hadn't planned for questions. Still, this one would help.

"Before we answer," Grits said, "why us? Out of all the detectives in Miami."

Pérez knew. He didn't want to say it. He offered a partial truth. "You've worked with Bill Jones. And my *tío*—Arturo Santos."

"That's all good," Gravy said. "But not an answer. If we're going to work together, we have to be honest. Why did you really call us?"

Pérez didn't want to admit it. Didn't want to say that whatever killed Jennifer Barrett wasn't human. But if these two could stop it and keep Miami from tearing, pride had to go.

"I called because you two take the freaky cases," he said. "Weird stuff. Haunted houses. Monsters. Like *Scooby-Doo*."

They hated the cartoon comparison, but let it ride.

Grits leaned in. "There's one thing you need to accept, and it's not easy. The things that go bump in the night? They're real. They live alongside us. Usually the worlds don't cross. When they do, we step in."

"Like what things?" Pérez asked.

Gravy ticked them off, flat as a grocery list. "Vampires. Werewolves. Goblins. Leprechauns. Easter Bunnies. Witches. Warlocks..."

"Am I missing a metaphor," Pérez said, "or do you mean werewolves and vampires?"

"Unfortunately not a metaphor," Gravy said. "As real as you and me."

Pérez tried to process that and what it meant for his case. The kid in the slide was still staring. Definitely stuck.

"You helped Jones on that 'suicide' that turned murder," Pérez said. "What was the real story?"

"The owner paid a voodoo priestess to curse his rival's food," Grits said. "When we put that together, we convinced him to confess to poisoning."

"How?"

"We told him we'd tell the priestess he ratted her out if he didn't," Gravy said. "Witches don't put up with snitches."

"What happened to the priestess?"

"We settled out of court," Grits said, dry.

"And my uncle's 'haunted' house?"

"Your uncle thought a hippie wizard from the '60s was after him," Gravy said. "He wasn't entirely wrong. But it was an Easter Bunny in the house. Supposedly they ward off vampires, though I've never seen it. Mostly they're in the way, so we ran the rabbit off."

"Easter Bunnies. Ecch," Grits muttered.

"And the wizard?"

"We addressed that off the record," Gravy said.

"What's any of that got to do with Daffodil Phil?"

Time to be direct. "A werewolf killed Jennifer Barrett," Grits said. "And the hooker. Probably the others. The wounds pointed us there, but we confirmed it because both were stuck between life and death—undead. In that state, we can talk to them. That's how we learned Deborah-Dawn's pimp's name. She told us."

Pérez took a long pull of milkshake. Impossible. And somehow it felt true.

"All right," he said. "Werewolves and the undead. What do I need to know?"

The Talk had taken. They could work.

"Most movie rules hold," Gravy said. "The curse passes by bite. Full moon powers them. Under the moon, they change—strong, hard to kill. You kill them with silver—bullets if you've got them— and, like most things in the shadows, it's wise to take the head."

"Does that mean Jennifer Barrett becomes a werewolf?" Pérez asked.

"That part's sketchy," Grits said. "If you're bitten and live, you turn at the full moon. If you're bitten and die, sometimes you come back; sometimes you're stuck in between."

"But two murders were on non-moon nights. How?"

Gravy had hoped he'd let that slide. He was impressed he didn't. "That's the piece we need to figure out."

"What is it about you two that lets you talk to the dead? Or undead. Whatever."

They didn't want to dump everything at once—namely, that both had been dead before.

"Call it previous experience," Gravy said.

Pérez was near his limit, but one more question had chewed at him since the day the new owners took over the Stone Detective Agency.

"How'd you get into this line of work?"

They shared a quick look. There were different versions of this story. He'd get the short one.

"A few years back we were in Hollywood for a celebrity roller-disco contest," Grits said. "Vampires got involved. We killed Dracula."

"It made an impression in their community," Gravy added.

"Of course," Pérez said, laughing despite himself—and realizing for the first time today that Gravy wasn't wearing a shirt.

"After that, L.A. got too hot. We headed east," Grits said. "Cliff Stone found us for a strange case. More vampires. Then he sold us the agency before he passed."

"When things get weird," Gravy said, "people find us."

The Talk works best when it ends before the client asks the questions he'll regret. Grits was about to steer them out when Pérez lifted a hand.

"You told me what I need to accept for us to work," he said. "Here's what you need to know about me.

"I love Miami. When my parents left Cuba, Miami took us in. My wife and I were married at Gesù. My daughters were born at Mercy. We can't just pick up and go.

"These last years—drugs, murders, lunatics—I don't know how much more this city can take.

"Drug dealers shooting each other is one thing. But that girl this morning—she wasn't a junkie. She wasn't a streetwalker. That could've been my wife. My daughter.

"This isn't a game. I'll do whatever I can to stop it. But I need to know you're not playing games. I need to know you can help me stop whatever we're up against."

People thought Grits and Gravy were aloof. It was how they kept from going crazy knowing what lurked past the edge of light. Pérez had that read, which is why he saw it when they let the masks drop.

"Detective," Gravy said, "we're not just going to find what did this and stop it. We're going to destroy it so it can't do it again."

They walked Pérez to his red Impala and shook hands. "By the way," he said, sliding in, "the milkshakes were a nice touch."

As he pulled out, the last thing he heard was Gravy yelling toward the employee door, "Hey, you. Yeah, you. Somebody needs to help that fat kid—the one stuck in the tube slide. He's a big one. You can't miss him."

———

Golyam sat on a leather couch in a quiet lobby no one could reach without a private elevator. If you could magically appear here, you'd never guess Miami's hottest club throbbed four flows below.

The young receptionist ignored him—as she ignored most of what happened at Midnight Miami. She answered phones for two names on this floor: Nina Karanovo to the left, Victor Karanovo to the right. She wondered how many messages were ever read. She could feel the big man's stare press on her skin. She pretended to journal and wished him gone.

The intercom buzzed. A deep voice said he would see the guest.

Golyam crossed to the door and stepped inside. The lock snicked behind him. The receptionist exhaled, reached for *Petals on the Wind* and a pack of Virginia Slims.

Victor Karanovo sat behind a massive desk on a raised platform designed to make every visitor feel small. Golyam didn't sit— not out of deference to the stagecraft, but because Golyam was never asked to sit.

On the shelf behind Victor, a black onyx box caught the fluorescents. The inlaid wolf-god of their clan glinted; anyone facing Victor had to feel the eyes of the wolf.

Victor didn't look up at first; when he did, it was only to confirm the silhouette. He spoke to the ledger. "How did our latest experiment go last night?"

"Exactly as planned," Golyam said.

"The White Room?"

"Perfect."

"The recordings?"

"We got everything we wanted."

Victor finally met his eyes. A tiny tremor ran through Golyam's knees.

"And his... performance... outside the club. Was that recorded too?"

"Yes."

Victor's face held stone three beats, then broke into a real smile. Golyam tried to return it and produced something like pushing his own teeth forward.

"Good boy," Victor said.

Golyam waited for dismissal.

"I want to meet with the fat Italian tomorrow morning," Victor said. "Contact him directly. Do not use the receptionist."

Silence stretched. Then: "You remember why we chose Miami, don't you?"

"The prophecy," Golyam said. "Light and shadows together to rule over all."

Victor nodded, slow, certain. "It's coming true. And now that the injection formula is correct, I'm as sure as I've ever been. Saturday night, we take what's ours. Prepare accordingly. You've done well, son."

He waved. Dismissed.

In the doorway's shadow, Golyam tried another smile and almost found one. He couldn't tell if that was good or bad.

6

PLAN B

Wednesday, 6:55 PM
Christy's Restaurant
3101 Ponce de Leon Boulevard, Coral Gables

AFTER LUNCH WITH DETECTIVE PÉREZ, Grits McCoy and Gravy Watkins burned the afternoon getting ready for their "date" with Nina Karanovo—reservations courtesy of FBI Agent Ronald Wilson.

Back at the office, they briefed Eleanor Stone, handed her a copy of the file, and asked her to ping her PD contact about the impounded Cadillac from Virginia Key. Eleanor actually liked those requests—normal, compared to yesterday's "rush a cord of lumber to a deserted stretch of beach by 5 PM." As soon as she thought she was clear, they hit her with *Love Boat* questions; she opted for an early swim at the YMCA and escaped.

They met outside Christy's at exactly 6:55. Quick huddle: Grits runs at Nina; Gravy handles Dee Wheatley later. Contingency for Wilson if he's dumb enough to show.

"Think they stopped serving salads after we asked them?" Gravy asked.

"Only one way to find out," Grits said.

The moment they stepped inside, heads turned. Staff whispered: Grits and Gravy.

Grits wore a tan double-breasted sport coat, the same white shirt from this morning—two buttons undone instead of three—brown trousers, camel cowboy boots. Gravy rocked red suspenders over blue jeans, black steel-toes. Shirtless. Naturally.

The maître d' lit up. They were good tippers.

"Mr. Grits, Mr. Gravy—welcome back." He checked the book, frowned, then, "Reservations for three?" He pointed subtly toward the bar. "Your third? The undercover agent?"

At the bar, Agent Ronald Wilson was "undercover" in the same navy suit—now accessorized with a neon "Miami" floral tie, rose-tinted aviator glasses, and a toy-store mustache.

"He'll blow our cover before we order water," Grits said. "Plan B."

They slapped a few quick signals. Gravy peeled off toward the bar. Grits turned to the maître d'.

"Change of plans—reservation for one. But I'd love that same table." He floated a crisp hundred.

"Of course, Mr. Grits."

Gravy appeared at Wilson's elbow, lifted him off the stool with one hand, left a Franklin by the three-quarters-full beer with the other, and shouldered him through the kitchen to the alley.

"I don't know what you think you're doing, I'm—" Wilson started.

Gravy raised a finger. "Everybody in there, including the maître d', fingered you as a Fed. This town is crawling with cops and Feds who can't blend. If you don't fix that, you're going to get yourself—or someone else—killed."

Wilson wilted like a scolded puppy.

"I've got an idea," Gravy said. "Payphone."

On Malaga Avenue, Gravy made a quick call. When he came back to Wilson, he said, "Friend in Little Havana—Arturo. Haberdasher. He'll make you look local. He'll meet us at Versailles after he closes his shop. Then we'll head over to his store, so nobody sees your monkey ass."

Wilson straightened to recover pride. "I'll get a cab?"

"No need. I'll drive," Gravy said.

"Where's your car?"

Gravy smiled. "Who said anything about a car?"

The hostess led Grits to the table Wilson had booked—right beside Nina Karanovo.

Nina wasn't pretty; she was beautiful—the kind that sticks. Mediterranean more than Slavic: medium dark hair, clean makeup on sun-touched skin, almond eyes. The kind of beauty that doesn't have to be announced.

They locked eyes. Awkward, palpable.

Before Grits could fish up a clever opening line, she beat him to it. "Do you mind if I join you, or are you saving those seats for the surveillance team?"

"They're not due 'til dessert," Grits said.

She stood, a brown pinstripe jacket and skirt over a white pussy-bow blouse, slung her purse, grabbed a half-bottle of Löwenbräu, and moved. Grits stood to pull her chair.

A large shadow rose behind her—Golyam. Guard dog in a suit.

"Golyam, I don't need you tonight. Go somewhere else," she said.

"But your father—"

"My father can watch me himself if he's worried about dinner. Leave. Now."

The big man dead-eyed Grits, then sulked away. The dismissal felt a touch theatrical.

Nina sat; Grits eased her in.

"Where I from, everyone listens. Very good at 'blend in,'" she said, English shaped by a Russian cadence. "Since I come to America, many men spy on my father, but very bad at blend in."

"We don't get many Soviet arms dealers down here," Grits said. "Give us time. It's the American way."

She looked offended. He realized he'd shown his hand.

"You are race-car driver, but also secret agent?" she teased.

"Something like that. Used to race. Now I'm a private detective. Stone Detective Agency."

"Your partner—the black, yes?"

"That's one way to put it."

"And you pretend to be detectives and follow people like me in restaurants?"

"Pretend is harsh. Cops and Feds like us because we can get into places they can't. How do you know so much about me?"

She dropped the "foreign girl" routine and slid into American, as Gravy would say.

"Save me the bullshit. You're famous, but not for the Feds. You're famous for chasing ghosts—haunted houses, witches, Easter Bunnies, goblins, vampires." She made finger fangs. "You're like Scooby Boo-Boo, except instead of a hippie and a van with white whores, you have a black and a race car. Vroom vroom."

"It's Scooby-Doo," he said mildly. "And maybe ease up on the 'black' talk there, Archie Bunker."

The waiter arrived with specials. Grits poker-faced through the famous Caesar, somehow still on the menu. Nina puffed her cheeks: BOR-RING.

"Eight-ounce filet. Medium," she said. "Blue Eyes here will have the same. Two Löwenbräu. And don't ask him about salad. He'll think you're trying to pick him up."

Grits nodded: she wasn't wrong.

A shirtless black man on a Harley FXB Sturgis turns heads anywhere. In Little Havana, Gravy turned heads and drew confusion—thanks to the blue-suited agent koala-hugging his waist.

Gravy parked at Versailles, "the world's most famous Cuban restaurant," then sat Wilson on the patio by the street. "Sit your honky ass down and be quiet." He crossed to greet his old friend, Arturo Santos.

Wilson, who'd only ever driven through this neighborhood, tried to eavesdrop. He thought he heard "Soviet," and watched the older Cuban's posture ease.

"Hey, Papi," a husky voice said above him. "You all by yourself? You want a date? You an undercover man? I like that. What agency, Papi?"

Wilson—Boise-born, Boise-raised—looked up. Not a transvestite so much as a man in a dress: blonde wig askew, two-day beard, chest hair for cleavage, an impressive bulge at eye level.

"Cut it out, Sweetpea," said a sunburned white guy at the next table, tropical shirt open, *cafecito* and cigar, eyes on the *Miami Herald*: "Magic City Maniac Strikes Again!"

"Leave him. He's here with Gravy. And look at you—are you even trying anymore?"

Sweetpea ripped off the wig, flopped into Wilson's chair.

Ricardo "Sweetpea" Castilla had been one of Miami-Dade's best vice cops for years. Drag wasn't a preference; it was a tool—and he was excellent. People cracked wise. He pointed to his pants and reminded them what their aunts and sisters called him: *Pinga Dulce*—sanitized to "Sweetpea."

But since Mariel, the streets were flooded with she-males who could pass under booking lights. Sweetpea had been ice-cold.

"I am trying, Murphy!" he yelled, placing the bulge inches from Wilson again. "New look—go the other way. Obvious. Wild. Desperate. Some sickos like that."

"You got desperate down," Murphy said, not looking up.

The tubby Irishman wasn't too worried about his partner. He could only feel so bad for a guy with an extra arm in his pants. Mostly, he just enjoyed getting Sweetpea worked up.

Gravy reappeared, half-hugging Sweetpea while instinctively keeping hips apart. "Sweetpea, my man. Senior year at Jacksonville A&M, first two games I didn't crack a hundred. Thought I was cooked. Kept my head down, did the work—bam, next game 347 yards. School record. Still there. And most importantly—you still got that huge jank in your pants."

They howled. Wilson stood.

Gravy looked almost surprised to see him. "Good news. Arturo's going to hook us up. We'll pop across, get your measurements, then he'll pull older stock so you don't look fresh off the rack."

Street noise swallowed Sweetpea and Murphy arguing about who wore the dress better.

Grits admired how Nina put away a steak. No dainty act. He admired more how straight she asked questions.

"Out of all detectives, they pick you," she said. "Is it because of the wolf?"

"Because of what?"

"Wolf," she said, impatient. "Big dog. Howls at moon. Awoooo!"

Heads turned. She didn't notice.

"In the old country, people are superstitious—witches,

demons, vampires..." She flicked a look at him. "...and werewolves. In my father's trade, you want fear, so you choose a symbol."

She showed a large onyx ring on her pinky—rectangular, knuckle to hand. A wolf in a pharaoh headdress flashed before she withdrew it.

"You know my father was a bad man around bad people," she said. "He didn't use lawyers. He used action. Action that made fear. With fear, respect."

"Was a bad man?" Grits said. She talked like he was past tense.

She flagged the waiter. "Two more Löwenbräu. He's paying."

When they moved on, she answered. "He was... is no saint. But he's out. I don't know what deal he made with your government, but we are legal. I was shocked the CIA didn't throw us in a van. He didn't come to sell guns. He came to free us."

She was good. It almost rang true. Almost. Grits couldn't tell what the play was, only that there was one. What he could tell was —against judgment—he liked her: rude to staff, racist every other sentence, ate like a farmhand... and somehow he felt funny around her.

"I'm bored," Nina said, loud. "Let's go. I want to see your vroom-vroom race car."

The waiter arrived with the check. Grits tipped heavy; the man earned it. Nina stood, chugged her beer, slammed the bottle, and belched like a longshoreman. Half the room snapped their necks to stare.

"Grits McCoy," she said, grabbing her purse, "take me to your race car. Let's see how fast you really go."

The visit to Arturo Santos's shop was quick. The *tío* of Detective Pérez said little beyond "Turn" and "Again," vanished into the back, returned with a travel bag holding three outfits.

Back at Versailles, Sweetpea and Murphy were packing up.

"All right, Sweetpea," Murphy said, loud. "Time to get you and that fine ass back on the boulevard."

Gravy and Wilson swung onto the Harley. Murphy called, "FBI, right? That blue polyester gives it away."

Wilson's eyes fell to a wind-stuck *Herald* front page at the light pole: "Magic City Maniac Strikes Again!" Subhead: "Young Woman's Mutilated Body Found in Alley. Police Puzzled."

Agent Ronald Wilson smiled. Let them laugh at the "bad undercover" act. Let them hand him Arturo. Let them underestimate him. Let them see what he does when the full moon comes.

7

———

A NEW MYSTERY TO SOLVE

Wednesday, 8:32 PM
Monty's Raw Bar
2550 South Bayshore Drive, Coconut Grove

GRITS McCoy TOOK the long way—north to the tail of the Tamiami, then back down South Dixie—so Nina Karanovo could "feel a real car." When traffic opened, the Charger howled. Nina did the South Florida thing: head out the window, one-finger salutes, a flash of breasts at least once. Grits wasn't impressed, but it did make him nostalgic for race week in Daytona Beach.

As usual, he drew attention walking into Monty's. Even if folks didn't know the résumé, the hair and the eyes said famous. Grits didn't notice. Nina did—answering lingering looks with more one-finger salutes.

He'd hoped the tiki-hut view of the bay would take the edge off her.

It did not.

"Thanks for not taking me to the Mutiny," she said. "I don't have time this week to catch chlamydia from a bunch of drug-snorting beaners."

Grits had been at the Mutiny at Sailboat Bay, Miami's other hottest night spot, last week on a case. Sure, there were plenty of cocaine cowboys and sniffles. But also bankers, politicians, celebrities. He'd seen Al Pacino and Brian De Palma listening to a gap-toothed man in black hair deliver a rant. Maybe Kenny Loggins at another table. Two light-skinned black guys were talking animatedly—probably DeBarges, though Gravy's invented "Stan DeBarge" had him second-guessing.

"What makes Midnight Miami better than the Mutiny?" Grits asked.

She gave him a look like he'd asked if water was wet, then switched to sales mode. "I've seen real clubs. Midnight Miami brings Europe here. You build a place for the young, beautiful, and cool—money follows. If it works here, we go national. Midnight New York. Midnight Chicago. You want a club, you come to the Midnight. You want to sniff cocaine and farts and give each other crabs, you go to the Mutiny."

The waitress arrived right on "crabs." Nina didn't blink.

"Two rum runners and two Löwenbräu," Nina said. "And no oysters. I'll handle the clams here—if you know what I mean."

She turned back to Grits. "Did you know the Mutiny is the largest buyer of Dom Pérignon in the world? We can't get any. My father had to call the local meatballs, get them to lean on New York. Only way we got stock."

"Meatballs" was a term Grits heard from Gravy often enough to translate. Maybe that was why Victor Karanovo sniffed around the Frusciantes.

Drinks hit the table fast. Nina knocked both rum runners like medicine; the heat came down a notch. Grits risked a question that wouldn't trigger another South American broadside.

"Of all places—New York, L.A., Chicago—why Miami?"

She smiled, almost sincerely. "The sun. I wanted a place where the sun always shines. Back home we were always hiding—houses, woods—moving in the middle of the night. I got packed like luggage. Smuggled like stolen goods.

"And my father is... traditional. My family has a legend—he says prophecy. The queen of shadows joining with a king of light. He wanted to leave the darkness and find me a husband. What better place than a city full of sunlight? I think that is why he made a deal with your government. He could bring me here and give me a start in the sun."

It cost her something to say that out loud. Grits also realized he liked her far more than made sense. Miami had plenty of gorgeous women without being drunk, vulgar, racist daughters of a Communist arms dealer who might be a werewolf—meaning she might, too.

"So, Mr. Vroom-Vroom," she said, "what brought you to Miami?"

"Honestly? Don't know. I just know this—Miami's the longest I've lived anywhere." He saw she was listening, so he kept going. "I'm an Army brat. My dad kept moving up; we kept moving on. I've been everywhere and nowhere. Cars gave me a fast way to make friends when I landed in a new town."

He'd never said that out loud. She might be the only person he knew who genuinely understood.

"Speaking of the sun," he said, surprising himself, "my house has a great view of the skyline at night. You have time for one more stop?"

"I think I can make time for my Scooby Boo-Boo and his vroom-vroom race car," she said, coy.

He paid, tipped heavy. Before the waitress left, Grits raised a hand.

"Ma'am, one last thing. What mayonnaise do you serve here?"

She blinked. "I can check with the kitchen."

"No need." He produced a small jar from his pocket. "Duke's Mayonnaise. The delicious richness puts springtime flavor in your food year-round—for sandwiches, cakes, or for salads if you're a woman. You can depend on Duke's."

When NASCAR banned him after the wreck that killed four other drivers, every sponsor fled—except Duke's. He never forgot.

A month later, NASCAR tried to reinstate him. The president offered a lawyered apology; Grits took the podium with a jar, thanked Duke's, then said the president could take this jar—and the reinstatement—and shove both up his ass.

Grits McCoy never raced a Winston Cup event again. Duke's did not renew.

Nina watched him. "I was told you were as stupid as you are handsome," she said. "I'm starting to think they were wrong."

Forty minutes later they pulled up to his place off Harbor Drive on Key Biscayne. He'd bought the place six months back, kept the furniture, added a 50-inch projection TV so *The Love Boat* looked the same at his house or Gravy's.

They cut straight through to the back. Two pit stops on the way—Big Daddy's for beer, Burger King for a late snack—gave them something to hold and a reason to not linger inside.

Biscayne Bay spread out from the deck; only the dock and speedboat spoiled the line. They took chairs at the far end of the pool, bags of food on their laps, beers in hand. American cuisine, deluxe.

"Road fries were a great idea," Nina said, mouth full. "Eat 'em separate, then the fries for your burger are still hot when you get home." She punctuated her statement with a loud burp.

"Alright, Mr. Mystery Machine Vampire Detective," she said. "You've asked questions all night. My turn."

"Fire away."

"You were a big-time race driver, but not for long. I don't want to be rude—"

"You? Rude?" he said.

"—but how do you afford this chasing ghosts?"

He should've expected it; everyone in town wondered. The Stone Detective Agency paid the bills, but not this. The truth was simple and impossible: killing Dracula made them heirs under the Laws of the Shadows. Dracula's fortune was theirs. Also, the reason why vampires like Prince Wym would never stop coming.

His hesitation told her enough. She stood, drained a Löwen-bräu, and pitched the bottle into the bay—end over end, splash.

"You can leave empties on the table," he said, still shocked by how her boorishness somehow aroused him.

"Shut up," she said. "I want to swim."

The blouse and skirt went. A beat later, the rest. She stepped into the light—honey skin, soft where she needed to be soft, and firm where she needed to be firm—turned a full circle so he got the complete inventory, then cut a clean drop into the pool.

"Come here, Scooby Boo-Boo," she said. "I have a new mystery for you to solve."

He undressed fast and not particularly gracefully—he was glad he'd kicked off the boots earlier—hit the water, pulled her in, kissed her. She kissed back.

Desire surged like he'd never known. He didn't just want her. He wanted to devour her.

"Nina!"

He turned toward the voice. Golyam stood on the pool deck, holding one of Grits's terrycloth robes.

In that instant, Grits had never felt more vulnerable—or

dumber. Naked in a pool. Closest thing to a weapon was a part of him that was rapidly losing its advantage.

But, if this was it, there were worse ways to go.

"Your father needs you. Now," the big man said.

Nina climbed the ladder without shame. She turned for the robe; Golyam draped it. She gathered her clothes, crossed to the table, and fished an envelope from her purse. She dropped it on the table and grabbed the remaining two Löwenbräu.

At the door, she looked back. "Thank you for a wonderful evening. We're having a fundraiser tomorrow night at Midnight Miami. I left four tickets. Bring your black and your secret undercover agent. Also, bring Eleanor Stone as your date. I would love to meet her."

She mouthed, *Goodbye, Scooby Boo-Boo.*

"Okay," he said lamely. "See you soon. You two find your way out. I'm just going to stand here a few more minutes."

He stood naked in the pool and started the list. How did he let himself get here? How did the big guy know where he lived? How did he get inside and find a robe without Grits hearing?

And the one that bothered him most:

Why did Nina Karanovo bring up Eleanor Stone?

8

DETECTIVE STONE

Wednesday, 9:03 PM
University of Miami
Otto G. Richter Library, Coral Gables

ELEANOR STONE TOOK a breath and let the library smell hit her. There was something about slow-rotting paper she'd always loved.

The Otto G. Richter Library was all concrete and hum. With campus mostly deserted for the summer, the buzz of fluorescent tubes filled the quiet. As she headed down to the lower level, the air picked up a dank note—mold and dust—like a warning label for scholars.

At the microfilm desk, Eleanor flashed her membership card. She hadn't been in for a few years, but she'd kept up the research pass—twenty-five bucks a year for access to a fat run of national and foreign newspapers was a bargain, even if she didn't use it much.

After going through the Midnight Miami file Pérez and Wilson had provided—and knowing Grits and Gravy were "interviewing" their female leads—Eleanor felt obliged to pull her weight.

She signed the clipboard and told the librarian she needed the library's Bulgarian papers. The librarian, a homely, expressionless girl who looked born to shush, asked about the topic. When Eleanor said, "Bulgarian arms dealer," the girl explained that while the library had plenty of microfiche—*Rabotnichesko Delo, Otechestven Front, Narodna Mladezh* ("People's Youth")—they were all Communist Party rags. Eleanor would have better luck learning about Karanovo at the nearest bus stop.

Eleanor remembered the other words that had been on her mind: Austrian. Prince Wym. Vampire.

"Alright," Eleanor said, pivoting. "What about Austria's business press?" If Karanovo was fronting a club, then whatever "Prince Wym" was, he likely had a legitimate front of his own in Miami.

Soon she had an armful of fiche cards—Austria's business papers—plus the *Miami Herald* Business section and the *Miami Business Journal.* She fed the first card into the bulky reader, twiddled the dials, and muscle memory returned: focus, zoom, frame advance. Back on the microfiche bicycle.

The Austrian hunt fizzled. With Prince Wym's last name—Blutmesser—finally pinned down from her old meeting notes, she chased the big word but came up empty.

Switching to the *Herald* and rolling backward, she hit pay dirt fast.

A real-estate roundup noted a new lease: Eastern Alps Medical Supplies moving its U.S. headquarters from Los Angeles to Miami. The privately held firm—"an Austrian company specializing in medical equipment for the transport and storage of blood"—was taking several floors in One Biscayne Tower downtown. The item added that the company had contracts with the five largest hospital systems in the country.

She checked the date. Barely a month after Grits and Gravy became the new owners of the Stone Detective Agency.

Eleanor pulled the *Miami Business Journal* fiche and found the directory entry: Eastern Alps Medical Supplies—Wym Blutmesser, Chief Executive Officer.

Her stomach rolled. She palmed her purse to feel the .38, then touched the crucifix hanging by her throat.

Without re-filing the cards, she rose and walked out fast without quite running, ignoring the librarian calling after her.

The librarian was still puzzling over the exit when a young man's voice at her shoulder made her jump. "How could that woman be so rude?"

When he wanted to pass for human, Wym Blutmesser looked like a gaunter, better-looking David Bowie. Tonight, he wore a sharp black suit and a white oxford—stylish but welcoming. He strolled to the abandoned reader and saw his own name on the screen.

He smiled. He preferred the shadows, but Eastern Alps was a real company and a profitable one—a lifeline that kept the House of Blutmesser afloat after the loss of Dracula's unfathomable hoard.

He'd been tracking Eleanor more and more these last weeks. With her partners out prowling, her sudden departure from her Surfside condo after eight had piqued him. The only thing staying his hand from taking her blood and her life was timing; he wanted the greatest possible pain for Grits and Gravy, who still hadn't given Eleanor the courtesy of explaining why her life was in constant jeopardy thanks to their sins against his family.

Wym slid the *Business Journal* card from the machine, gathered the rest, and dropped them into the bright yellow basket the librarian had issued.

He hadn't fed yet tonight, and hunger was chewing at him. Good thing Eleanor had fled; appetite could ruin a careful plan.

Setting the basket on the desk, he recognized how easy it would be to bend this bland, lonely woman to his will and fill his need for tonight.

As she thanked him for returning the cards, Prince Wym Blutmesser said, "Have you had dinner yet my darling? I haven't— and I must say, I'm starving.

And I would love to have you."

9

ONE OF THOSE FACES

W ednesday, 9:48 PM
Midnight Miami
1555 Collins Avenue, South Beach

GRAVY WATKINS DRESSED for the club the way he dressed for everything—red suspenders, jeans, steel-toed boots, no shirt— and rumbled his Harley up to Midnight Miami.

Perk of being famous on a motorcycle: any curb was valet. He rolled past the rope under the marquee:

W – Ladies Night sponsored by Löwenbräu

Th – Freestyle Dance Party / DeeLeon (Industry Showcase)

Fri – Miami Sound Machine

Inside, it was Dolphins training camp with neon. Coaches, trainers, bubble players—back slaps all around, except from running backs trying to keep jobs. Gravy kept moving.

He had to admit: the Karanovos built this joint right. First floor —almost all dance floor, ringed by raised banquettes so everyone could look down on the day-glo herd trying to be *different* in the exact same outfits. Your eye got pulled to the second-floor stage floating over the far wall. Private rooms glowed off the mezzanine. One sign hummed like a bug zapper:

The White Room.

"Gravy, my man!" a young brother yelled. "Tell me you ain't here 'cause Petey Maymoore might show."

Gravy couldn't place the name, but the build said former ball. He was glad he hadn't heard the rumor—otherwise he'd have to lie. "I'm here for Dee Wheatley."

"You and everybody," the guy laughed. "Petey set their showcase for tomorrow. Might pop in tonight. Might be at the Mutiny playing in the snow." He pantomimed a bump and peeled for the third floor.

Gravy took the elevator to the showcase level—separated from the chaos, small stage for suits with clipboards. He muscled to the rail through a corridor of handshakes.

At 10:10 the emcee popped: "Before their big night—give it up for DeeLeon!"

Dee Wheatley and Leon "Juicy" Robinson slid into the twin mics, cornrow braids threaded with neon to match their jackets. Dee sang clean; Juicy sang and strummed rhythm. The band kicked a sped-up, keyboard-bright "Ain't Nothin' Like the Thing," half electro-boogie, half freestyle.

Eight bars and it was obvious: Dee was the star. Clear voice, easy authority. Juicy worked, but he was already at his ceiling— reaching for high notes, slipping on key changes, compensating with spins, guitar twirls, and enough sweat to water the palms.

Classic Ike/Tina math—if Ike wore white leather.

Two uptempo numbers in, they huddled. Ballad time. Dee came back smiling. "We thought we'd have a special guest on this one. Maybe tomorrow. For now, give it up for Juicy Robinson."

A girl in a purple halter next to Gravy leaned in. "Petey was supposed to duet. He's in town—just, you know."

They launched "Heat in the Sheets." Juicy did an acceptable Petey; Dee took the Mayo Davies part someplace better. Gravy knew every word to both parts. *I could've done Petey better,* he thought.

For the closer, Juicy waddled to center, mopped his face, and wheezed into the mic. "Ladies and—ah—gentlemen—ah—give it up for Dee Wheatley!"

A stagehand slung a guitar on Dee. Juicy hacked, then tried showman again. The band hit a high-tempo original. Dee set rhythm. Juicy let his *dancing* loose—spins, bunny hops, deep pelvic thrusts—his white leather pants praying for mercy.

On a split, the pants surrendered. The rear seam detonated, white shrapnel fountained, and Juicy howled like a man who'd just learned he could do the splits and simultaneously should not. The room broke up.

Gravy watched Dee, not the disaster. For a heartbeat: mortified, sympathetic, exasperated. Then she sprinted to him, laughing like it was planned—kind, not cruel. Stagehands dragged him off. Last the crowd saw of Juicy: polka-dot bikini briefs framed by the remains of his white leather pants.

Dee planted center, clapped along, rode the laughter down. "Y'all give it up for my man Juicy. He's so crazy." She turned, shouted to the band. The lead guitarist mouthed, *We didn't practice that.* Dee said something that read, *Then learn now.*

She counted three. The band slammed Prince's "Why You Wanna Treat Me So Bad." Twenty seconds in she looked right at Gravy, and he couldn't help grinning back.

House lights on the button. For the first time all night he saw her face clean. The recognition hit like a body shot. He grabbed the rail to keep from folding. There was no mistaking: Dee looked just like Her.

The backstage green room smelled like beer, cigarettes, and victory. A Dolphins trainer iced Juicy's groin. Band kids smoked and bragged. Club staff moved through with trays and towels. One passed close—a thin guy in a black vest, silver name tag, and a dull gray lapel pin that almost disappeared until he turned. Gravy's eyes flicked—fast, sharp: a wolf in a pharaoh crown.

He filed it. Kept moving.

Dee held court in back in a University of Miami tee and jeans, braids still neon-threaded, cigarette in hand. She looked at Gravy the way you look at somebody you're sure you've met. "Don't I know you? You look familiar."

"That's Gravy Watkins!" a bandmate announced.

Her face lit. "*The* Gravy Watkins! My brother had your posters all over our bedroom."

Gravy had braced for this moment. He'd seen monsters and myths, died and come back, been everywhere and beyond—but reincarnation never made his list. Still, here she was, the outline of a dream—*Her*—he'd lost years ago. Even the way her eyes shined when she smiled.

She touched a finger to his chest. "I know I've seen your picture for years, but I feel like I know you from somewhere else."

He felt it deep and used the line that saved him when faces blurred. "I get that a lot. I just have one of those faces." He didn't want to linger on this subject. "Y'all were great. Loved the Prince closer. Think Petey's gonna be mad? You know those two hate each other."

"If Petey's got a problem, he can say it to my face." She dragged, exhaled, stepped in. "He's in town. Put this whole thing together and won't rehearse. Word is he hit the Mutiny and vanished."

Perfect opening.

Gravy flashed an embossed brass card: *The Mutiny at Sailboat Bay.*

"I happen to be a member. We could go find him."

She made a face. "Why you got a Mutiny card? You one of those freaky swingers?"

The disgust impressed him. The Mutiny started as a swinger den before *yeyo* changed the game. "Nah, baby. I'm a private detective now. I go where the action is—just not that kind." He grinned. "I'm all about clean living. Whoppers and cocoa butter."

The Dolphins trainer glanced up. "Petey ain't at the Mutiny. Said he saw a vampire, freaked, and split. Heading to a party on Key Biscayne."

Gravy didn't rule out the vampire. He did appreciate skipping the Mutiny. More time inside Karanovo's ark.

He leaned to Dee. "I've never had the grand tour here. You wanna show me around?"

She looked for reasons to say no and found Juicy on an ice pack in polka dots. She also noticed Gravy wasn't wearing a shirt.

"I'll meet you at the elevator in five."

Six minutes later they drifted the first-floor perimeter, pausing every six feet for somebody to grab Gravy. The distraction let Dee scan the raised tables. Faces she knew from the club; others from the paper. Nobody met her eyes—busy doing what people do at tables.

Then she saw him.

Little Angelo Frusciante sat across the floor, elevated, perfectly placed to watch everything. Two Colombians in cowboy suits to his right. Two small, wolfish Cuban "teens" in chalk-stripe hand-me-downs and ratty tees to his left.

Little Angelo stared at her with dead black eyes under a too-tight bowler.

Dee refused to drop her gaze. Three giant Dolphins wedged in for Gravy's autograph and blocked the view. When they shifted, Little Angelo and his pair were gone.

Before she could process it, the players swore they'd seen Petey upstairs—maybe in VIP.

The second floor was marginally quieter. In the lounge, Gravy slid into detective cadence—but a sight nicked him first: a pin on a waitress. Another wolf dressed like a pharaoh.

"You good leaving your man upstairs? He looked hurt," he asked.

"Juicy is *not* my man," her eyes said before her mouth. "We grew up in Jacksonville. He started the band with my older brother, then I joined."

"Your brother—?"

"Donald. He was in the band, but now he's doing fifteen in Otisville. Wrong crowd, wrong time, wouldn't snitch, so they buried him. Somehow he's the only one who got buried."

"You get to see him?"

She stiffened. "Not really. They sent him far to keep him away from family."

He saw how it ate her. Wilson could turn that screw. *Not if I can help it,* Gravy thought.

"How'd Petey get involved?"

"Juicy's dad is a D.J. at W.E.R.D in Jacksonville. Knows everybody. We jammed with Petey. Hit it off. Juicy's dad worked the manager and got this showcase."

She watched him watch her. "Juicy's a really good musician. Great, even. He pulled this together. Without him I'm a waitress at Huddle House."

Hollywood taught Gravy to hear between lines. "They already trying to split you two?"

She almost smiled. "You could say that. How'd you know?"

"You're a star. Juicy or no Juicy. And I've been out west. I know the drill."

"They're a bunch of vampires," she said, not knowing how right she was.

"You got that right," he said. "That's what brought us back east."

She lit a fresh cigarette for the courage to ask, "You really... chase ghosts? Like Scooby-Doo?"

Gravy was getting tired of the Scooby-Doo comparison. "First of all," he said, "every famous detective had spooky business—Sherlock had the Hound of the Baskervilles, and then the Hardy Boys, Nancy Drew, Kolchak, Miss Marple, Fish on *Barney Miller*—"

Her face told him to downshift. He did. "World's strange. Most of the time it's smoke, mirrors, and narcotics. Not always."

Her eyes widened—not at him, past him.

Gravy turned.

Little Angelo stood three feet away. The "teens" flanked him—Doctor Fun and Cheryl, if Wilson's file was right. They jittered like kids needing a bathroom.

Little Angelo wasn't tall, but he was wide. Sicilian heavy—olive skin, black eyes, blacker hair. Dressed like Capone in July; the wool and Miami heat kept him in a permanent sweat sheen and fever.

He looked past Gravy and fixed on Dee like she was a steak.

Gravy stepped into his space. Dee watched the muscles in his back rise with his breath. The red suspenders bit his shoulders.

"Little Angelo!" Gravy intoned—a greeting dripping with insincerity. "Man, I've heard all about you. I like that suit. Is it wool?"

He let the question linger before adding, "Has nobody told you Eye-Talians about linen? Shit!"

Gravy was not trying to de-escalate.

Before the giant Italian could answer, glass broke and two neon peacocks started a shirt-pulling match by the bar. Bouncers poured in.

Little Angelo glanced. When he looked back, Gravy and Dee were gone.

The line at the door still wrapped the building. Gravy was impressed the club kept filling as Wednesday night prepared to turn into Thursday morning.

He hustled Dee toward the sidewalk.

"You seen him before?" he asked.

"Little Angelo? He's here all the time. Always with those little creeps. He spooks everybody. I think he's in with the owner."

Time to level. "Listen—Grits and I were asked to check this place out. Cops and Feds think something's cooking. Maybe tied to the Magic City Maniac."

They kept moving. "Is that why you came to see me?" she asked.

Gravy laughed. "No. I came to meet Petey Maymoore." He looked at her a half-beat too long.

She stopped. "Why do you keep looking at me like that? Like you're my dad or something."

He kept his voice even. It was tough when he thought of Her. "You remind me of somebody I knew a long time ago."

She smiled sly. "I get that a lot. I just have one of those faces."

They reached the Harley. She found a way to wrap herself around him, and they slid into the humid dark toward Washington Street. At her walk-up, she kissed his cheek and promised tickets at will call—like he ever needed them.

Gravy rode off with that bad feeling settling in. He was setting himself up for trouble.

And he was right.

10

CARLOS VAZQUEZ DOESN'T HAVE TIME FOR THIS DARN STUFF

Thursday, 7:49 AM
Collins Avenue, Miami Beach

CARLOS VAZQUEZ MOVED through the first floor of the stash house on Collins, slow and careful. Late Tuesday he'd off-loaded 155 kilos —just over ten million—at Black Point, hustled the yeyo into a van, then into this little two-story. He'd parked it neatly in the empty dining room, left six well-armed men to babysit it for a day, and gone home.

However ...

There was no yeyo. There were no men. There was just ...

"Aw... shucks," Carlos said, yanking his right foot out of a slick of red goo. Whatever was left of the six was now paste.

Manny Martinez offered a towel. Carlos waved him off, found a small reading-nook rug mercifully untouched, and scraped his sole clean until the squeak came back.

From this angle the dining room looked like somebody had heaved a water balloon full of blood into it. The splash had painted everything—the walls, the ceiling, the bricks of coke. The only dry spots were neat rectangles where the kilos had sat, islands of wood in a sea of viscera. Most of it had crusted, which meant the party happened closer to Tuesday night than this morning. Here and there, still-wet clumps told another story.

The blood didn't rattle either man. Carlos and Manny had rocketed up the Medellín ladder in the last few years. Violence was a time slot on the daily schedule.

What threw him was the missing corpses.

Killing was easy. Machine guns turned it into clerical work. Getting rid of bodies sucked time—chop, burn, carry, mop.

Kitchen and bath were clean. No bleach, no ash, no hacksaw teeth.

Carlos was doing math on weekly body-disposal hours when his shirt stuck to a wall smear. He peeled away and snapped, "Aw, heck!"

Manny eyed him. He'd been biting the question for days. "Carlos, what's with the way you're talking? Every time you get mad you sound like *Leave It to Beaver*. What's going on?"

Carlos looked tired. "It's Camila. She keeps giving me sh—... crap about how I talk in front of the kids. Says I swear too much, the boys are catching it. She wants us to blend in America. Says our kids can't sound like they're drug smugglers."

Manny nodded. He got it. Last week he'd told a killer joke about Olivia Newton-John and the Pope, which had the table howling. Everyone except his girlfriend.

"Forget that," Carlos said. "We've got bigger issues. We've got a hundred fifty keys that aren't here—and whoever took it ate our crew."

The word "ate" hung there and both men thought of Little Angelo.

"What about the fat Italian?" Manny asked. Word on the street was Little Angelo was sniffing around Karanovo.

"That fat monkey?" Carlos said. "He's too stupid to tie his own shoes, if he could see 'em. He couldn't find this house, and he couldn't get it out without us noticing. And no way he takes six of our guys."

"He's got those two retards," Manny said. "And if somebody told that fat meatball where the house was ..." He let it trail; Carlos picked it up.

"You think Karanovo wants in with the wops and uses Little Angelo as his hammer?" Carlos said. "That's not how the Frusciante play. They like quiet."

"That's Old Man Frusciante," Manny said. "What if Little Angelo's tired of the old way?"

Carlos nodded. It made sense. It also raised more questions, and all of them smelled like Karanovo.

They took the stairs to the second floor, slow.

"My cousin Gordo told me a story," Manny said. "About Karanovo. Says he worships a wolf. Egyptian god. Back in Russia, you crossed him, a wolf sign showed up on your house. Everybody knew you were dead."

Carlos rolled his eyes. "Gordo always talks nonsense. Last week he told me an Easter Bunny was at Arthur's Eating House. Said the bunny tried to pay in jellybeans and the bounced out the front door."

Manny remembered seeing Grits McCoy with Karanovo's daughter the night before. "What about the gringo? Grits McCoy?"

"The race car driver?" Carlos said. "I heard he's a detective now with that big black football player. They investigate haunted houses like the Hardy Boys."

"We saw him last night. Driving a race car with Nina Karanovo. And for once, the big bodyguard wasn't with her."

Now that was useful. It reminded Carlos that Victor and Nina Karanovo were never seen out in pubic without the big guy, and that they were never seen in public together.

Carlos also knew more about Grits and Gravy than he wanted Manny to know. He'd heard they lived like money, way more than two retired jocks should. Angelo couldn't pull a lift like this. Grits and the muscles, with Karanovo behind them? Different story.

Upstairs was a bust. They turned back down. On the second-to-last step Carlos planted into another hidden smear and slipped, grabbing for anything. His hand closed on a cable.

He steadied, looked at the coaxial cable in his fist. It had been painted into the wall, but he'd ripped it loose. He followed it up and saw a small camera, half-hidden in the ceiling, now gaping at him.

He tugged. The cable ran down the stair wall, turned right, stapled low above the baseboard, and disappeared into a pantry door that was locked from inside.

A few kicks and the door gave. Inside was a little closed-circuit rig, tidy and quiet. On the main panel, a symbol of a wolf dressed like a Pharoah.

"We put this in?" Carlos asked, knowing the answer.

Manny shook his head. "No."

Carlos dropped into the chair, rolled the footage back twenty-four hours, and watched. When the tape hit the part where his men and his yeyo left the story, his progress on profanity took a few steps backward.

He stood, stepped out, shut the pantry. He kept moving. Manny followed.

They blew out of the driveway. Manny finally asked, "So what'd you see?"

"Enough," Carlos said. "Enough to know we need a special solution."

"What's that mean?"

Eyes on the road, Carlos said, "I'm calling in the Brazilian."

11

MORNING MEETINGS

Thursday, 10:02 AM
Stone Detective Agency
80 West Flagler Street, Miami

THE THREE EMPLOYEES of the Stone Detective Agency gathered in the conference room to swap notes from last night and plan the day.

Before Eleanor Stone arrived, Grits finished catching Gravy up on his amorous adventures.

"You do realize you nearly had sex with a woman who probably *is* a werewolf?" Gravy said.

"Yeeesss, but..." Grits made a two-handed gesture that could've been arthritis or big breasts.

Gravy nodded, all sympathy. "The boobies will get you."

"Every time," Grits said.

Eleanor stepped in and started the meeting with her update.

"Before you got here this morning, I got a call from a man named Earl Mayfield. He says he has information on the Magic City Maniac."

She slid a worn manila folder to the middle of the table. Inside were yellowed clippings. One featured a shaggy man with a full beard and a flannel shirt under the headline: "Local UFO 'Expert' Accuses Dade County of Cover-Up."

"Normally I'd pitch a call like this," Eleanor said, "but he isn't a random nutjob. My father used him on a few cases. The most recent was in '78—looked like hippies torn up pretty bad, same kind of damage you two are seeing now."

Grits looked annoyed; Gravy looked like he was trying to remember something important that kept slipping away.

Eleanor headed them off. "Yes, he looks like a kook, but Dad trusted him. He's expecting you at 2:30, and he was adamant that both of you come. He's about thirty miles north in Broward, out by the swamp." She handed over an address.

Grits and Gravy shrugged. In their line, odd characters were part of the job.

Grits recapped his dinner with Nina Karanovo—leading with the fact she knew she was being tailed and knew all about Stone Detective Agency. He covered the Karanovos' arrival in the States, the family's wolf connection, her claimed reason for working with the Frusciante family, and the four tickets for tonight's showcase at the Midnight Miami. He conveniently left out the near-romp and the part where Nina mentioned Eleanor by name.

"I don't believe a word she says," Grits summed up, "and I know she's hiding something. But everything she told me... it all tracks."

Gravy ran through taking Agent Ronald Wilson to Little Havana for normal clothes, then shared his read on the Fed.

"There's something about this Wilson I can't put my finger on," Gravy said. "I had Arturo Santo's give him a once-over. He agrees with me. Wilson's off. Not just 'Fed' off—bad mojo." He didn't add that he was most worried Wilson would push Dee Wheatley into something dumb to help her brother.

He closed with Dee's performance and his trip to the Midnight Miami. The big takeaways: Little Angelo is an Eye-Talian and a fat creep, and a vampire was spotted at the Mutiny by Petey Maymoore—maybe Prince Wym, maybe not.

Any time that Austrian's name came up, the room tightened. After reading Wym's name at the library last night, Eleanor felt the same.

She decided to drop what she'd learned. "After I went through the folders from Pérez and Wilson, I did some digging on my own. Nothing solid on Karanovo, but I did find something on Wym Blutmesser."

She gave them the quick version of Eastern Alps Medical Supplies—moving in right after her sale to the boys, and Wym listed as C.E.O.

Grits and Gravy exchanged a whole conversation with their eyes. From their faces, this was news. "Thank you," Grits said, then pivoted. Wym was off topic for the rest of the meeting.

"Nina gave us four tickets to a benefit at the Midnight Miami tonight," he said. "Eight o'clock. A special showcase for Dee's band. Fundraiser for Mariel refugees. Paper says every local bigwig will be there, and Petey Maymoore might show."

Gravy stood, thumped an imaginary bass, and hummed the bassline to Petey Maymoore's "Funk in the Trunk."

"Gravy, I think we should bring Wilson," Grits said. "We can keep him close while we're busy. You watch him, I'll bring Eleanor to round us out."

Since last night Grits hadn't stopped thinking about how casually Nina had dropped Eleanor's name. He took it as a veiled threat. He wanted Eleanor close without spooking her.

Gravy waved them off. "You two figure Wilson and the tickets. Dee left me some, and I'm working on my own date for tonight." He went back to air-bass.

Eleanor and Grits traded a look. Gravy's "mystery dates" were always true mysteries. None had ever been less than a ten, but the ages and social status pinballed from elderly socialites to cashiers in their first week at Burger King.

Sensing the meeting slipping, Eleanor snapped it back. "At two, you two regroup here and head for Broward to see Earl Mayfield."

At the door, Gravy paused. "Don't think I've forgotten *The Love Boat.* I'll call after noon for an update." He hustled out, singing down the hall: "That ain't no junk... she's got funk... in the trunk."

Grits stood. "You ready to go?"

Eleanor blinked. "Go where? I've got a stack of paperwork."

"The paperwork can wait," he said, grinning. "You and I have a new car to pick up."

———

IN THE FOURTH-FLOOR lobby of the Midnight Miami, Little Angelo Frusciante sat on a couch and stared at the ceiling. The eyes, empty and distant, said "nothing upstairs"—but that wasn't true.

For months the young capo had pushed his uncle Sal's Miami crew to move into cocaine. The family was doing fine—gambling, prostitution, union rackets, fencing, pornography. With home video coming, smut would only get fatter—no more sleaze houses; people could watch in their living rooms if they had a VCR.

The Frusciante way had always been to go light on dope; it brought heat from politicians and Feds they didn't need when other rackets paid. That was the old way. And Miami didn't respect the old way anymore.

Little Angelo watched Colombians and Cubans rake it in and flaunt it—sports cars, speedboats, water houses, champagne hot tubs, blowing lines at dinner. And these filthy spics were animals —shooting each other in the street like the eggplants. No shame and nobody stopping them.

His middle path: let the Cubans and Colombians draw the heat and use the Frusciante network to quietly expand. The Feds would target the guys in Lamborghinis shooting each other in daylight, not the ones in the shadows.

He'd pitched it for months. The family didn't want to rock the boat. Then he found a kindred soul.

Victor Karanovo opened his office door and waved him in. Normally the receptionist ran this theater, but she always took a long smoke break when Little Angelo showed. In a rare display of grace, Victor didn't blame her.

Little Angelo stood; behind him were the reasons she left—his two Mariel maniacs, Doctor Fun and Cheryl.

Doctor Fun stood against the wall, eyes shut, grinning like a devil. Six feet in front of him, Cheryl—equally manic—threw a knife. It thunked into the wall two inches above the good doctor's head. The drywall was a pincushion.

Like their boss, both wore wool suits—bad ones. Too tight here, baggy there; no shirts or ties, just filthy tees. Doctor Fun sported Donny Osmond; Cheryl's just read "69" in giant print.

For months, Victor had courted the Frusciantes through Little Angelo—mostly to keep busy while he waited for the prophecy to ripen: light and shadows joining to rule all. Victor believed the time had come. But first, he needed the one man who could stop it out of the way.

He led them past the desk to three chairs set before a small screen. They sat without being asked. Golyam slid in silently and disappeared into a closet. The lights dimmed. A VCR whirred. Snow gave way to black-and-white security footage of a man dancing with three women. He wore a sport coat; something on the lapel caught the light and winked.

"Remember the jacket," Victor murmured.

More footage—drinking, snorting. A shot of one of the women driving a big metal syringe into the man's backside. The lapel kept flashing. In the dirtier moments, Doctor Fun and Cheryl whooped and smacked each other in the face.

The footage jumped—from the club to a living room. Six men with MAC-10s ringed a stack of white bricks—kilos of cocaine. There was sound now. Spanish. Colombians.

They were jumpy. A loud bang—like something heavy dropped. The men flinched. So did Doctor Fun and Cheryl, then they laughed.

A blur ripped through the room. Three Colombians hit the floor. Dark liquid pooled. Kilos scattered like a kicked anthill. The remaining three swung their guns wildly. A shriek of feedback from the mic. Another blur. Then a clean frame:

A thing stood center room—bodybuilder welded to wolf. The sport coat was on it; the lapel still twinkled. With both arms it hoisted a Colombian overhead, then tore him in half like paper. Blood and guts painted the room. Someone screamed high and thin. The tape stopped.

Doctor Fun and Cheryl cheered like the Dolphins won the Super Bowl. Little Angelo sweated harder.

Lights up. Victor faced Little Angelo. "As of this morning, I have claimed the approximately ten million dollars of cocaine you saw. Enough to start you on your own. Your uncle and your family need not know. By the time they do, you'll be too big to stop.

"As you've seen, I can turn a normal man into a killing machine. I'll give you protection and enforcement the cartels—and your family—can't match. You'll be untouchable."

Victor took Little Angelo's sweaty silence to indicate that he wanted to know more, so he continued.

"In the Old Country, when I wanted to give a person this power, the process was long and arduous. Messy. Bloody. Night. A bite. And then, to wait for the full moon."

Victor turned to his desk to grab something from it. When he turned around, he showed Little Angelo a large metal syringe, like the one in the video."

As he held out the syringe, Victor said, "First, I found a way to replace the bite." Then he pointed to a strange looking flashlight on his desk and said, "Then I found a way to have my own full moon."

A few quiet beats hit where Little Angelo should have asked for the catch. When he realized that the question wasn't coming, Victor said, "There is one man in our way. I need him eliminated. Once he is gone, I'll give you the address where the cocaine is hidden. It's yours, no strings—save one: take out this man. Today."

He held up a surveillance photo of Gravy Watkins taken at the Midnight Miami last night. To Gravy's right was the pretty little singer that Little Angelo thought about day and night.

The large Italian forgot the wolfman. He forgot about bites and the moon and whatever else Victor said. Little Angelo grinned, broad and sweaty, and nodded.

Before he could say a word, Golyam slid up behind him and stuck a big metal syringe in his neck. Doctor Fun and Cheryl squealed, grabbing the two remaining syringes from a table, and jabbed each other.

Golyam handed Victor the oversized flashlight from the desk. Victor thumbed a switch; it came alive with a sound no flashlight ever made.

The white light hit Angelo and ran through him, tearing everything it touched. He was exploding from the inside out. His last clear thought, before everything changed forever, was that maybe his uncle had a point about being cautious.

12

ITALIAN WEREWOLVES ON VESPAS

Thursday, 10:56 AM
Burger King
3601 NW 27th Avenue, Miami

AT THE EDGE of the Burger King lot—his current favorite, close by the airport—Gravy Watkins sat astride his motorcycle and worked through three Whoppers with Cheese. He'd slid in just before the 11 A.M. switch to lunch, not that it mattered; he was friendly with a young lady behind the counter who, in his words, looked like "a Cuban Vicki Lawrence." If he wanted Whoppers all day, he'd get 'em.

He wore his uniform: jeans, boots, red suspenders. Aviator goggles rested on his forehead. A silver dagger rode in each boot—souvenirs from the vampire Cadillac. As it approached its noon height, the sun threw a hard Miami sheen across his bare black shoulders.

The suspenders matched the paint on his new Suzuki GS1100,

cherry red. He had a gut feeling he wanted speed today, so he left the Harley at home. His gut was correct.

He took a bite, glanced down at the *Miami Herald.* "WHO IS THE MAGIC CITY MANIAC?" The piece tried for tabloid heat but landed soft, full of "experts" guessing Mariel refugees, Colombian hitters, lone-nut honkies. About as insightful as a stick of butter.

His mind stayed stuck on FBI Agent Ronald Wilson. Something about the man itched under Gravy's skin. Was it just Wilson circling Dee Wheatley? That didn't help, but there was something else. Something hiding in the open.

———

Grits McCoy and Eleanor Stone rode the elevator from the seventh floor down to the Stone Detective Agency's private vault in the basement at 80 West Flagler. Before they fetched the new car, Grits wanted cash.

They stopped at a steel door. Grits keyed it, glanced at Eleanor. "Wait here."

The door swung and, for half a second, she saw the rumor made real: a mausoleum-sheathed vault ringed by cement crosses, like someone had parked a small Catholic church under the building.

Two minutes later Grits reappeared with a briefcase and the grin of a kid with two dollars burning a hole in his pocket at a candy store.

Moments after, they shot out of the garage toward Prestige Imports on West Dixie Highway.

"What exactly is wrong with this car?" Eleanor asked, perched in a passenger seat padded for Gravy's frame. She felt like a toddler trying to sit upright on a leather sofa.

"Nothing," Grits said, carving lanes like he was back on the track. "But Miami's a new show. This car is too 1970s. That decade is over. I need something that says, 'Ladies, we're ready for the Eighties.' More current. More extravagant."

"A car that makes you look like an asshole?" she said, smiling.

He braked hard at a light, turned, and grinned back. "Exactly."

———

GRAVY BALLED the last wrapper and flicked it. Across the street at a gas station two kids sat their Vespas—he was pretty sure it was Little Angelo's boys from last night. Their scooters were not stock —dual tailpipes, slammed stance.

More important: both faces were a dog's nightmare—furred ears, velveted snouts. Wolf.

Gravy kicked the Suzuki to life and shot out, cut through four lanes of traffic like he owned them. Horns bellowed. He stopped nose-to-nose with Doctor Fun and Cheryl—full wolf, eyes yellow, strings of spit dribbling. One wore a cardboard crown.

"You Eye-Talians up for a race?" Gravy taunted.

The two Cubans bristled at being called "Eye-Talian," but recovered quick and threw their heads back in a duet howl.

"I'll take that as a yes," Gravy said, dropping the goggles over his eyes. His rear tire screamed. He blasted out. They followed.

———

PRESTIGE IMPORTS TREATED Grits like royalty. He was everything they desired in a customer—a national celebrity with a knowledge of cars and plenty of cash. Some customers paid in cash, but those were dealers and wiseguys demanding features only coked-up imagination could invent.

Eleanor watched from the lobby. From the look of it, he'd pre-ordered. So what was the holdup? She watched faces instead of words. Smiles at first. Then Grits' expression soured; the salesman went defensive, lips repeating the same phrase. Eleanor closed her eyes to tune her hearing.

"Lamborghini... Countach."

Then, just like that, Grits lit up. Heads bent together, conspiratorial. Nods. A handshake. The salesman ducked through a service door. Grits strode to her.

"Let me guess," Eleanor said. "He kept pushing the Countach, which ticked you off, until you figured out why—the commission. You asked the delta and found a way to make him whole."

His smile gave him away. "Well done, young lady. You should own a detective agency. Come on—let's see my new toy."

———

On NW 36th Street, Gravy opened up the Suzuki. Even with traffic he held eighty, easy. A stock GS1100 topped out around ninety-four; a best friend who'd driven Winston Cup meant no machine stayed stock for long. He kept a little in reserve for the pedestrians who hadn't planned on a werewolf scooter chase before lunch.

He snaked east, hopped the center line, punched gaps. An ancient 1920s Cadillac loomed head-on—driver in a chalk-stripe suit, Al Capone hat, wolf face. Gravy threaded the needle and wondered how far back Little Angelo was.

Intersection coming. Right to Little Havana—more pedestrians, more cops. Left to Liberty City—fewer pedestrians, fewer cops. After last year's McDuffie riots, the police had mostly abandoned it.

He leaned hard left.

NW 12th Avenue northbound, Gravy tried to buy some breathing room. He wanted to pick the ground for when this turned into a fight.

Behind him: sputtering two-strokes. In his mirrors the progression played like a flipbook—first the boys running their Vespas like kids pushing scooters, next the boys sprinting at inhuman speed with the scooters overhead, then a Vespa airborne and coming for his spine.

Impact. Metal clanged across his back—no physical damage, but the hit kicked the bike sideways. He fought the slide, saved it, and let it lay into a controlled skid.

Goggles off. He surfed the sliding Suzuki. They came at him faster on foot than on those hot-rod Vespas. The cardboard crown stayed glued to one head.

Gravy sprang, met the lead wolf with a right cross to the snout. A normal skull would've been soup. This one came out cartoon-flat, features pancaked like a frying-pan gag. The crown still perched on his furry head.

The second wolf came in switching fists and claws. The kid wasn't used to his new body, but with every miss he got better.

Gravy shelled up. He slipped and pivoted, fed back a kick or two—nothing. The crowned wolf closed from behind. Gravy back-kicked the knee. On a human it would've made a permanent greater-than sign. Here it buckled for a beat. The king would be fine in seconds.

Claws raked his right pec—four clean surgical lines. Blood welled. Gravy felt his stomach drop. He was in deeper than he liked.

He took inventory. Deserted intersection in Liberty City, two crushed corner groceries, a ring of tired shotgun houses. Escape meant dragging a family into this mess. Not happening.

He flipped back to buy space, dove across a parked car for

cover, rolled to his feet, and remembered the boot blades. Silver in each hand, he waited.

He didn't wait long. The crowned wolf heaved the car aside and roared.

Gravy shot low, rolled under a swipe, came up cutting, and laid the silver deep into the right thigh. The king let out a noise halfway between toddler and dying dog and sprang to a roof, clutching his leg.

The other wolf didn't blink. He booted Gravy in the gut and launched him ten feet. Gravy hit, bounced up. Lucky for him the feet were more man than wolf—no claws. Otherwise, he'd be dealing with a gaping hole in his midsection.

They squared. Gravy figured he'd get one clean try. He'd make it count.

The wolf pressed. Jab, slash, slash. Gravy saw the rhythm in the kid's hands. There—the tell.

He ducked the left jab, dropped into a squat, crossed his blades. At the punch's peak he snapped his arms up and open like scissors.

The silver sheared the forearm clean below the elbow. The hand and half-arm twirled end-over-end in the late-morning light.

The wolf howled—more pain than fury—stumbled backward, toppled a chain-link fence, and sat in a front yard staring at the emptiness where his arm had been. Seasick.

Gravy rose, wheels turning—crown-boy on the roof, angry and a little green; the one-armed wolf across the way, dazed. Time to go.

His Suzuki lay in a puddle of oil in the intersection. Maybe she'd run. Maybe enough to get clear.

He jogged. A sting fired across his left shoulder. Blood slicked into his waistband. He touched the wound, grimaced, and admired the one thing that had survived: the red suspenders.

He hauled the bike upright.

A howl rolled down the street like thunder.

He looked up into eight feet of wolf in a chalk-stripe suit. Little Angelo Frusciante had outgrown the vintage threads. A porkpie clung to his skull; furry ears poked through.

On each flank, Doctor Fun and Cheryl cackled.

"Good thing I had that third Whopper," Gravy said. "Looks like I'm gonna need it."

———

GRITS cut Eleanor through an EMPLOYEES ONLY door, back through offices to the service garage.

Eleanor had been raised on the old detective rule: your car should blend. This one would be the opposite.

Canary-yellow 1981 Ferrari 512 BBi. Triple-coat *Giallo Modena* over glossy black lower panels. Beige leather inside—the only sane choice under Miami's nuclear sun.

"I like the *Giallo Modena,*" Eleanor said. "Close to Duke's Mayo, too."

Grits blinked, impressed. "How do you know *Giallo Modena?*"

"I've got a fat payout coming when I retire," she said. "Maybe I want something loud to tell the Eighties I'm ready."

The word "retire" hung between them. Both felt the twinge.

A burst of radio shriek cut the moment—police band static— from Grits' Dodge across the garage. Grits had parked the Charger so the mechanics could look it over. A young man with an oil-covered jumpsuit sat guiltily in the driver's seat, hand half-off a switch.

Grits leaned in as the dispatcher's voice punched through.

"All available units, motorcyclist at high speed northbound

NW 12th Avenue toward Liberty City. Black male on a red motorcycle..."

Tires howled in the background. Then:

"...and he is being pursued by two wolfmen on Vespas?"

———

GRAVY STEPPED TOWARD LITTLE ANGELO. An Italian mountain of fur. Doors cracked open, then slammed shut. Liberty City knew when to stay inside.

Little Angelo ambled in Gravy's direction. The two smaller wolves paced him, throwing in giggles that broke into pained huffs. They'd let the big suit make the first move, then pile on like hyenas.

Gravy studied Little Angelo. This was the picture book—half man, half wolf, angry, powerful, higher and heavier than the man would be. So big he completely blocked the fact that a yellow Dodge Charger was bearing down from behind.

The Charger smashed into Little Angelo. He didn't go under; he went up—several full somersaults, then face meeting asphalt with a wet, final slap.

Doctor Fun and Cheryl howled laughter.

Grits had triangulated from the radio call and guessed the route. He'd guessed right. He braked to a stop beside Gravy, perfectly lined for a passenger to jump. Gravy slid in.

"Thanks, brother," Gravy said. "Gun?"

Grits reached right, handed over a Beretta. "Chambered."

They shot the intersection again. As they blew past the fallen Suzuki, Gravy leaned out, took one clean shot at the tank.

The bike went up.

"I don't want those Eye-Talians hanging around," he said,

settling back in. "Even here that'll draw cops." Having three more GS1100s in his garage made the decision easier.

Grits flicked him a look. "How bad?"

Gravy Watkins' body was special for many reasons. In addition to the incredible physical shape due to the former football player's continuous weight-training regimen, Gravy's body had an unnatural ability to recover from damage. He did not necessarily heal, but his body always returned to the state it was destined to be. Gravy once likened this ability to throwing a large rock into a lake: the water would be disrupted for a few minutes but then would return to its normal constant state.

He checked his chest. The pec was already pristine. "I'm okay now," he said. "If you hadn't shown up, they might've made it stick."

Grits nodded at the floorboard. "What's on your back?"

Gravy felt something snagging his waistband. He reached, pulled up the culprit.

Doctor Fun's left forearm.

Grits smiled. "You don't see that every day."

"You sure don't," Gravy said, and tossed it into the back seat like a towel into a hamper.

"As long as we're out," he added, "lunch?"

"You read my mind."

"Burger King by the airport. I'm starving. And have I told you about the girl who looks like a Cuban Vicki Lawrence?"

13

____

MERRILL MOMENTS AT MAYFIELD'S

Thursday, 2:29 PM
Earl Mayfield's Residence
US-27, Broward

WHILE GRAVY WATKINS ordered (and shamelessly flirted with Cuban Vicki Lawrence), Grits McCoy found a payphone and rang Eleanor at Prestige Imports. She'd wrapped the Ferrari paperwork on his behalf. He caught her up on the morning, then, when she complained she was stranded, reminded her she was holding the keys to a brand-new 512 BBi.

New plan: meet at his Key Biscayne place before the Midnight Miami showcase. She had a spare key back at the office.

Eleanor, efficient as ever, had already briefed Detective Pérez and Agent Wilson on last night and told them Grits had tickets for the showcase—they could sit with her and Grits. That tidied up the "who goes with whom" question.

———

AFTER LUNCH—AND one more pass at Cuban Vicki Lawrence—Grits and Gravy pushed the Charger north on US-27 toward Earl Mayfield. The place sat forty miles out, Everglades to the left of it, Alligator Alley over its shoulder.

On the drive, Grits wrestled with the talk he'd been ducking. Gravy's festering anger toward Italians, which, based on what Grits knew of Gravy's past, made no sense. However, when Gravy blamed a surprise red light on the "Eye-Talians," Grits knew it was time. Time for a Merrill Moment.

"Gravy, I am requesting a Merrill Moment with you," said Grits.

The two best friends had established a protocol for difficult conversations. When the stakes were high, they talked like *The Love Boat's* Captain Merrill Stubing would—square and kind.

Gravy nodded solemnly. "I'm listening."

"It's your thing with the Italians. You're running hot. I need you thinking straight, not mad."

Gravy's jaw set. "I hear you, brother, but *Rocky II*—"

"It stinks," Grits said. "We agree. But is this about *Rocky* beating Apollo, or about you not landing *Rocky III*?"

A few months back Gravy had read for a role—charismatic, muscular, black, just his lane. The "no" had poured gas on his Eye-Talian fire. He flicked his eyes left, right, searching for a comeback. Grits let it ride.

"Let's put this on the sideline for later," Grits said gently. "Right now—eyes on the prize."

Gravy nodded, and the matter was settled for now. They did what Captain Stubing would do in a situation like this one: focus on the matter at hand.

They turned off 27 onto a long gravel throat of driveway. Low ranch house. Cars rusting into sculpture. Random heaps of metal. The air felt damp enough to drink.

"This looks exactly like where a crazy honky would live," Gravy said, voicing both their thoughts.

The door opened. Earl Mayfield stepped out—older than the clipping, same beard, red flannel, overalls, green fly-fishing boots. Grizzled, yes, but the eyes were bright.

They climbed out. Gravy carried the canvas sack of silver—plus the werewolf arm, which he figured might serve as an icebreaker with a silversmith.

Earl came down two steps and studied them, then broke into a wide, honest smile. "Gentlemen, gentlemen. A pleasure to meet men who've fought the shadows and lived."

The warmth took them off guard. Both men felt a bit of shame for judging a honky book by its grizzled cover.

Instead of ushering them in, Earl set them at a picnic table on the porch, then reappeared with lemonade and a plate of chocolate-chip cookies. They were still warm.

Once each man had a cookie, Earl said, "Gentlemen, gentlemen, I've tracked you for years. Miami was a great choice for your move. Long sunny days to keep the bloodsuckers at bay. Of course, once you killed Count Dracula and claimed his fortune under the Laws of the Shadows, you knew they'd hunt you till doomsday."

Grits and Gravy traded a look—relieved he knew their file, embarrassed by their accidental inheritance.

"You're wondering why I called," Earl said. "The papers' 'Magic City Maniac'? I've been following it. I figured you'd be involved. You boys know your vampires. What do you truly know of werewolves?"

Grits laid out the last forty-eight hours—undead victims, killings off the moon, this morning's dust-up with Little Angelo and his pups. Gravy added Victor Karanovo's dossier and the family wolf sigils.

Earl listened, then reached for their bag. He drew a dagger, turned it in the light.

"Gentlemen, gentlemen, I am so glad that you brought these gifts to me. This is superb vampire craftsmanship. I believe this is from the House of Krenn."

He tilted the pommel into a sunbeam. A hair-line crane glowed.

"Krenn—German for 'crane,'" Earl said. "Old vampire family. Famous for stretching their necks when they feed—or when they are sexually aroused by other male vampires."

"Oh," said Grits and Gravy together.

Gravy muttered, "Explains the leather vests."

Earl went on. "These weapons were made for killing were-wolves. Silver's poison, but don't count on bullets and blades alone. Yes, yes, to finish a werewolf, you take the head. And don't make a habit of killing them wholesale. Many are victims who got bit and bent. Wound them, drive them off, save your silver for the clan leader. Kill the head wolf—release the innocents."

He paused, met both sets of eyes. "When you kill the leader... finish the job."

He mimed a throat-cut, then laughed lightly, easing the lesson. "Well, what do you think of my cookies?"

The porch became a classroom. Between sips of lemonade, Earl mapped the night country—his knowledge broad, a little wild at the edges. They could tell he'd spent many years focused on what occurs in the darkness, probably to the detriment of other areas of his life. This point became obvious when he strayed from esoteric subjects. From his periodic off-topic rants, Grits and Gravy learned Earl had very strong opinions on seemingly random subjects, including tomatoes as condiment, the inclusion of Alpine skiing as an Olympic sport, and the decline in quality of South American soups.

Then he slid back to the point.

"Vampires are old money—aristocrats, smug and blind to what's in front of their faces. Werewolves?" He snorted. "Hillbillies who hit the lottery. New money in Trans Ams and speedboats. They score big, never learn to keep it."

Most movie rules, he said, still held: a bite that doesn't kill will curse you; the full moon turns the whole tribe and makes them damn near indestructible.

One big difference. Silver bullets can kill them, but it usually isn't enough. You must take their heads.

Then Earl cocked his head like a strange idea had invaded his mind.

"You said you fought a trio in sunlight this morning. What made you sure they were werewolves?"

Gravy handed over the forearm. Earl's face tightened. "Indeed, indeed." He vanished inside and returned with a bulging notebook.

"Years back," he said, thumbing clippings, "I caught wind of something ugly. Vampires studying the moon." He saw their confusion. "Sun kills them. Moonlight is just sun bounced off a rock. It powers werewolves but leaves vampires alone. The bloodsuckers fiddled with moon rocks hoping to 'cool' sunlight—to walk in the day. They failed, but an unintended consequence: they learned to fake moonlight. Perfect full-moon frequency."

He tapped a page. "Rumors said the wolves stole that trick. Your story says those rumors were true."

Grits and Gravy both nodded. Daylight transformations. Full-moon carnage on off-nights. Pieces clicked.

Earl stared out at the sawgrass, thinking deep. Gravy watched him like a man on the lip of a question.

"Will either of you have the opportunity to explore this night-club—this Midnight Miami?" Earl asked at last.

"Tonight," Gravy said. "Tickets. No sneaking."

"We've got the building plans," Grits added, fishing the folder. Earl scanned, energized.

"Yes, yes. Here." He tapped the fourth-floor suite. "Two offices, secret passage between, and a concealed exit to lower floors. Father and daughter, I'd wager. Use these points to move unseen."

Then he set homework: find clan symbology—he could use it to name which wolf family had come to town—and keep an eye out for any odd light fixtures. "Moon machines will look wrong next to nightclub gear," he said. "Bulky. Purposeful."

Gravy's internal clock struck five. He stood and told Earl they needed to leave.

After sharing goodbyes, Earl stood silently and looked at Gravy. The prolonged silence began to make the race car driver very uncomfortable. When he could no longer take it, Grits broke the quiet. "Earl, how did you learn so much about werewolves?"

Earl's smile turned inward. "February '45. Outside the Ardennes, after the Bulge. I was sent on a special errand and met my first werewolf. The world never looked the same. Been studying the dark ever since."

He glanced at Gravy. "And if I recall, you were there too?"

Before Gravy could answer, Earl shook himself like a dog after a bath. "Gentlemen, gentlemen, it's already five o'clock. You've got a night ahead. We'll continue this soon, I'm sure."

He returned the canvas bag—lighter by a few pieces—and said it was past time they built their own kit. Then he hurried out with a parting gift: two gleaming silver revolvers.

"Six pure-silver rounds in each," he said. "Save them for the worst of it. If one of you is bit, do not let the other turn."

They thanked him and headed for the car. In the rearview they saw him waving, then shaping one last instruction with both hands:

"And remember—silver's not enough. You finish the job."

He drew a finger across his throat again and again, a grim little pantomime against the swampy gold of late afternoon.

Halfway down the drive, Grits couldn't help himself. "Gravy, you gotta let me try some of that cocoa butter."

Gravy tried not to laugh. Failed. Their laughter braided with the skitter of gravel as the yellow Charger pointed south on 27.

14

COME OUT FIGHTING

Tuesday, February 27, 1945, 0900 hours
Roscheid, Germany

IT WOULD BE an understatement to say the last few weeks for Corporal Earl Mayfield—and for the world—had been eventful. After the Allies turned back the German assault in Belgium's Ardennes Forest—the Battle of the Bulge—their momentum carried through the Siegfried Line. Mayfield's 11th Armored Division helped crack it and roll up a string of strongholds, including Roscheid here in western Germany. The end was finally visible.

The division had been granted a rare pause in Roscheid, but Earl knew it wouldn't last. So when Major Jeffrey Forbes sent for him, Earl assumed it was about the next push. He belonged to the 41st Cavalry Reconnaissance Squadron. Despite the "Cavalry" name, he scouted from a light tank. He was humble about it, but he was good.

Major Forbes, behind a makeshift desk, opened with questions.

Where are you from, Corporal?

Sir, Pembroke Pines, Florida.

Near Miami?

Sir, twenty miles north.

Are you a silversmith?

Sir, a silversmith and blacksmith.

Can you ride a horse?

Sir, yes.

How well do you speak German?

Sir, conversational, not fluent.

How well do you understand it?

Sir, very well—spoken and written.

Was your brother Sherman Mayfield?

Sir, yes, sir.

One of the POWs executed at Malmedy?

Sir, yes.

Do you hate Negroes?

"Sir?" Earl said, blindsided. He'd fought alongside the blacks these last weeks and respected them. It was not the question he expected.

"Corporal Mayfield," Forbes barked. "Simple question. Do you hate Negroes—yes or no?"

"Sir, no, sir."

"Corporal, do you like Negroes?"

Earl sifted what he knew about Forbes. The Major was known to be welcoming to the black battalions—too welcoming for some mess-hall whispers. Earl answered truthfully.

"Sir, I like anyone who wants to kill Krauts."

Major Forbes broke into a real smile—the man, not the rank. "At ease, Corporal. Have a seat."

Earl sat carefully. Forbes fished two glasses and a flask from a drawer. One burn of campsite bourbon told Earl he'd guessed right.

"Corporal Mayfield," Forbes said in an uncle's tone, "our official conversation has ended. Anything we discuss next did not happen."

Earl must have looked confused. Forbes gave a little hand wave that meant, "Just listen." Earl did.

"As you know, on December 17, during the push in the Ardennes, an SS unit executed at least eighty-four American POWs outside Malmedy. Your brother was among them." Earl nodded once—heavy.

"What you may not know," Forbes went on, "is that the same day, in Wereth, Belgium, eleven Negro soldiers of the 333rd were sheltered by a friendly family. A German soldier's wife informed on them. Another SS unit dragged the men to a field, tortured them, then murdered them."

Earl sipped. He didn't know why this part had to be off the record. Forbes made it clear.

"We've received word the Kraut and his tramp wife from Wereth, along with some other SS scum, are hiding in a hamlet called Hurenmaul not far from here. Our orders are to rest and prepare. An official mission of painful, righteous justice will not be permitted."

Earl saw where it was going. There were a hundred men with the same ache who were more qualified. Why him?

Forbes slid a folded paper across the desk. "You have a skill set we need. Given the proper materials, can you fashion what's on this list in the next few hours?"

Earl scanned the items—odd, one circled as "Most Important" —but all doable if supplied.

"Yes, sir," he said, keeping the paper when Forbes waved

him to.

"Sergeant Williams," Forbes said.

From behind the desk flap stepped the biggest Negro that Earl had ever seen.

At the time, the man was calling himself Ernest Williams—Staff Sergeant Ernest Williams of the 761st Tank Battalion, the Black Panthers.

Earl half stood, half saluted, and sat again, doing all three poorly. Sergeant Williams calmed him with a palm-down "easy."

"Corporal Mayfield," Forbes said, "this is Sergeant Williams of the 761st. You will report to him for this mission. I can't give you more. This mission is not authorized. If you're captured, you're on your own. This is your chance to walk away with no consequence, because this conversation never happened. But if you're going to walk, you must do it now."

Earl could feel Williams sizing him up. Fair—see how the kid handled pressure. Earl thought of his parents losing another son. What would hurt them more: losing him, or learning he refused a chance at vengeance?

"Sir, it would be an honor."

"On your way out," Forbes said, "you'll find a box with your initials. Materials you need. Finish the list and report to the 761st at 1500 hours with the items in hand. From there, Sergeant Williams will tell you what you need to know."

Earl nodded to Forbes, then to Williams, who returned it and stepped back into the canvas fold he'd come from.

"Corporal, you are dismissed," Forbes said, looking back down as if the meeting truly hadn't happened.

Earl knocked back the bourbon, saluted, and was halfway out the flap when he paused. "Sir, permission to ask a question."

"Granted."

"Please correct me if I'm wrong, but I don't believe Sergeant Williams was wearing a shirt."

Forbes cycled through bewilderment to amusement. "You know what? I think you're right."

At 1500, Earl walked into the 761st's encampment. The Black Panthers were an independent tank battalion—assigned out, not fixed to a division—and unusual for being almost entirely Negro. Segregation meant their own camp.

Awkwardness climbed Earl's spine: only white face in sight, toting a heavy box of oddments that threw off his gait. Otherwise, it was any Army corner—equipment being tinkered with, soldiers smoking or reading. A light-skinned man with a pencil-thin mustache looked up from a tank and called, "Sarge, he's here."

Sergeant Williams emerged from a tent, afternoon sun sparking off a monumental pectoral. He was indeed still shirtless. Boots. Olive drab trousers. Suspenders. Standard issue—if you ignored the lack of a shirt.

Williams nodded Earl toward the tent. As Earl passed, he noticed a soldier hosing out a small animal cage—the kind they used for circus tigers. It was empty now, straw clinging to the bars.

Inside, Williams pointed to a table. Earl set down the box. Williams inventoried quickly: an ammunition tin with twenty-four silver rounds—approved with a grunt. A gleaming silver machete—Earl was especially proud of that. Williams swung it through air like a man who'd done that before. Lastly, Williams checked the "Most Important" without fully exposing it, then nodded.

He handed Earl a pile of filthy civilian clothes. "Put these on."

"Sir—permission to speak?" Earl gagged a little. The clothes smelled like they'd lost a fight with a barn.

"We're off the books," Williams said, stern but calm. "Drop the 'Sir' and the 'Mother, may I.' I'm Williams; you're Mayfield. I'll tell you what you need to know, when you need to know it. No chatter. Put on the nasty clothes. Uniform over there. Dog tags off."

It made sense. If captured, he'd have nothing useful to give. It didn't make the stink better. As Earl dressed, Williams swapped his own trousers for a more worn pair.

Earl settled a floppy cloth hat on his head and looked in the tent mirror. He'd made himself into a peasant shepherd. Which was the idea.

Williams came up behind him, meeting Earl's eyes in the glass. "You're too clean. Face needs to match the clothes. Go cake yourself in mud. There's a hose outside."

Earl stepped out. The cage was empty; the man with the hose was gone. Earl made a fresh puddle away from the runoff and slathered on mud. Better too much than not enough.

Back inside, Williams was loading the silver into four older but well-kept revolvers, spinning cylinders with practiced flicks. "Private DeBarge!" he called without looking up.

The light-skinned soldier appeared. "Yes, Sarge."

"Package ready?"

"Yes, Sarge."

"Leave it by the bike."

Williams finished loading, then picked up a pump garden mister. "Close your eyes. Hold your breath. Cover your mouth. Pinch your nose."

Earl obeyed. A cool mist hit his face, chest, and—"turn"— back, then his crotch. When Williams told him to breathe, a faint tomato-plant smell hung in the air.

"What is that?" Earl asked.

"You don't want to know," Williams said, almost smiling. He handed the mister over. "My turn."

Sprays completed, Williams packed the four revolvers, the machete, and the "Most Important" into an olive-drab rucksack, then passed the pack and a German-issue canteen to Earl. "You carry the bag. And that's all the water we've got—go easy."

Out back sat a green BMW R75 motorcycle with sidecar—probably captured. Beside it, an enormous olive-drab duffel. Williams hoisted it like a bookbag. The canvas sagged; his shoulders did not.

He kicked the bike to life. Earl remembered Forbes asking about horses and decided not to ask. He climbed into the sidecar, and they rattled off into the fading late-afternoon light.

The first mile reminded Earl that he had no goggles. Grit sandpapered his eyeballs. "Sorry," Williams shouted over engine and wind, his own eyes shielded by aviators. "No spare. Use the pack as a windbreak." Earl hauled it up and shielded his face. Despite the noise and many bumps, Mayfield found the fresh air intoxicating and was soon asleep.

He woke to the engine dying and the smell of pine. Sun was a sliver in the west—call it 1730. They were at the edge of a forest, green even in February. He stretched.

"Light's wasting," Williams said. "Grab the pack." He walked the motorcycle just inside the trees, drew a machete from a compartment—not Earl's silvered one—and tarped the bike in camouflage. The giant duffel stayed on his back.

They moved through the forest—Williams sure-footed in the gloom, now and then swiping a limb, calling "log" or "hole." Night fell. Earl lost all sense of time. He glued himself to the duffel; it was the only thing he could see.

Just as he was about to complain he couldn't see at all, they stepped into a clearing, and the moon shouldered through the clouds.

It felt like a children's book. The forest hummed and sparkled like a living thing stuffed with elves. Grimm country.

"This is some real Hansel-and-Gretel shit," Williams said, eyeing the rising moon. "We're almost there."

Ten minutes later they looked down on a hamlet. Williams stopped and had Earl pass the ruck.

Williams distributed the tools: three revolvers for himself—one slid into each boot, and one tucked behind his belt. Earl took his revolver and mimicked Williams's belt move. The "Most Important" disappeared into the waistband behind the duffel on the giant black man.

Williams handed Earl a small wooden placard. In a moonbeam Earl read the inscription in German and translated aloud. "My name is Dieter. I am mute."

When he looked up, Williams had buckled a collar around his neck. Chains wrapped his wrists.

"What is this?" Earl whispered, the words bouncing off the trees.

"Shhh. Work with what you can find. You're Dieter, and you're mute. You're a shepherd or some shit and you've captured me. We walk into town, find a house with a red light, knock, you hand them the card, make the money sign, point at me. I take it from there." Williams rubbed thumb to fingers to demonstrate the money sign.

Earl was forming a nod when the duffel yawned.

"What was that?"

"What was what?"

"Don't 'what' me. The bag just yawned."

"No, it didn't," Williams said, deadpan. "That was my stomach. I was thinking about cheeseburgers. Now quit stalling. Let's go get some Krauts."

Earl opened his mouth to protest. He couldn't see how any of this got him the chance to kill Krauts. He could only imagine himself dead, and the men who did it thinking his name was Dieter.

"Just get me in the house," Williams said. "I'll take it from there."

And off to grandmother's they went.

The town sat on a hill with three roads like stripes. The top two were houses; the bottom held shops. Storybook, if the story ended with witches and children in the oven. Cloud breaks let moonlight pour over everything.

On the middle road, almost dead center, glowed a window of red glass, candles behind it—an oven door in the night. Earl pointed. "There."

"Great," Williams said. "Eleven minutes." Earl didn't know what that meant. Williams did. He was a living clock.

They didn't run, but they moved with purpose. As they neared the door the din of merriment grew. The red light meant what it usually means.

The two men stood at the front door. Williams and Mayfield looked at each other. Williams had the same expression that Mayfield had seen since they met earlier in the day. An expression of seething anger that was tempered by the cool and quiet confidence of its owner. Mayfield, on the other hand, could feel his heart start to race, its beat rising in his chest.

"Remember," Williams said quietly. "Hand them the card. Make the sign for money. Point at me. I'll take it from there."

The bag on Williams's back made a quiet growl. It squirmed.

With his hands bound, Williams banged on the door.

"That was not your stomach," Mayfield said.

"Three minutes."

"What does 'three minutes' mean?"

"Get the card ready, Dieter."

The door opened, and six sets of hands grabbed the two men and yanked them inside.

Earl Mayfield had never been inside a whorehouse, let alone a Nazi whorehouse, so he couldn't say for certain that this was one. But if he imagined what a Nazi whorehouse would look like, it wouldn't be far from this.

While the exterior of the house looked like a house, the inside resembled a saloon from a cowboy western movie. A bar. A piano. An upstairs balcony with women in stockings and garters hanging on the arms of scruffy men. The inside was lit by a combination of candles placed throughout and moonlight shining through large windowpanes on the second level on the western side of the house A few crucial differences between a cowboy saloon and this house of ill repute would include the large quantity of Hitler Youth graduates and more Nazi flags than were hanging in *der Führer*'s garage.

Guns snapped up—a dozen at least—aimed at Earl and his "captive." Fear helped him find Dieter. He raised the card. A blond man read it out, and the room laughed. Earl rubbed thumb to fingers and pointed at Williams.

The guns dipped. The crowd split for a woman in a red dress and a blond man in a shredded SS uniform.

Earl had never seen a washed-up whore, but this was what he would've imagined: obvious wig, makeup spackled onto a lost face, a red dress forcing her into a shape she used to own. He felt sorry for the seams.

The blond man kept an arm around her. He wore an SS uniform like he'd slept in it for weeks. Drunk now and puffy from nights of drink.

Earl's gut said these were the Wereth pair. Williams took a long breath that confirmed it.

The woman in red approached. Earl did the Dieter routine

again—card, money sign, point. She tugged the chain at Williams's neck and, in German, asked if everyone wanted to watch her "test" the black. The crowd whooped. Williams, in perfect German, suggested that would be like throwing a bratwurst into an empty beer hall. Louder whoops—except from the husband.

Earl wanted control. He slapped Williams and repeated card, money, point. The room howled. Red Dress laughed and pointed at Williams, so Earl slapped her too, then did card, money, point again. More laughter—except the husband, who slurred something ugly. Red Dress and Earl looked at one another and slapped the husband in tandem. The place shook.

The husband shoved Red Dress down, then dragged Earl by the elbow and Williams by the chain to the center of the floor. Four SS goons—also frayed—joined him.

"One minute," Williams murmured.

Earl fought the urge to speak.

The five Germans argued about what to do. Red Dress found her feet. The duffel on Williams's back grumbled and shifted. Guns lifted again.

Two goons leveled rifles while two more heaved the duffel off Williams's shoulders and plunked it onto the bar. The bag shook.

"When it happens, grab Red Dress and get her out," Williams said.

"When what happens?" Earl said in English. Dieter time was over.

A bright white light washed Earl's face. He looked up. The full moon cleared the windowpane.

Two huge, furred legs kicked through the bottom of the duffel. The bag stood on the bar. The thing inside tripled in size in a heartbeat. Canvas exploded.

A giant werewolf threw back its head and howled.

Earl dove onto Red Dress and covered her with his body.

He shut his eyes and heard screaming, gunfire, breaking glass, furniture splintering—and wet sounds, slicing meat, bone between teeth.

He heard Williams yell, "Get Red Dress out of here—and don't lose her!"

Earl dragged her toward the door. She didn't fight.

Outside, she broke free and tried to run downhill—wrong way. Earl yanked her back toward the forest entrance at the bottom road.

They both stopped dead. The houses on the bottom street were collapsing one by one. A Sherman tank was driving through them.

Behind them, an explosion; up top, another Sherman plowing the upper row.

Red Dress bolted again, but Earl caught her. She clawed for his face; he dropped her with a quick right to the chin. He'd never hit a woman, but he also didn't count Nazi whores as women. After two tries, he got her ample body across his shoulders and headed for the trees.

A man crawled from the wreckage—another SS uniform. He raised a pistol at Earl, but a wolf launched at the officer and devoured him in four seconds.

Earl found himself nose to muzzle with the beast, Red Dress still on his back. The wolf stepped in, sniffed twice, and vaulted away. Earl remembered the spray Williams had misted onto him. Seconds later came more screams and the sound of chewing.

Williams appeared, blood-slicked but steady. He nodded at Earl. "Almost finished," he said, pointing to the forest mouth.

At the edge, Williams said, "We gotta put our doggy down before we leave." He had Earl lay Red Dress against a tree, then bound her with the chains.

"You still got that revolver?" he asked. Earl showed it. "When he comes, fill him with holes. I'll take it from there."

Two canteen splashes brought Red Dress back to her predicament, and she screamed appropriately. Bait.

Williams and Earl stood on opposite sides of the tree, pistols out. Williams fired six into the dark. A naked man slid to Red Dress's feet—emaciated, bug-eyed, with four holes in his torso. Without fur, he looked stranger than he had as a monster.

Williams pulled him up by the hair. "We bagged this bastard last month on our first German visit," he said. "I saved him for something special."

He met Earl's eyes. "Hopefully you never need this, but silver alone won't do it. You have finish it."

He drew the silver machete from Earl's ruck and took the head cleanly. Earl finally vomited—long overdue.

When he could stand again, Williams had the "Most Important" in hand and passed it to Earl. A nearby ruin was burning. Earl readied the tool—his finest work of the day: a cattle brand with the 761st insignia, a black panther and the motto.

COME OUT FIGHTING.

Williams tossed the head and torso into the fire. Then, in a slow, steady voice, he said the names of the eleven murdered men of the 333rd. When he finished, Earl added, "Private Sherman Mayfield."

He pressed the red-hot brand to Red Dress's forehead.

A Sherman tank rumbled up. Williams unchained Red. He and Earl climbed aboard. Earl recognized the driver—another Floridian. Captain Cliff Stone at the controls.

Before they moved, Red Dress staggered up and screamed that they couldn't leave her there alone.

Williams's eyes brightened like he'd remembered something. He reached into the pack, brought out a round object, and tossed her the decapitated head of her husband. "Tell your boy all about it."

He slapped the turret twice. "Time's wasting, Stone." The tank clanked off into the night.

Away from the screams, Earl finally asked, "What was in that spray that kept the wolf off us?"

Williams smiled. "You don't want to know."

"No, really."

"Wolfsbane—diluted with my urine."

"You son of a bitch," Earl shouted.

"I told you you didn't want to know."

Earl switched lanes. "Why ask if I could ride a horse?"

"Because guys who can ride horses are cool."

Earl laughed too hard and too long at that. When he finally stopped, Sergeant Ernest Williams talked the rest of the ride about cheeseburgers.

That night began Earl Mayfield's long study of werewolves. He never saw Sergeant Ernest Williams again—until a Thursday afternoon in the summer of 1981.

15

IRISH SECURITY SYSTEM

T hursday, 6:05 PM
280 Harbor Drive, Key Biscayne

ELEANOR STONE CHECKED the scrap of paper on her lap to make sure she had the address right.

Normally, in a place like Key Biscayne, she'd have been self-conscious about her car. Her daily ride was a decommissioned-police Plymouth Gran Fury—great for keeping trouble at arm's length. Today, though, she was behind the wheel of Grits's brand-new, canary-yellow Ferrari, one she'd paid for—in cash—a few hours ago. Not her cash, granted, but counting bills out of a briefcase had been fun.

She passed the Nixon Helipad, ticked off numbers on Harbor Drive, and turned in. No guard gate. It figured—this was Grits McCoy's house. He probably had an Easter Bunny on a leash or something equally strange.

Walking to the front door with her garment bag and a small valise, Eleanor revisited the question that haunted her at odd moments: how could Grits afford a place like this? Yes, he and Gravy had bought the Stone Detective Agency and its real-estate holdings—cash, full ask. They were ex-pros, not paupers, but they weren't Rockefellers either.

She decided, again, not to think about it.

Her key turned. Inside was an open-plan first floor—stairs up, then living room and kitchen flowing to a wall of glass. Sun poured in. Whatever Grits's sense of home décor was, this wasn't it. Aside from the 50-inch projection TV, everything looked like it had come with the house.

The surprise was the cleanliness. She'd braced for a giant smelly dorm room—socks, beer cans, Burger King bags—yet the bar top passed a finger test. No dust.

Relieved, she draped her black cocktail dress over the back of the couch, set her bag down, and drifted toward the sliders, drawn by a view of Biscayne Bay and the downtown skyline. She cracked the door for a better look—and got one she hadn't planned on.

A young blonde stood there, topless, a beach towel over her forearm.

"Hi, I'm Patti from Daytona Beach," she said. "I'm Barry's girl-friend. I was getting some rays before my shift."

Eleanor got her name out and kept her eyes north of the equator. Patti from Daytona Beach looked like she'd stepped out of a *Playboy* centerfold. Before Eleanor could ask who the hell Barry was, Patti spoke again.

"Nice to meet you, Eleanor. A man stopped by earlier and left something for you and a guy named Grits McCoy." She pointed at the patio table, where two plastic-bagged garments hung from the umbrella frame.

Patti from Daytona Beach breezed past her into the house. Eleanor crossed to the pool deck.

Two dry-cleaned items, each wrapped and papered. A note was taped to one.

For tonight so you don't dress like a bum.

XOXO, Nina

PS – I included a gift for Eleanor.

Eleanor rolled her eyes and checked the clothes. One hanger held a black tux. She nudged the wrap aside and found the label: Borgonuovo 21—Armani's black label.

The second hanger held a dress. She peeled the plastic and tissue back and lifted a black evening gown—no label—into the light.

It was stunning. She'd brought a reliable little black number; next to this, hers felt like her Pontiac parked next to Grits's Ferrari.

She held the gown against her. From the hang, it looked like a perfect fit.

Grits McCoy stood at the sliding glass door at the back of his house. He looked at Eleanor holding the black dress against herself, trying to imagine herself in it. He found himself doing the same.

From the first moment he saw Eleanor, Grits knew that he had to deny any attraction or feelings for her. Grits firmly believed that romance and finance were two areas that needed to stay as far apart as possible.

Ignoring her physical beauty wasn't easy, but the situation was manageable. The hard part came in having to interact with her daily. Her charm, intelligence, and confidence exceeded her physical qualities. These attributes were the obstacles that Grits had yet to figure out how to overcome.

Grits decided to alleviate the budding sexual tension growing within him the best way he knew how: by opening his big, dumb mouth.

He quietly slid open the door and called out, "You know that you're welcome to change inside?"

She looked up. He was at the slider, watching her and the dress. She wasn't embarrassed; she knew the gown did her favors.

He mouthed "wow" at the tux, then, instead of saying what was obvious about the dress, he glanced down and found two shoeboxes she'd missed. He handed her the feminine one—inside, black stilettos that made his calves ache just looking at them. His box held glossy black oxfords.

"Did you do all this?" he asked.

She passed him the note.

Eleanor wasn't sure if he blushed, but he did a poor job of hiding a smirk.

"So how much fun did you have last night?" Eleanor said.

"Nothing too exciting. This is a case, you know. I'm a professional."

A pair of panties, caught by the bay breeze, skittered along the pool deck and twirled in the air. Both of them watched the aerial exhibition.

Eleanor raised an eyebrow. Grits said, deadpan, "I told Mama she's gotta stop using the clothesline when she visits."

"And who is Patti from Daytona Beach?" Eleanor added. "Did you not see her jiggle past you when you came in?"

"Patti from Daytona Beach? That's just Barry's girlfriend. She's one of the Mutiny Girls." He sighed. "Listen, we've got a real problem. That's twice a Karanovo's been inside my house in the last twenty-four hours without so much as a chirp."

He gathered the clothes and nodded for her to do the same. Back inside:

"I'm sorry your security system failed," Eleanor said, "but whoever's cleaning—"

She didn't finish. A small redheaded man—in a leprechaun get-up because he was, in fact, a leprechaun—popped from nowhere and started shouting at Grits.

"Where is it? Where is my gold? Give it to me! Give it to me! Give it to me now!"

His eyes bulged. Spit foamed at his mouth.

Eleanor looked to Grits. He wasn't scared. He was annoyed.

"Dammit, Barry," Grits said. "First, like I tell you every day, the gold isn't here. Second, it isn't your gold and you know it."

Barry's fury switched to OFF.

"Who's the lady?" he asked in a thick brogue. He looked Eleanor up and down, then met her eyes and waggled his eyebrows.

Grits spread the tux across the dining table. "Barry, this is Eleanor Stone. Eleanor, Barry the Leprechaun."

Barry did a jig, tipped his hat, and went back to eyebrow calisthenics. Eleanor didn't run, but she made sure to stand on Grits's side of the room.

"For reasons known only to Barry," Grits said, "he thinks I have his gold, which I don't. He shows up every day, we do this song and dance, and then I reset his clock for twenty-four hours."

Barry gave Eleanor a "you-got-me" shrug and blew her a kiss.

"Gross," she said, out loud.

"Drink?" Grits asked, heading for the fridge.

She shook her head.

"Barry, all I've got is Bud in a can. That work?"

"Sure, McCoy," Barry said. It was the first time Eleanor had ever heard anyone call him by his last name.

Grits lobbed the can. Barry snatched it, tipped his hat, and slurped loudly.

Grits patted the sofa. Eleanor perched.

"Barry's why the house is clean," Grits explained. "He shows up hunting gold and ends up vacuuming, mopping, doing the windows—inside and out. Washes and folds my clothes. Better than any cleaning service in Miami."

Barry paused mid-slurp to nod, then returned to his work.

"He's also my unofficial security system," Grits went on. "He pretends he lives here. Patti from Daytona Beach thinks this is his house. He scares off anyone who isn't a hot blonde."

A thought tugged at Grits. "Barry, where were you yesterday? We didn't talk. Someone's been in here twice since then."

Barry paused. "Would've been rude to interrupt when you were trying to fornicate with that woman in the pool last night."

Grits ignored Eleanor's look and was saved by the next revelation. "Other than her—and Patti from Daytona Beach—it's just been me and your new dog."

Grits and Eleanor traded a glance. "What do you mean?" Grits said. "I don't have a dog."

Barry sniffed the air like a bloodhound. "Sure you do. Don't you smell him?" He set his beer down, dropped to hands and feet with his backside in the air, and tracked scent toward the stairs.

"Barry," Grits called, "not now. Just hang here tonight and handle anyone who comes by. I don't have a dog. If you see a dog, it isn't a dog—it's something after your gold. Deal with it accordingly."

Barry snapped a salute, bounded back to the living room, and tossed off another jig.

Grits crouched and stage-whispered, "You can't be in here while the lady's here. You're creeping us both out. Go play in the pool."

Barry locked eyes with him and belted the first verse of "Danny Boy," spun on his heels, sprinted for the slider, and plowed into the closed glass. He bounced to his backside, stood, opened and shut the door properly, then started running laps around the pool, whistling what might have been an Irish shanty.

"The guest suite and bath are upstairs, right," Grits told Eleanor. "You can't miss it."

"I don't want any magical visitors when I get out of the shower," she said. "Do I need to worry about him?"

"Nah. Barry's good for hours."

They both looked over to the pool in the backyard. Barry was bouncing on the diving board. He had stripped off all his clothes but was wearing Nina's panties as a bathing suit. He executed a perfect cannonball into the pool.

They both showered and dressed in about the same time. Grits made it downstairs first, which worked out, because he got to watch Eleanor descend in the black gown.

This time, he didn't fight the look. You don't walk past the *Mona Lisa* without a pause.

He met her at the last step and took her hand. "Eleanor, you always look incredible, but ..."

A loud thud hit the back glass. They turned. Barry had his face mashed to the slider, eyebrows pistoning, still in his makeshift trunks.

The moment fizzled. "Looks like I've got competition," Grits said. "We should get going."

Barry's cartoon routine took the edge off whatever had been gathering between them. Still, Eleanor felt like she owed him a line.

"Don't worry," she said. "I'm not an eyebrows girl."

16

A PRINCE OF THE SHADOWS

T hursday, 7:21 PM
Midnight Miami
1555 Collins Avenue, South Beach

VICTOR KARANOVO SAT behind his desk, scanning invoices and fantasizing about the soon-coming day when this sort of small-time nonsense would no longer touch him.

A low "grrrr" rolled through the office. Victor looked up. Golyam was on his feet across from the desk, nostrils flared, growling like a junkyard dog.

A beat later, Victor felt it too—pestilence. "You can show yourself now, vermin," he said.

Something thin and pale peeled out of the rear shadows. The man's face had a soft, bony quality—like a gaunt society matron. Instead of his imitation David Bowie look—he hated that guise— he let rodent features dominate. Blond hair slicked back. Eyes both red and yellow. A contemptuous smile that bared elegant canines. The air of aristocracy—and the certainty you were beneath him.

Prince Wym Blutmesser.

Golyam barked. Victor flashed a palm—stay—and the big man went silent.

Wym was vampire royalty, a prince of one of the oldest houses. When the families wanted vengeance carried out with taste and terror, they sent Wym. Everyone in the shadows knew his obsession: the messy, exquisite deaths of Grits McCoy and Gravy Watkins—and, with their bodies cooling, repossession of the immense fortune they'd taken from Wym's line.

His obsession, but not his only assignment.

Wym, in a voice like a knife stropped on velvet, began, "Are you calling yourself Victor Karanovo these days, or are you calling yourself—"

"What do you want?" Victor cut in.

Wym ignored the question and strolled, talking for his own pleasure. "A clever strategy. You move your clan to a city with filled with sunlight. You ring yourself with Italians, Roman Catholics forever draped in crosses. You flirt with those legendary vampire hunters—Grits and Gravy." He tasted the names like something rotten.

Victor remained unimpressed.

"And then," Wym went on, "you turn humans into hidden weapons—the perfect killers—men who don't know they're killers until after the deed."

He stopped, smiling to himself. "I've followed your work closely. I watched each dishwasher progress on his path, from the first derelict to this week's Colombians. I hate to admit it, but it's... impressive."

Victor's face did not change.

Wym dropped into the chair opposite. "So impressive I made sure you got credit."

He produced a handful of Midnight Miami matchbooks and scattered them across the desk. Victor had heard about the matchbooks turning up on bodies and wondered how. Now he knew: Wym had gotten there first and salted the scenes.

"I also solved your scent—what you used to mark the victims and the cocaine. When I saw you were sending out a new dishwasher, I ran my own test." He tossed the late edition of the *Miami Herald*. Jennifer Barrett's photo stared up from the front page.

Victor said nothing. Wym finally reached his point.

"You stole our research—the power to make moonlight," the prince said. "I can absolve you. Settle your debt to my family without your blood being spilled."

Victor could hear how pleased Wym was with himself. "And?"

"During this weekend's full moon, when you are at the height of your power, you will capture Grits and Gravy alive and bring them to me."

The play was clear enough. With the matchbooks and whatever else he'd manufactured, Wym could hand the police a neat package that ruined Victor's Miami identity without exposing the truth—and destroy his plans for Saturday night. But for all his pride, the prince still hadn't grasped what Victor's work was pointed at, even with the answer right in front of him.

Victor decided to answer in a way even an aristocrat could understand. He flipped a small metal cover on the desk, tapped a recessed button.

Concealed fixtures around the office flared to life, pulsing pure white every three seconds. The light of a full moon.

Victor's and Golyam's bodies twitched and bubbled; lupine features pressed up under their skin. Wym stood quickly and leapt back toward the rear of the office where the video footage was viewed, fanning his coat to shade his neck and face. He landed beneath an air grate. He'd probably used the ventilation to traverse the building safely while there was still sunshine outside.

"My answer is no," Victor said evenly. "Come near me again—or touch my clan's work—and I'll drive the stake through your heart myself. Be gone."

Wym hissed and vanished into the ductwork. The patter of a dozen rats raced through the vents and faded.

"What time is it?" Victor asked.

Golyam checked his thick watch. "Seven thirty-nine."

"Wait by Nina's door. Bring her down at eight-twenty. Then await further instructions."

The big man left without a word.

Alone, Victor let the room settle. Dewayne Shelby had become a liability; that needed remedying. And after Little Angelo's fiasco yesterday, there was still the matter of Gravy Watkins.

Then a calmer thought: Wym's arrogance had blinded him to the true reason the Karanovos had come to Miami. A reason that should have been obvious from the beginning, yet one Wym could not comprehend through his mammoth hubris.

The prophecy. The coronation of the King of Light and the Queen of Shadows.

Grits McCoy and Nina Karanovo. Their marriage. And with it, the unlocking of the unfathomable fortune held by Grits and Gravy.

17

TOM TORPEDO

T hursday, 1:41 AM
Turf Pub
22 Ocean Drive, South Beach

As usual, Gravy Watkins nosed his Harley into a spot close enough to taste the neon across from Midnight Miami. He liked a quick exit. Tonight, he liked an even shorter walk—for his passenger, who was balancing on five-inch heels.

"Gravy, you sure about this?"

Sweetpea Castilla, in a white sequined ball gown, adjusted his crotch and tried to look casual.

"Sweetpea, you know you got it," Gravy said. "I wouldn't bring you here otherwise."

AFTER DROPPING Dee Wheatley earlier that same morning, Gravy did what he did most nights: he rode. For good reason—Gravy Watkins never slept.

After finding that his dreams were reruns of his life's worst moments—especially his last night with Her—one night in '67 he decided to see how long he could go without shut-eye and just ... kept going.

Cops all knew the football legend in red suspenders on roller skates—or lately, a Harley. The only thing they ever hassled him for was an autograph.

But this ride had a point. In the shuffle with Detective Pérez, a simple angle got missed: Deborah-Dawn Teats had a pimp. If she had a pimp, he might've brushed shoulders with the Magic City Maniac. So Gravy went hunting Daffodil Phil.

Ocean Drive gave him his first bite. As he rolled past the Turf Pub—a former English joint now serving a different cut of meat— the door flew open and two bodies hit the sidewalk: a Cuban in a dress and bad blonde wig, and a portly Irishman in a Hawaiian shirt. Sweetpea Castilla and Murphy O'Neill from vice.

Gravy killed the engine, swung off, and hustled over. In the doorway stood a tall, lanky white guy with a swimmer's build, wearing nothing but black bikini briefs and a sombrero the size of a billboard. The man was flanked by two bleached blondes in tiny jean shorts and even tinier sombreros strapped under their chins.

"I don't want any cops hassling my customers!" the man barked. "And if I see you again—"

The man stopped as he noticed the muscled man in red suspenders also standing outside this early morning.

"Gravy Watkins, is that you?"

Gravy squinted, then grinned. "Gary Parker? Well, I'll be."

They traded fives like they were celebrating a touchdown.

"It's been a while," the man said. "By the way, I don't go by Gary Parker anymore. You can call me Tom Torpedo."

"I can see why," Gravy said. "You got a minute?"

Tom Torpedo looked sternly at the two blond men in tiny sombreros. "My muses—stay." He ushered Gravy inside.

In the dim, Tom laid it out: he didn't want trouble with the cops, but he sure didn't want uniforms scaring off his crowd either. Gravy pointed out that bouncing two officers wasn't exactly risk management. Still, he told Tom he could likely smooth it—if they could talk somewhere private.

A few minutes later, Tom snapped twice. The muses slunk inside. Gravy waved Sweetpea and Murphy in with a quiet, "Heads down, eyes forward. Don't say a word."

They threaded through to the back while Fatback Band's "Backstrokin'" rattled the barstools. In a stockroom, two tiny-sombrero waiters reappeared with a pot of coffee and two cups, set them down without so much as a glance at the vice boys, and vanished.

Gravy poured. "All right. What happened?"

Murphy O'Neill spoke first, already hot. "We walk in, we're just looking. Dumbass here sits at the bar and starts putting out the vibe to some guy. The guy yells he's a cop. Sweetpea denies it, the guy yanks the chain and says, 'Then what's this?'—and he's holding Sweetpea's badge. This genius wore his badge on a string. Look, he still has it on!"

Sweetpea flushed and tucked the shield down into a thicket of chest hair.

"Sweetpea, you're a mess," Murphy said—not unkind, but not gentle. "I know you're in a slump, but you're gonna get us killed if you don't lock it in." He took a bracing sip.

Gravy looked at Sweetpea. Beneath the dress, beneath the wig, was a cop with guts and a clean ledger in a dirty detail. Gravy decided to prove he believed in him.

"I've got a thing tonight at Midnight Miami," Gravy said. "I need someone undercover I can trust." He pointed at Sweetpea. "I need you as my date."

Sweetpea started listing reasons it couldn't be him. Gravy cut him off.

"Listen. I need the best. And dammit, *Pinga Dolce*—you're the best."

Hearing his nickname in his native language lit something behind Sweetpea's eyes.

Gravy peeled off five hundreds and pressed them into his hand. "I need you looking right. I can't have the Miami elite thinking I'm chasing chicks with *pingas*. My reputation's on the line—" he paused for emphasis, "—and so is the future of my penis."

Sweetpea nodded solemnly, a man accepting a sacred charge.

———

THE ODD COUPLE hit the Midnight Miami entrance a little before eight. Gravy wore formal black slacks, black loafers, and his formal black suspenders. No shirt. His nightclub best. It worked.

Sweetpea brought his A-game. Fresh shave timed to outrun shadow. Chest waxed at dawn. With Gravy's cash, he'd hit a vice-friendly boutique for a white sequined ball gown and a sharp black wig that didn't scream K-Mart Halloween. Big fashion sunglasses to soften the angles. A white leather purse to match—and to ride shotgun over the bulge.

Most important, the confidence was back. Adam's apple and all, Sweetpea believed he was the hottest woman in the room. Somehow, it worked.

At will-call, Gravy murmured, "Keep the purse in front."

A uniformed attendant led them through the empty first-floor dance floor—rarely seen without a crush of bodies—past the second-floor DJ perch centered on the back wall, and into an elevator.

"Cocktails and hors d'oeuvres until eight-fifty," the man said. "Then we'll seat you and the show starts at nine."

As the doors slid shut, the attendant's gaze stuck to Sweetpea and finished with a come-hither eyebrow wave.

Sweetpea caught it and tried not to beam. He glanced at Gravy.

Gravy nodded, grinning. "Just keep that purse where it needs to be."

18

THE BALLAD OF
CATHERINE MELLENCAMP

Thursday, 8:21 PM
Midnight Miami
1555 Collins Avenue, South Beach

GRITS MCCOY and Eleanor Stone were already on the third floor, taking inventory of the crowd. For a new ownership group, the turnout impressed: councilmen, bankers, socialites—exactly the sort of Miami faces you wanted at a fundraiser. A handful of sharp suits they couldn't place read music-business by posture alone.

To kill time, Grits floated his Top Five *Love Boat* co-stars list for when—never *if*—he got on the show.

"...and for the fifth and final pick: the Mandrell Sisters," he said.

"Wait," Eleanor said. "All the Mandrells? Not just Barbara?"

"I hope so. The Pointer Sisters were on this season as Isaac's backup group. There's precedent."

"I guess we'll find out soon," she said.

She needed another topic and found the small Irish man in a green suit. "So, really—who is Barry? And why is he dressed like a leprechaun?"

Grits pondered his options. Before Cliff Stone sold the agency to them, they'd asked Cliff how to handle explaining their *real* work to his daughter. Cliff had said Eleanor would figure it out eventually.

But she still hadn't. Grits decided to be a little more direct.

"Because he *is* a leprechaun. And, in a way, we do have his gold."

"What? How does that happen?"

"It's...complicated."

"I imagine so."

"We've got gold that used to belong to him. So in that sense, it's 'his.' But we came by it fair and square—from someone else. I think they sent him to pester us."

The name of Prince Wym flickered through Eleanor's mind. She was on the verge of assembling a puzzle that made no logical sense.

Before she could press, Gravy Watkins arrived with his date. Grits did a double take—then the smile came wide for Sweetpea Castilla.

Eleanor, who'd only met Sweetpea a few times—never in drag—managed a polite smile. She wondered what Cuban Vicki Lawrence would think if she saw Gravy's date.

"Grits, Eleanor, this is..." Gravy stalled; they'd never settled on a cover name.

Sweetpea stepped in, voice smooth with new confidence. "You can call me... Meeeeee-shell."

Across the room, Detective Rafael Pérez and Agent Ronald

Wilson appeared. The wardrobe upgrade had taken: light-brown suit, dark-blue cabana shirt—odd on paper, sharp in person.

Grits leaned to Gravy. "Let's see if we can get Wilson to hit on Sweetpea."

The three men peeled off, leaving Eleanor alone.

"Dumdums," she muttered.

"Eleanor Stone?"

The woman's voice at her shoulder startled her more than she let show. Eleanor turned to find Nina Karanovo. Two instant notes: the girl was genuinely pretty—and she was wearing the same black dress as Eleanor.

Back at Florida State, Eleanor's father had hated that she joined a sorority. He thought sororities—and fraternities, for that matter—were just excuses for drinking and screwing.

Of course, he wasn't entirely wrong.

But he never understood the training value: a finishing school in psychological warfare against the most ruthless opponents alive —Lindas, Joans, Barbaras, Christines, Jacquelines.

The Lindas. They were the worst.

From that war, Eleanor learned the primary skill: not caring what other women said. On paper, simple. In practice, years of drills. Don't react. Don't even acknowledge. If the words don't exist, they can't cut you.

And if all else fails, sleep with Linda's boyfriend.

Nina approached. Up close, she read more Mediterranean than Eastern Bloc—maybe the Miami sun. She carried herself like royalty, but what kingdom? Head high, tasteful but generous cleavage, a practiced strut. Confidence, yes—but it was performance, not essence. Like a sorority girl she once knew. What was her name...

"Eleanor Stone, that dress looks better on you than I ever imagined it could," Nina said.

Eleanor ignored the barbed bow. "Thank you for the dress. I was impressed you guessed my size so well." Credit where due—the matching-dress ambush was a classic move. Effective, too. Not that Eleanor would tell her.

Nina didn't meet her eyes; she pinched the fabric at Eleanor's hip. "Yes. I was afraid it would be *way* too small for you. Way too small. I'm glad it worked out."

Then eye contact—up, down—like she was pricing a side of beef. "I must say I am impressed by your restraint. I am surprised you have not taken Grits for yourself. You seem...capable. You went to an American college. Like *Animal House.* Yes, you know your way around a penis. Perhaps it is him—maybe he does not want a woman of your...vintage?"

Eleanor didn't bite. Nina kept fishing. "Perhaps men are not your thing. No, that is not it. Maybe it's the black. Yes! Do you prefer the black? He can be your—"

"Catherine Mellencamp," Eleanor said.

Nina blinked. She'd expected claws, not a random name. Eleanor went on.

"You're right. I went to college—Florida State. I had a sorority sister named Catherine Mellencamp. I think her real name was Chastity, but she went by Catherine. Family had money, just not the kind that buys respect—bootlegging, plus a string of 'nightclubs' in the Panhandle—strip joints and brothels. Catherine wanted respectability. She also wanted a husband with his own family money so she wouldn't be stuck when her folks' fortune dried up—which it would.

She found her target: pre-med, father a doctor, grandfather a doctor. Robert Something the Third, but everyone called him Trey—blecch. Anyway, snagging Trey was easy. Marrying him was harder. Catherine was smart. She knew the real courtship was with the mother. So she built a character—the respectable daughter of old money. Catherine had spent her life around rich girls; the girls saw through her, but she studied their mothers and older sisters. She learned the walk, the talk, the pearls. She became the part."

Eleanor paused to read Nina's face—stone. She continued.

"Eventually Trey's mother invited Catherine over alone. House to themselves. The speech was straight out of a TV movie—family reputation, Florida society, blah blah. Then the briefcase. Fifty thousand dollars to walk away. Opened it, fanned the stacks—the whole nine.

But Catherine had rehearsed for that moment. She acted like a lady of lineage: appalled, insulted. Catherine even wore pearls so she could clutch them. Then a door opened behind Trey's mother and out stepped Trey. Catherine thought, *This is it. Triumph.* But Trey said, 'You should have taken the money.' He'd known all along. To him, she was always gold-digging white trash. No costume would cover it."

Eleanor stepped close. "I don't know your endgame, and I don't care. A word of wisdom..."

She leaned to Nina's ear, as if to share a secret.

"...you're not fooling anybody. And those two clowns aren't as dumb as they look."

They both glanced across the room. Not far away, Grits and Gravy watched "Michelle" chatting up a balding man in a tropical shirt. Sweetpea shifted his purse just long enough for Agent Wilson to notice the bulge.

Wilson recoiled like he'd seen a snake—which, in a way, he had. Grits and Gravy cackled and elbowed each other like twelve-year-olds.

Eleanor looked back at Nina. "Or maybe they are. Either way, good luck, sister."

She took Nina's face in both hands and kissed her on the mouth, then walked off.

Behind her, Nina called, "It makes sense now! You are like Velma on the Scooby Boo Boo!"

19

HEAT IN THE SHEETS

Thursday, 8:57 PM
Midnight Miami
1555 Collins Avenue, South Beach

SHORTLY AFTER ENJOYING Agent Wilson's reaction to Sweetpea and his *pinga*, a uniformed female attendant approached Grits McCoy, hesitant but determined.

"Pardon me, sir. Are you Grits McCoy?"

Grits slid on what he called his Autograph Smile. "Yes."

"There's a phone call for you. A woman named Amanda Poker. She said it was urgent."

Grits stepped into the coatroom, followed the cord to a receiver lying off the hook, and lifted it to—dial tone. As he turned to leave, Nina Karanovo blocked the exit. There was never a phone call. And there sure wasn't an Amanda Poker.

"Weren't you going to say hi to me—especially after last night?" Nina asked, adjusting the top of her dress to showcase cleavage a blind man could land a plane on. She glanced around. "Coatroom, huh? I've got a fur you can hang."

"I have no idea what that means," Grits said.

"Oh, Mr. Race Car Driver, I have a place you can park your car," she said, and her right hand swept north to his crotch as she kissed him.

To his surprise, he kissed back before his brain yanked the wheel. He eased her away. "Listen, Nina. The night's young. We've got plenty of time to catch up. I want to introduce you to my friends—Gravy and Eleanor."

Nina's eyes narrowed. "I've already met Eleanor. Boooring." She sing-songed the word, then added, "But I'd like to meet the mighty Gravy." She mimed placing a gun to head and pulling the trigger.

Before Grits could bark, she grinned. "Lighten up, Scooby Boo Boo. I'm kidding. Let's go meet your best friend."

Grits walked her over.

"Gravy Watkins, I don't believe I've had the pleasure," Nina said, offering her right hand like a debutante.

Grits was amazed at Nina's instant shift to proper manners, though Eleanor wasn't. Gravy turned on his LBF—*Love Boat* Face—and took both of Nina's hands instead of one.

"Miss Karanovo, you're even lovelier than advertised." He flicked a lightning glance at her bosom, then sent Grits two quick eyebrow salutes.

Holding her hands, he turned them palm-down, studying the onyx rectangle on her left pinky. The light caught an inlay—an Egyptian wolf with a scepter, the same image he'd seen on the staff's pins the previous night.

Gravy's eyes lit; the image finally registered. He raised his gaze to Nina's—smile ready, compliment loaded.

Instead: "The Opener of Ways."

Nina's expression curdled. She recovered, almost. Everyone had seen the flinch.

"Pardon me?"

"Wepwawet," Gravy said, still smiling. "The Opener of Ways."

An attendant arrived and asked guests to take their seats. Another peeled Nina toward the stage.

At 8:50 sharp, everyone was down. Grits and Gravy were ten feet from the stage, dead center, dates to either side. The three center tables in front were label brass—Grits and Gravy both swore Berry Gordy sat there, which made sense since Petey Maymoore was Motown. A rumor floated that Quincy Jones was in the building. Gravy also insisted a few DeBarges were at the table; Grits, no soul expert but not clueless, was pretty sure there weren't any DeBarges named Stilton, Gouda, or Brie. Eleanor shushed him before he could say so twice.

House lights dropped. Spot hit center stage. Nina Karanovo.

"Ladies and gentlemen, thank you for coming to the Midnight Miami. We are honored you are here for this wonderful cause." She leaned into the accent. "My name is Nina Karanovo. My father, Victor Karanovo, is the owner. Unfortunately, he will not be able to join us this evening."

She spoke on the plight of the Mariel refugees, then announced totals, tipping her hat to a large Motor City-sized donation. The spotlight swung to Berry Gordy; Grits elbowed Gravy and murmured loudly something about Berry probably knowing Aaron Spelling. Eleanor shushed them again.

Back to Nina. "Now, ladies and gentlemen, put your hands together for our featured performers... DeeLeon!"

Curtain up. The band hit exactly as last night: a fast, sleek "Ain't Nothing Like the Thing."

As the second number kicked in, Grits slid from his chair, calm as a church usher, and headed down the hall toward the restrooms. Past them, a plain door posed as a utility closet—Earl's "clandestine passageway." It wasn't dead-bolted. Grits popped it with his Mutiny card, slipped inside, and found the rail. Dim light from below was enough to climb.

Fourth floor: a hidden corridor stitched the two office suites together behind the walls. A thin blade of light showed at eye level —a peephole. He bent to it. View: behind the receptionist desk. Lobby lit, empty.

Left should be the smaller suite—Nina's. Right: the larger— Victor's.

He ghosted to the left-hand panel, listened, pressed. It gave. Inside was black as a coal bin; if there were windows, blackout shades made them rumor. He waited, then thumbed a penlight.

Nina's office was a wreck—boxes everywhere, desk buried, more storage than workspace. Two rolling racks shoved to one wall. He ran the beam along them. One rack: men's suits, shirts, a sprawl of men's dress-shoeboxes on the floor. The other: women's garments, with more shoeboxes below. He spotted yesterday's jacket and skirt. At the rack's front hung a black cocktail dress— the dress Eleanor and Nina were both wearing. Catty didn't cover it.

Time was burning. He let the boxes be and slipped back into the passageway, then eased into the larger office.

More ambient light here. A big desk sat on an elevated platform. Behind the chair, mounted higher, an onyx display box the size of a small safe. From the front, guests facing the desk couldn't miss it; anyone seated there would have it floating over their head. He lit it briefly: the same inlay as Nina's ring—wolf in a pharaoh's headdress with a scepter. Wepwawet. The Opener of Ways.

A simple hook held the front closed. He considered flipping it, then thought better. Too big to pocket, too obvious to move.

His beam skimmed the desktop. Centered was a large, odd

"flashlight"—wrong proportions, distended at the base. Earl's warning about lights that weren't quite lights rang. Grits picked it up. Lighter than it looked, but dense. He thumbed the switch. The device coughed like an old Chevy and pushed a white sheet of light that seemed to fill the room. He clicked it off. Good enough. The Karanovos worshipped Wepwawet and owned moonlight toys. He slipped back into the wall and worked his way to the table.

Eleanor Stone was enjoying DeeLeon. Not her usual record shelf, but talent and charisma she could spot at fifty yards. Dee had both. The other singer, Juicy Robinson, was perched on a stool and hiding behind sunglasses bigger than Sweetpea's. Unbeknownst to the crowd, Juicy had cracked his femur in last night's split disaster. A Dolphins trainer had dosed him like a healthy 250-pound linebacker, not an overweight 250-pound singer with undiagnosed diabetes.

Between numbers, Dee stepped back and conferred with the band, her body language all questions, no answers. Eleanor also noticed Juicy nursing a coffee mug like it was oxygen.

Dee returned to the mic. "Hey, y'all—our original plan was to have a special guest for this next song, but he couldn't make it…"

"He got snowed in," someone heckled from the back, and the room cracked wise. Berry Gordy turned to find the mouth.

Dee steadied. "But I don't need a special guest when I have my own Juicy Robinson. You might know this one. It's by Mr. Petey Maymoore—it's called '*Heat… in the Sheets.*'"

Gravy had been running that record ragged. Eleanor could live with most of it; however, the title duet—with vanilla soulstress Mayo Davies—made her want to stuff napkins in her ears. Unfortunately, she knew it cold. She glanced at Gravy—concern sat on his face like a parent at a school play.

The band opened. They stretched the intro; later she would

realize it was because Juicy missed his cue. The male voice starts with a spoken passage—a fake-out. After *"When I leave the streets..."* there's a beat, then a long, high note. Anybody can talk the talk; only a singer can land the note.

Juicy spoke the lines, steady voice, melting posture. "Before anything else..." Dee's eyes said what Eleanor thought: no way he hits it. "...you made me change..." Eleanor looked toward Gravy. He was gone. "...how I worked my game..."

Juicy wobbled. He finished the last words—"When I leave the streets"— even as he slid backward off the stool.

In the heartbeat before the note, a dark, muscular arm caught Juicy. Another snatched the mic.

"I bring the heeeeeaaattttt... in the sheets."

Gravy Watkins stepped into the spotlight, mic in his right hand, Juicy cradled in his left like an oversized sleeping child. Dee didn't miss a beat, introducing him between lines. Gravy carried the male verses clean, then ceded the center to Dee for the Mayo parts. When the trade-offs came near the end, he returned and locked eyes with her. He knew every word and hit every note. The room forgot to breathe.

They also forgot he was still holding an unconscious Juicy.

The place stood and roared. Gravy and Dee kissed—quick but loaded. They both knew it meant more than either of them wanted.

While the applause still rolled, Gravy murmured to her, "Do like last night. Hit 'em with the Prince song." He eased Juicy out of the beam, raised a hand to the crowd, then lifted Juicy's limp arm to wave, too. The band cracked into "Why You Wanna Treat Me So Bad." Dee sang like it was hers. A star got born in front of a roomful of executives.

After the show, the third floor flipped back to cocktails. The mood was bright; the networking turned serious. DeeLeon's stock had just spiked. Their manager—also Juicy's father—worked the room grinning like a cat who just cornered a mouse.

Gravy kept his head down, wary of stealing heat. A few execs made a beeline anyway. He used the moment to angle for intel on how to get on *The Love Boat.* No bites. Yet.

Grits and Eleanor stood with Detective Pérez—black suit, same awful brown paisley tie as yesterday. Grits brought him up to speed on Earl Mayfield. Pérez agreed to meet back at the Stone office after the shindig.

Grits was about to ask where Agent Wilson had slipped to when DeeLeon emerged. The flock descended—executives, press, admirers. In the middle: Agent Wilson. Grits' neck went hot. He and Gravy moved at the same time.

They arrived as Wilson, too loud, said, "...and if you can give me something, I can maybe help your deadbeat brother shave some time off his sentence." Loud enough for every ear in range.

Wilson looked up at Gravy. "Isn't that right, Gravy?"

Dee snatched an abandoned highball and slung it in Wilson's face, then marched to Gravy and slapped him.

"This is the guy you're working with? The bastard who made sure they threw the book at my brother when he wouldn't snitch? And now you two just happen to be here to humiliate me on the biggest night of my life? Thanks for nothing." She pivoted and left to a chorus of whispers.

As eyes tracked Dee, a deep voice rolled in behind them. "Grits and Gravy. I need to talk to you."

They turned to Victor Karanovo—hulking and grave—with silent Golyam a step behind.

"Alone," Victor said. Wilson was happy to take the out; Pérez followed. Eleanor held her ground until Grits and Gravy each gave her small nods.

She drifted just far enough to watch. Gravy's body language

went big and mean—shoulders wide, chest high. Grits, oddly, looked puzzled, like he couldn't quite square what he was seeing.

When the trio had some privacy, Victor spoke. "I want to meet with just the two of you. Here. Tomorrow. Six o'clock. We have a common enemy. It is time to bring together the light and the shadows to end the affliction threatening both our families." He turned away and added, almost as an afterthought: "...Wym Blutmesser."

Grits and Gravy traded a look. Same thought. Grits said it first.

"I could really go for a Whopper right now."

20

AN UNEXPECTED VISITOR

Thursday, 11:13 PM
Stone Detective Agency
80 West Flagler, Miami

HOMICIDE DETECTIVE RAFAEL PÉREZ had agreed to regroup at the Stone Detective Agency after the showcase to take stock of Victor Karanovo, the looming full moon on Saturday, and the still-murky identity of the Magic City Maniac.

Gravy Watkins peeled off with Pérez to secure provisions. He'd worked out a deal with one of his Burger King lady friends to stash a sack for "police use only." It was going to be a long night, and the power of the crown would have to see them through till dawn. After his awkward scene with Dee Wheatley, Agent Ronald Wilson did the smartest thing he'd done all week—drive Sweetpea Castilla home.

On the seventh floor of 80 West Flagler, Grits McCoy fished for his keys. Eleanor Stone caught his arm.

"The cleaning crew always leaves a light on," she whispered. "It's pitch-black."

Grits nodded. He slid the Beretta from his shoulder rig as Eleanor drew her .38 from her purse.

The door swung open onto total darkness—then the room flared, washed in a cold, perfect white, like a full moon had sprung to life inside the reception area. The light was so pure it burned their eyes for a beat. When their vision cleared, Grits and Eleanor found themselves face-to-face with a fully changed werewolf: Dewayne Shelby.

Grits fired four quick rounds into the wolf's chest. The beast rocked back as if shoved by a strong wind and kept coming.

"Eleanor—kill that light!"

Grits snatched the freestanding coat rack—the relic from Cliff Stone's day—spun once for momentum and cracked the wolf under the jaw. Dewayne toppled, sprang right back up, and roared.

The breath Grits bought was enough to get a silver dagger off his calf. He drove forward for a slash, but the werewolf seized him and raised him overhead, ready to tear him in half.

The glare made it hard for Eleanor to find the source. The wash seemed to come from behind her desk—the receptionist station to the left of the fight. She stitched three shots toward the brightest glow; the third smacked metal and something glassy. The moonlight died.

Dewayne hesitated—a fraction—and Grits jammed the silver blade through his right eye. The wolf shrieked, dropped Grits, and staggered. Half-blind and half-washed in afterimage, Grits still managed to put two last Beretta rounds into the thing's face. Dewayne collapsed, shrinking back to human in a ruin of fur and skin, one white penny loafer still clinging to his foot.

"Silver bullets?" Eleanor asked, breathing hard.

"No," Grits said. "We need him alive to find out who did this to him."

Three seconds later the sound of a straw finding the last of a shake pulled their eyes to the entry. Detective Pérez stood there with Gravy behind him, a grease-stained paper sack in one hand and a vanilla milkshake in the other.

"Did we miss anything?" Gravy said.

On the sidewalk outside 80 West Flagler Street, Pérez spoke to a throng of reporters as an ambulance took away the wounded and shackled body of Dewayne Shelby. On the seventh floor, the three members of the Stone Detective Agency took the conference room. Cheeseburger wrappers, empty fry bags, and sweating shakes turned the table into a crime scene of their own making. Eleanor hated to admit BK was the right call, but after the exhilaration of seeing her first werewolf in person, it was perfect.

"Let's run the list Pérez and Wilson gave us," she began. "Nothing falls through the cracks. The Karanovos first. Gravy, what did you say when you saw Nina's ring?"

"That ring had an Egyptian god on it," Gravy said. "Wepwawet. The Opener of Ways—opens the road for spirits to pass to death. Not exactly a werewolf god, but he's in the family."

"If you wanted a reaction, you got it," Grits said. "She spooked hard. How'd you know Wep-wa—whatever?"

Gravy shrugged, coy. "Spent some time in Egypt a while back." The understatement of the night, considering his role in the discovery of King Tut's tomb.

Grits added, "Same wolf was on a black onyx display box behind Victor's chair. You sit down with him, you stare at the wolf. And there was a weird flashlight—wrong weight, wrong sound. Flick it on and the room fills with that white stuff, just like what hit us here."

Gravy said, "I'll update our werewolf expert Earl and get his take."

Eleanor moved on. "Little Angelo?"

"Gone underground since Grits bounced him off the hood," Gravy said. "We'll see him Saturday night—for sure."

"The Brazilian?"

"Nothing," Grits said.

"What did we actually accomplish?" Eleanor asked.

"I'll tell you," Gravy said. "We skipped the confetti, but we *did* bag the Magic City Maniac."

"Who put him in our office?" Eleanor asked. "Prince Wym?"

"No," Gravy said. "This building's vampire-proofed. Crosses, crucifixes, the whole kit. Easier for a bloodsucker to catch a tan at the Vatican than walk in here."

It took a moment for Eleanor to realize that Gravy had very casually confirmed that Wym was an actual vampire. After seeing her first werewolf, it was not a long reach.

"What else?" Eleanor asked.

"Agent Wilson," Gravy said. "Something's off."

"Gravy, maybe you're taking this a little—"

"No." He cut her off, calm but firm. "I care about Dee, but this isn't about that. That guy's been holding out since minute one."

"I'm with Gravy," Grits said. "Awful convenient he ticked Gravy off and then skipped the one meeting where a werewolf just happens to show."

Grits leaned to Gravy. "Should we hit Gesù tomorrow? Haven't seen Father Johnson in a while. The Maiden might be useful here."

Gravy grimaced. "Not on a Friday. She's always crabby. Didn't even thank me for that Whaler I brought her last time."

Eleanor let that go right past. "So. What's next before you meet Karanovo?"

"Easy," Grits said. "Have our resident werewolf expert, Earl Mayfield, check his notes."

"And we figure out who leads this pack—and what the plan is," Gravy added.

"Where do we start?" Eleanor asked.

Grits didn't hesitate. "Tomorrow morning, Gravy and I pay a visit to this Dewayne Shelby and find out who made him a werewolf."

Gravy added, "But tonight, we'll go find the one person that touches everything and nobody's talked to."

"Who?" Eleanor said.

Grits and Gravy, together: "Daffodil Phil."

———

JUST AFTER MIDNIGHT, Victor Karanovo called Golyam to the Midnight Miami rooftop to review the evening. During the showcase, Golyam had slipped Dewayne Shelby into the Stone office and set the moonlight projector to trigger on entry. When Golyam found him, Dewayne was back in the kitchen washing dishes and still dressed in the blood-soaked sport coat and single white shoe. Best case, Eleanor Stone would be a midnight snack; worst case, the detectives would trace the Magic City Maniac to a felon-turned-dishwasher and be done with him. Either way, Dewayne was no longer a liability Prince Wym could play.

The rooftop was convenient for Golyam; his crate—the big man's doghouse—was up there.

After the report, Victor smiled. "My son, by this time tomorrow, our future will be assured with the betrothal of Grits McCoy to my daughter."

The "son" warmed Golyam, but he couldn't square the confidence. "What about the mighty black, Gravy Watkins? Tonight he showed he knows our lineage. He won't allow the union."

Victor's smile widened. For all Nina could do with Grits, Gravy had been the puzzle piece he couldn't move—until tonight.

"By this time tomorrow," Victor said, "Gravy Watkins will be dead."

21

THE DEVIL RIDES OUT

F riday, August 8, 1969, 12:46 PM
Stone Detective Agency
80 West Flagler, Miami

CLIFF STONE WAS PLEASANTLY surprised by his unexpected guest. In his line of work, surprises rarely leaned pleasant.

He sat behind his desk and studied the man in the visitor's chair. They'd first met more than twenty years ago in France, World War II—"official" operations and a handful of the sort that never make the history books, the kind with enemies better suited to monster matinees than to after-action reports.

After the war they crossed paths every few years. The man across from him had helped on a few odd cases—strange business no detective course would cover. Cliff could remember one time he'd sought the man out; the rest, the man had simply...arrived. Coincidence, Cliff used to think. He didn't anymore—especially not with the visitor appearing right before Cliff's next appointment.

Cliff didn't know how or why, but the laws of nature didn't seem to apply to this man. Every time they met, Cliff felt a little pudgier, a little balder, a step slower—and the big black man with the sunshine smile hadn't aged a day. If anything, he looked younger. The only change Cliff ever noticed was that the man's muscles kept getting bigger, though today they were hidden under a tan trench coat—the rain from the summer thunderstorm drummed the windows.

"So what brings you to Miami?" Cliff asked.

The man who was calling himself Ernest Williams—the same name Cliff knew from the European Theater—took in his old friend. Cliff was a touch heavier and certainly balder, but he wore it well. The pencil-thin mustache and dark suit lent him a David Niven sort of polish that worked with the remaining hair puffed over his ears. The years had worked on Cliff's body; his mind, Ernest knew, only got sharper.

Ernest considered how to answer. He couldn't share the real reason: a meeting with the Maiden, his adviser on the peculiar. The Maiden provided more than counsel—new names and identities when the old ones got too "hot." England had been productive. He'd been due for a change; the name Ernest Williams was now attached to a dramatic reduction in pagan sorcerers west of the Channel.

Sometimes the Maiden created an identity from scratch. Other times she borrowed the life of a recently deceased man who bore a startling resemblance. "Just one of those faces," Ernest would tell people who swore they'd met him somewhere.

"I'm in town on some business," he said, the coy smile just shy of a laugh.

"I bet you are." Cliff smiled back. "While you're here, mind if I run the next appointment by you? Might be a case for your... special touch."

Ernest had expected as much. The Maiden's summons usually came with work. "I'd be disappointed if you didn't."

Knowing his next client would arrive any minute, Cliff got to it.

"Arturo Santos is a major figure in the Cuban exile community. He got out just ahead of the revolution. Like most Cubans here, he hates Castro and the Commies with every fiber of his being. But Arturo's not just talk—he gets his hands dirty. During the Bay of Pigs, he acted as go-between for the government and the Florida mafia families, helped supply the boys with weapons. He's kept his connections with both sides, but he hasn't let the access corrupt him. Arturo's clean. All he cares about is getting rid of Fidel.

But that kind of profile paints a target. There've been threats and attempts, but Arturo himself is well protected—private muscle for years. He's also made himself 'Tío Arturo' to every Cuban kid in Miami. Wherever he goes, he's surrounded by family."

Ernest nodded along. He'd seen kingdoms rise and fall; he wasn't sold on the United States (he remained, at heart, a French monarchist), but Communism, to him, was a special abomination —human cruelty rendered into policy.

Cliff went on. "He thinks someone's trying to get at him another way—through his family. He's got five kids: four daughters, all married to good Catholic, Commie-hating Cubans, and a son—Luis, the youngest. Twenty. A little older than my Eleanor. Between us, the boy's probably spoiled like most kids these days and a little gullible. Arturo thinks some group got their hooks in him. I believe it. Coconut Grove is crawling with a new crop of bohemian weirdos. These damn hippies. The latest generation of useful idiots."

Ernest knew the term and the type. He'd spent the last two

years in London—busy with a coven trying to resurrect King George to reclaim the colonies, of all things—so he'd missed the Summer of Love, but the aftershocks had crossed the Atlantic. Cliff wouldn't be calling him in if this were only bongo-beating beatniks.

Before Ernest could reply, the intercom buzzed. The voice of Stone's other detective—his wife, Marguerite—came through, a hint of France still clinging to her words. "Cliff, Arturo Santos is here to see you."

Before Ernest could ask how Cliff wanted to handle his presence, the office door swung open.

Arturo Santos was a handsome Cuban, not tall, not short, nearer fifty than forty. Black hair flecked with gray, the tan of a man who spent time among his people. Navy suit, white Oxford shirt, gold-and-brown tie—like a bank executive from the '50s. Ernest took the wardrobe to mean serious business.

Arturo didn't see the big black man at first and started when he did. Ernest didn't take offense; the man's nerves were frayed.

"Mr. Santos, this is an old associate of mine..." Cliff began, then faltered. Ernest handled it.

"Mr. Santos—Ernest Williams. Ernest Williams, Jr. My father served with Mr. Stone in the war. Mr. Stone calls me in on unusual work." He offered a warm hand. "Pleased to meet you."

"Likewise," Arturo said.

Cliff led them to the conference table. When they were seated, he said, "I've briefed Mr. Williams on your background and your status in the community, including threats against your life as an opponent of Castro. I've also told him your general concern about your boy, but I want the particulars from you. Be candid. Mr. Williams' specialty is the out-of-the-ordinary. You may need to share something embarrassing or just plain strange. Tell us everything. What doesn't make sense to you might matter to us."

Relief softened Arturo's face. He trusted Cliff. From long experience with Latins, Ernest knew talking about a son's failings was no small thing.

"My son, Luis—good kid," Arturo began. "A little quiet. Four sisters will do that. He's always struggled to find his place, be his own man. Not athletic. Good student, not great. But the last few years he found something—writing.

"This past year he's spent more and more time in Coconut Grove. At first it was good—other writers, encouragement, instruction. He started meeting girls. Finally not scared of them. Staying out late. Not good Catholic girls, but still—things were going well. Until last month. Something changed.

"He started spending all his time at one place. The way he talked about it, I thought it was a coffeehouse or jazz bar—some waitress he was chasing. Then I saw the address on a slip of paper. Residential street. I went to look.

"Middle of the day, and I couldn't believe it. Not beatniks or musicians—hippies. Dirty hippies. Everywhere. The place was a commune. I made some calls, learned the owner's name— Cavendish Vervain. Sounded fake. I reached out to an old FBI contact."

Arturo's mouth tightened. "He called back quickly. Cavendish Vervain's real name is Charles Lilac. Chemistry professor in California. Fired for cooking LSD in the university lab. Also kept a harem of coeds and skimmed money from the science department.

I asked how a man like this could live so openly; my friend went quiet. Said he couldn't tell me more and hung up.

Two days later a package arrives—no return address. Inside were these."

He upended a manila envelope. Pamphlets fanned across the table. Ernest spread them out. Most were standard fare—END

THE DRAFT, MAKE LOVE NOT WAR. He'd seen the type in London.

But two things were different. First, the psychedelic art hid occult symbols everywhere—things you notice after you've spent two years hunting warlocks. Second, Cavendish Vervain's name and face were plastered all over—a bland white man with beady eyes draped in oversized Celtic robes, compensating for his uncoolness. The hair he had left he'd grown long—like a garden overtaken by vines.

Cliff lifted a leaflet. "Arturo, this word—what's it mean? I'm not familiar."

Arturo looked sick. "The word is vegetarianism. It means you only eat vegetables because eating meat is evil."

A loud crack spun both men toward Ernest. He'd snapped the arm of his chair without realizing it.

He smoothed his coat and asked, "What does your son say?"

Arturo didn't look any better. "I haven't spoken to him. That's why I called Cliff. The same day those pamphlets came—Luis didn't come home. A week today. I think he's at the commune. I can't prove it."

Ernest took a breath. Hippie propaganda soaked in occult symbols; an outfit pushing that Dutch-sounding V-word; a ringleader named for witchcraft herbs—Lilac, Vervain. It all stank of black magic. What he couldn't see was how it tied back to Castro.

"The package also had these," said Arturo as he pulled two more items from his inside pocket.

The first was a *Los Angeles Times* clipping about the disgraced UCLA professor, with yearbook photo of Charles Lilac. The second was a photograph of the same bland man in fatigues—standing next to Fidel Castro.

Ernest stayed put while Cliff walked Arturo out. When Cliff returned, he asked for Ernest's read.

Ernest pointed out the occult symbols in the pamphlets and the witch-herb names. The Castro connection he hadn't expected. Cliff had a theory.

"At first I couldn't believe it either. How could the FBI let a guy with those ties run around loose—let alone in Miami? Then I thought: say they busted Lilac at UCLA and learned about his Castro pipeline. He's in perfect position to cut a deal. The Bureau loves infiltrating radicals. As 'Cavendish Vervain,' he's a gold mine —kids, drugs, Commies. Forget infiltrating a group—he can build one for them. Feed them real intel when it suits, tell them what they want to hear when they need an excuse to move on an enemy. You and I know that's how the world works. No point explaining it to Arturo. To him, anything touching Castro is black-and-white."

As always, Cliff's insight impressed Ernest. It made sense. Still, something darker moved at the edges.

"What do you want to do?"

"First, find out if Luis is in danger. If he is, we get him out. If he isn't, we get him out anyway. Bring him home, let his parents hear from him. If he wants to drop out and be a hippie, he can say it to their faces. Meanwhile, I want to see what these folks are really up to. Maybe it's just pot and terrible music. I want to make sure that's the worst of it."

Cliff went to his desk, grabbed a manila folder, and handed it over. "I had my daughter Eleanor do some reconnaissance in the Grove. She's heading back soon to Florida State for her sophomore year—blends right in. Nineteen. Looks like her mother, so the boys talked plenty. She's a Criminology major with Bureau dreams, so I'm not worried about them recruiting her. Hell, she probably hates hippies more than I do. She got wind of a big party at Vervain's tonight."

Inside the folder was a flyer: LOVE-IN FREAK-OUT across the top, THE REVOLUTION BEGINS TONIGHT across the bottom, an address in between. More occult art. Admission required the flyer. Two were in the folder.

Cliff said, "No way a guy like me gets in. You and my daughter could. I think you and Eleanor should go, find Luis, and see what's what. Either way, you pull him out—and maybe punch a couple of stinky hippies on your way."

Ernest respected Cliff's confidence in his girl. If she was a Stone, she'd be the real deal. He liked the plan, with one change.

"I'll go in, find Luis, and get him out—no problem. One condition: I go alone." He lifted a finger to forestall the objection. "It's not about your daughter's ability. If she's a Stone, she's better than you think. But you should know—I've spent the last two years in England doing very off-the-books work in a very off-the-books way. If your girl wants a Bureau future, you don't want any record of me near her, let alone being seen together."

He let that sink in, then added, "And there's something else. For months I've felt a foreboding. In all my years I've never felt anything like it. Something dark is coming. It's no accident I'm here now, and it's no accident everything around Vervain reeks of black magic. Even if the FBI uses him, that doesn't mean he's walking straight. Working for them gives him license to do whatever he wants in plain sight."

Cliff frowned. He knew his friend was right. He'd remember this conversation five months later, when two FBI agents came asking after an Ernest Williams—Person of Interest in a dozen London murders.

"These kids dress strange," Cliff said finally. "You got clothes to blend?"

Ernest smiled. "I've spent two years in Swinging London. I can look the part. My only concern is if some hippie is dumb enough to bad-mouth cheeseburgers in front of me. Damn."

He arrived a little after ten on a hot, swampy Friday. The first thing Ernest noticed was the smell. Skunky wet weed, the incense meant to hide it (only made it worse), all of it steam-cooked by body odor. Hippie hygiene was one thing; pack a house full of them in a tropical August and it becomes its own trip.

"These damn hippies need to wash their butts," he muttered.

The second thing helped distract from the first. Boobies. Everywhere. For every long-haired boy, there were two young women shedding undergarments. Tie-dye tees and spaghetti-strap sundresses worked hard; a not-insignificant number went without tops. The bikini girls looked like prudes.

The London scene had been scanty, too, but the British girls had disadvantages—bad teeth and blotchy skin you didn't notice until you left nightclub lighting. The Poinciana Avenue crop had no such flaws. Grain-fed, fluoridated, sun-kissed—enough to make a man reconsider the U.S.A. He hadn't abandoned the divine right of kings, but a nearly nude sorority of coeds will make a monarchist think twice.

The men were shirtless, too, Ernest included. He'd dressed to fit in: red suspenders clipped to custom trousers sewn to look like they'd been cut from Union Jacks, white leather Chelsea boots. No shirt. Cocoa butter glow.

He worked the ground floor twice, then drifted out back—another crowd gathered at the kegs. He forced himself not to take a theatrical lungful of the humid night.

If word of a giant black man spread, he wouldn't need to draw more attention. He kept his ears open. Everywhere the same talk: Cavendish Vervain—how brilliant he was, how he knew the "real" workings of the world, how he'd ready them for the revolution, how special it was to be summoned. He was here, they said, but upstairs in his inner sanctum.

No sign of Luis.

Admission upstairs required being interesting enough to be

invited. Ernest could punch his way up and take the boy, but he wanted to see what else the man was peddling.

Leaders like Vervain always noticed another male orbiting the prettier planets. Jealousy and professional curiosity—they wanted to know the competition's tricks. Ernest picked his spot near a girl he recognized from the line out front. She'd introduced herself earlier as Crystal Blue.

Two kegs sat side by side. A paper on one read BEER, the other: BEER AND ACID.

Crystal Blue looked twenty, like the rest. Bikini bottoms and an Indian vest instead of a top. Blonde and sun-browned—like the Coppertone kid grown up and gone hippie.

She waved Ernest over and introduced him to her friend. "Ernest, right? Ernest, this is my friend Valencia. Valencia, this is Ernest."

"Valencia? Like the orange?" Ernest said.

Valencia stared a beat, then lit up. "Like the orange? What? No way! I mean—yes. Like the orange. Far out!"

She had a big smile, a glorious head of curls, and the eyes of someone under multiple influences. She held a coffee mug— Ernest had noticed mugs stacked by the BEER AND ACID keg.

She set her mug down, gazed at him, and made waxing motions over his chest. As her arms moved, fresh aromas wafted from under the poncho that appeared to be the only thing she wore.

"Whoa, Ernest—your aura. That's wonderful. I've never seen anything like it. The way it flows from your skin—your muscles. Oh, wow."

"That's just the cocoa butter doing its thing, baby," he said.

"No, it's more. Cavendish told me so. He said I could see auras, and I can use it to help when the revolution comes."

Perfect opening.

"I knew a guy in 'Nam who could see auras," Ernest said. "Didn't help him see Charlie sneaking up behind him before they cut him down. That's why I deserted. Didn't want to fight the Viet Cong—I want to fight the revolution."

Both girls breathed an impressed "ohhh." Good. Word would travel upstairs. In the meantime, he played casual.

"I don't want to talk about 'Nam. Let's try this 'beer with acid.'"

He doubted anyone could dose a whole keg. Suggestion would do the rest. And if it was laced, he'd survived warlocks' potions more than once.

They drank from mugs while Valencia kept the conversation humming—her style was to ask a question, then answer it herself with a wild *non sequitur*. ("Crystal Blue, did you go to high school here? When I was in high school I had a crush on a janitor. I used to stuff the toilet with garbage so he'd have to fix it. Then everybody thought I had bowel problems.") Between bits she testified to the greatness of Cavendish Vervain.

She was cute and entertaining. The problem was the gestures —every excited sweep of her arms released a new bouquet of funk from beneath that poncho.

As Ernest eyed the yard for a hose, a tall, muscular hippie approached. This one looked tougher than most. Moment of truth: fight or invitation.

"Valencia, who're your friends?" he asked. His tone said he hadn't decided which way this was going.

"Oh hey, Donald—wow, your aura. Better, but it's still really brown. It reminds me of the toilets at my high school," Valencia said. "These are my friends Crystal Blue Sensation and Ernest T. Bass."

Donald blinked, then looked to Ernest and Crystal Blue. "Donald was the name the owning class stuck on me. Now I'm Leaf. Nice to meet you, brother. Cavendish heard you left the

Army. He thinks that's far out and wants to meet you. He wants to see all of you, hear your thoughts on the revolution, man."

Upstairs, Cavendish Vervain had been expecting interlopers. Reports throughout the evening had singled out the giant black man in Union Jack pants and the blonde in the vest—especially with Valencia in tow, the easiest mark in his widening circle. He sent his main enforcer—Donald-turned-Leaf—to collect them.

Leaf eyed the big Negro warily; he could handle any other guy in the house, but this one was worrisome. The man's slurred agreement soothed him. Maybe he was almost as loaded as Valencia.

Leaf threaded them through the house. At the foot of the stairs, the black man slipped and fell on Crystal Blue. He helped her up, then toppled the other way into a bookcase. Leaf and Valencia had to haul him up the steps.

At the top, Leaf noticed Crystal Blue hadn't followed. No matter. Once they were inside, the show would begin.

Leaf shoved the pair into the room and threw the bolts—then wrapped them with a chain and clicked a padlock. No one would enter or exit without permission.

Ernest didn't know what to expect from Vervain's lair. The room was big—likely two bedrooms knocked into one. The king bed sat far to the right. The true master had been turned into a stage.

Cavendish Vervain stood at the back wall in a purple hooded robe scrawled with occult symbols—pentagrams, goats, triangles —like a Hammer horror costume.

A dozen very stoned, very pretty half-naked girls sprawled on the floor worshipfully. Several shirtless "guards" tried to look menacing and didn't.

On either side of Vervain, iron manacles were bolted into the wall. The set on the left was empty. The right held a young

Cuban who looked a lot like a junior Santos—white cult robe and all.

Valencia screamed his name—"Luis!"—with honest fear as Leaf grabbed her arm and hauled her to the empty irons.

Hands clamped on Ernest's arms. He wobbled, playing drunk. The stairwell pratfalls had a purpose—whisper to Crystal Blue to get out, topple a bookcase as cover, and sell the "loaded" act hard.

Luis shouted, "Leave her alone! She's done nothing. Take me. I'm the one you want!"

Both kids were shackled by the time Ernest met Vervain's beady eyes. The robe's sleeves bellied grandly as Vervain raised a stone-handled knife and declaimed like a ham actor.

"Hah-hah-hah! You fool! Did you think you could enter my house unseen? When will you capitalist pigs learn—"

Ernest tried to hold the man's gaze, but the robe kept pulling his attention. It was so familiar. A Hammer picture—Christopher Lee, but as a good guy for once...

"—and tonight, when I sacrifice this reactionary, the world will see the revolution—"

Two realizations hit at once.

First: *The Devil Rides Out.* He'd seen it at the Odeon in London last summer. Vervain's costume was a straight lift.

Second: Cavendish Vervain was a decoy. A puppet meant to distract Ernest from the real shadow he'd felt for months. Something dark was coming; this clown in a robe was just noise.

Ernest got angry. Time to close the curtain.

He shrugged off the two "guards" and walked toward Vervain. Leaf stepped in and ate a right cross that left him horizontal in the air—then on the floor.

Ernest drove a boot into Vervain's gut. As the man folded, Ernest grabbed the robe at the back of the neck and ripped it over Vervain's head. For a brief moment, they appeared to be in the world's grooviest hockey fight. Ernest spun him so his flock could see what was under the purple robe: boxer shorts. White with red hearts.

Whatever hold Cavendish Vervain held over these hippies was permanently severed.

Ernest faced the roomful of kids—stoned, wide-eyed, waiting for orders. He wanted to be mad but felt mostly sorry—gullible children lured into decadence with the promise of no consequences. He wouldn't waste the moment.

"Listen up, you smelly honkies. Look at this clown. This 'leader,' this 'revolutionary,' is a two-bit con. A fraud who used beer and drugs to see all your boobies and peddle his lies. And speaking of lies…"

He paused, let it land.

"…this is what happens when you start believing hippie nonsense like *vegetarianism.*"

He clamped one hand on the back of Vervain's neck, the other still full of purple robe, and hurled him through the second-story window. Glass exploded into the yard. The resulting shattered pelvis and vertebrae landed Cavendish Vervain in a wheelchair for the next two years.

The room was silent, eyes wide. Ernest knew exactly how to finish.

He pulled a fat wallet from his flag pants. "Who wants to go to the Bayshore Inn—drinks are on me!"

The cheer rattled the house.

A tide of hippies—led by a shirtless, muscular black man in Union Jack pants—hustled through Coconut Grove. Ernest kept Luis Santos within arm's reach, but the boy had no interest in running—home was the only direction he looked. Closer still clung Valencia, dreamy-eyed. Even with all the chemicals, Ernest could tell her heart had lit. Offering himself in her place will do that.

During their journey, Ernest explained to Luis about Cliff's involvement. Luis, red-faced, admitted he'd fallen under Vervain's spell—house of smelly delights and all. That ended last Thursday when he stumbled on a folder about his father. When he confronted Vervain, Leaf clipped him from behind. They'd kept him locked in the lair ever since.

At Monty's Bayshore Inn, Ernest found owner Monty Trainer, explained his sudden generosity, and slapped down a deposit that would cover the tab for hours.

He grabbed a pay phone outside where he could still watch Luis and called Cliff.

"He's fine," Ernest said. "One warning—he's bringing a girl. Your next case is getting her to un-hook herself from your boy. Whether he likes it or not, Mr. Santos may have a bride. Also, you got a convertible? They both smell like hot balls. It's terrible."

He almost hung up, then remembered the most important part.

"Tell Eleanor that even though I picked her out the second I saw her, she did pretty well. 'Crystal Blue' is a solid cover, outfit was good. But she's way too clean to pass as a hippie. Next time—smellier. A whole lot smellier."

He'd been expecting her. If she was Cliff's child, she'd be there. Her eyes and her nose—both her father's—made his job easy. At the stairwell he'd fallen "accidentally" onto her and whispered, "Eleanor, you're not fooling these smelly hippies. I'm going to make a distraction. Take your monkey ass home before I carry you out. Say hi to your mama for me, too."

"One more thing," Ernest added to Cliff. "I won't be there when you pick up Luis. And it may be a while before we see each other again. Next time I'll probably have a different name and a different life. But we'll see each other. Whatever my name is—you'll always be my friend."

The following Monday, Ernest met the Maiden beneath Gesù Catholic Church, just a few blocks away from Stone Detective Agency. By then the country was waking to the Tate and LaBianca murders. The Maiden agreed: Cavendish Vervain had been a distraction designed to keep them from stopping the coming horror—and the evil influence that came with it.

It wasn't the end of the fight, just a new chapter. While Ernest would spend the early '70s hunting down every Manson wannabe he could find, the Maiden developed a new plan to help draw out the true evil—and the real reason—that the man now called Ernest Williams had been granted a new life after his death.

And he would do it under a different name.

That same Friday night, as Ernest walked the Grove, a young man just north of the Florida line was thrown from his car when a front tire blew. He died instantly. His mother had passed months earlier; there was no other family. According to the Maiden, he looked a great deal like Ernest Williams.

His name was Ernest Watkins. His friends called him "Gravy."

When Cliff hung up, he told Eleanor what Ernest had reported. She had to admit she was impressed he'd spotted her in the crowd. She could count at least two dozen girls who looked just like her—though almost all of them surely smelled worse.

"How do you know this guy?" she asked.

Cliff chuckled. "Would you believe I fought with him in World War II?"

Eleanor took a long moment, then asked, "Dad...do you know where we can buy cocoa butter?"

22

———

DAFFODIL PHIL

Friday, 1:41 AM
Dade County Medical Examiner
1050 NW 19th St, Miami

BECAUSE OF PRIOR CASES, Grits and Gravy were already friendly with the night desk at the morgue, so they slipped inside without fuss.

They were also better prepared for their second visit with Deborah-Dawn Teats.

"I was wondering where you guys went," the undead street-walker said as they roused her.

Gravy handed her a crisp twenty. No small talk. "We're looking for Daffodil Phil. Where can we find him?"

She snapped the bill from his hand, studied the paper like she might grade it, then asked, "Why you wanna see Daffodil Phil so bad?"

"We think he can help us find who killed you," Grits said.

"Hmmm. I don't know about all that. Daffodil Phil don't like nobody in his business. He might get mad at me."

Grits and Gravy traded a look. She hadn't quite processed her... change in circumstance. One wrong sentence and she'd go slack-eyed on them, and that would be that.

Gravy squatted to eye level; his voice soft but direct. "Listen, lady, I don't want to be insensitive, but you're dead. You're on a gurney in a morgue. The only reason we can talk is you're stuck between here and the great beyond. Daffodil Phil's business ain't our concern. You are. Help us figure out who put you here so we can help you get out."

Deborah-Dawn sat up a touch and took in the stainless, the tile, the toe tags. No screaming fit—just a small, tired, "Aw, man."

Grits cleared his throat and rubbed finger and thumb. Gravy produced another twenty. This time the bill worked like intended.

"Daffodil Phil works out of a gay bar off Washington called the Tijuana Cat. Keeps a booth in the back. You can't miss him—wears all yellow when he's working."

Gravy nodded, slid her a third twenty—a charity he would not have offered a living lady of the night.

"Anything else about that evening?" Grits asked.

She pinched her chin, eyes drifting to Gravy. He groaned and peeled one more twenty. She yanked it and finally said, "Same as usual. Phil told me go to my room at the Banana Bungalow—Collins and 23rd. Only thing different was a German man outside my door. Said his friend was inside but nervous I was a cop. Gave me matches from Midnight Miami to show his friend I wasn't."

Grits and Gravy exchanged another look. Prince Wym's finger-prints—planting matchbooks to splash Karanovo.

Grits closed his eyes to summon the Maiden's instruction on sending a spirit back to sleep. Before the first step returned, the morgue rang with a metal "bonk." He opened his eyes to see Gravy palming back the twenties while Deborah-Dawn settled, eyes closed once more.

"Time's wasting," Gravy said. "She ain't going anywhere. We'll catch her later."

————

ELEANOR WASN'T sure the boys truly understood the word "gay." Not that they had anything against homosexuals; it just didn't compute. Grits and Gravy really, really liked women. Anything outside that lane slid off their brains—this in a city where, since the Mariel, half of Washington Avenue was feathers and eyeliner.

So when they headed to the Tijuana Cat hunting Daffodil Phil, she figured they'd define a gay man as either "a guy who just doesn't like girls that much" or "a vegetarian."

Two o'clock closing spilled a river of bodies onto Washington. It felt like a festival—horns, laughter, perfume, cologne—so the detectives in their evening wear blended in well; Gravy in black slacks and formal suspenders, Grits still in his tux.

They'd heard of the Tijuana Cat but couldn't place it. Flyers on poles steered them in the right direction. The first read "warm," the next "warmer," the third "oh yeah getting close," each with a cartoon cat in a sombrero. The last said "come on in now." (In their heads they corrected the spelling of "come" and inserted the implied "on in.") By it, a steel door with an eye slot.

Gravy knocked. The slot slid, took him in—suspenders, shoulders, and the wad of wrinkled bills in his fist—and opened.

They cut through the dark bar toward the back and were surprised at the attention. They were used to eyes on them, just not at this intensity.

"These guys must really like sports," Gravy muttered.

"No kidding," Grits said. "Guy on your left must love horse racing—he's got a bit and a saddle. That's dedication."

They spotted Daffodil Phil at the same moment: yellow polyester suit, yellow Oxford, bleached hair plastered in Brylcreem, acne-red cheeks and a thin brown mustache only a thirteen-year-old boy would dare in public.

They were already in the opposite booth when he finally looked up from a book of *Mad Libs*.

Daffodil Phil's eyes went wide, and he started to rise. Gravy's hand set him back down. "Easy, man. We want to ask about one of your girls. Deborah-Dawn Teats."

"With a hyphen," Grits added.

Daffodil Phil trotted out his pimp routine. "Man, who are you two jive cats to be axin' me, and—huh huh—where that bitch at? She be owin' me money, you dig?"

Both men leaned across and yanked him forward.

"That *woman* you put on the street's been dead almost a month," Grits said through his teeth. "We're trying to find who killed her. Start talking before I make that stupid voice go up a few octaves. Permanently." He pushed the Beretta into Daffodil Phil's lap for punctuation.

A large shadow fell over the table. "Gentlemen," a voice said, cool and stern. "We have a problem?"

All three turned. Tom Torpedo—black bikini briefs and a sombrero the size of a kiddie pool.

As Tom's torpedo hovered, Grits felt like he'd walked into a 3-D movie.

"Now the hat makes sense," Gravy said.

They released Daffodil Phil. The mack, emboldened, rattled off indecipherable high-speed jive capped with a triumphant "Dyno-mite!" He assumed Tom would back him. Daffodil Phil assumed wrong.

As owner of both the Turf Club and Tijuana Cat, Tom Torpedo tolerated the lowly pimp strictly as a future offering to law enforcement. With Gravy on the premises, the future had arrived.

Five minutes later, in the Tijuana Cat's kitchen, Daffodil Phil hung upside down over a double deep fryer, ankles lashed in a bull-rope lasso looped over an I-beam. Positive motivation.

Gravy held the rope with one hand and ate fried okra with the other. "I'm not a vegetable guy, but I gotta say—this okra's got something."

Grits, leaning on a stainless counter, grunted agreement around a mouthful. The okra impressed him almost as much as how fast Tom produced a coil of bull rope.

Daffodil Phil squeaked out more nonsense. Gravy loosened the rope just enough to drop him an inch. The fryer hissed. The pimp whimpered.

"Listen, you honky bitch," Gravy said evenly. "You're gonna tell me what you know about Deborah-Dawn's last date. Slowly. And in American. And if I hear one more 'jive turkey' or any reference to pork products or watermelon, I'm gonna let go of this rope and make you the newest appetizer at the Tijuana Cat."

English returned to Daffodil Phil along with his memory. He'd been approached by a big man—spoke English with an Eastern European accent. Wanted a girl new to town. When he named the price, the big man doubled it. Daffodil Phil knew nothing about a German, or anyone else close by.

And the big guy liked to talk—complaints about running every errand for his father and sister at a family nightclub; everything in his life revolved around the sister; the father only cared about her. The real reason they were in Miami was to see her married— family choices guided by some ancient prophecy. The bride would marry a rich man. Not just rich—some kind of king. The King of Light.

When Daffodil Phil finally ran out of steam, Grits and Gravy figured they'd squeezed him dry. They winched him away from the oil and set him down. The big man sounded just like Golyam, so they'd tied Karanovo to the play and also given them the shape of the family plan.

They let him pick at the knot on his ankles. As soon as he was loose, Daffodil Phil exploded into gibberish again. Gravy grabbed a frying pan and started forward.

"No," Grits said.

"Why not?"

"Because I want to do it," said Grits as he took the frying pan from Gravy.

Grits and Gravy deposited the unconscious Daffodil Phil in the outside garbage bin. Tom Torpedo met them in the alley; they thanked him—especially for the okra.

They strolled down Washington. Grits had his new bull rope slung over one shoulder.

"What was Tom's name before he changed it?" Grits asked.

"Gary Parker."

"Why you think he switched to 'Tom Torpedo'?"

"Probably 'cause of his huge dick."

"I was thinking the same thing."

Gravy popped another piece of okra. "Say what you want about vegetarians, they're onto something with this fried okra."

23

A TYPICAL VISIT TO THE HOSPITAL

Friday, 7:29 AM
Parkway West Regional Hospital
17290 NW 7th Avenue, Miami Gardens

BEFORE SPLITTING UP EARLY FRIDAY, Grits and Gravy set a time to introduce themselves to Dewayne Shelby. They wanted to hit the hospital at shift change—late enough not to spook anyone, early enough to miss any brass, especially Agent Ronald Wilson. Pérez knew the plan and agreed to run interference. Neither man was worried about the rank-and-file guarding Shelby; they trusted their own charm to carry them through to the Magic City Maniac.

They also reminded each other: bring Earl Mayfield's silver-bullet six-shooters and a couple of silver daggers. Gravy had grown fond of tucking daggers into his boots—practical in their line of work and, in bright sun, cool as hell. Grits added one more item: the moonlight projector left in their office. Eleanor had shot it, but he'd coaxed it back to life.

They rolled into Parkway West just before 7:30. Skipping the front desk, they took a back stairwell to the unmarked wing where the hospital hid high-profile or dangerous patients.

Dewayne's door was easy to find. The surprise was Detective Pérez and Agent Wilson parked outside it—and just as surprised to see them.

"What are you guys doing here?" Wilson snapped.

"We're here to see Dewayne Shelby," Gravy said. "What happened to security?"

Wilson strutted up, chin out. "We're the ones asking questions, you meathead. Now—"

He didn't finish. Gravy's right hand closed on his jaw and throat and lifted him off the floor. After last night and Dee Wheatley's reaction to Wilson, Gravy had no patience for the man's mouth.

Pérez threw his weight on Gravy's forearm and pried them apart. "We're trying to find out why our officers aren't here," he said. "There were supposed to be four on guard."

Grits didn't want the mystery of the missing uniforms to derail the reason they'd come. "That man in there is the missing piece," he said. "His sudden appearance is too convenient. We just want to talk to him."

"Good luck," Wilson rasped. "He's so doped you'd have to set his balls on fire to wake him."

"We'll take your word about his balls," Gravy said. "But you gentlemen are welcome to join us."

The hall was empty—perfect. They pushed into the room. Dewayne looked half machine, half man: wires, tubes, restraints. Out cold.

"What's your plan?" Wilson asked.

Grits held up the repaired lantern. "This. A full moon in a can." He thumbed the switch.

Nothing.

He rocked it back and forth. A thin hum, a puff of smoke from the base.

"It worked last night," he muttered, smacking the housing.

Wilson laughed. "Pérez, I told you these two were clowns—"

The lantern coughed, caught, and roared. White light flooded the room, pouring over Dewayne's face and chest. Everything went cold and silver, like the moon had risen indoors.

Dewayne sat bolt upright and howled. His skull and snout were already changing.

"Cut it off, man—cut it off!" Gravy yelled.

"I'm trying—it's stuck!" Grits fought the switch.

Dewayne tore lines and hoses free and wrenched one arm loose from the cuff.

Gravy stepped in and hammered him in the face, full power.

Grits wrestled the switch what felt like a week before the light finally died—but the damage was done.

"Do something!" Wilson's voice cracked. "Do something!"

"Shoot him like you did last night," Pérez barked.

Gravy kept punching. It wasn't helping.

"Grits—shoot him."

"I can't shoot him—we're in a hospital."

"You got a better idea?"

Grits yanked his Beretta. Two quick shots to his face.

But Dewayne sagged mid-transform. He looked like a guy who'd fallen asleep halfway through a werewolf makeup job.

"Silver bullets?" Pérez asked.

"No," Gravy said. "That would kill him. We want to know what Karanovo did to him."

"We've got silver on us," Grits added. "If he goes again, we use it."

The lantern sputtered to life on the floor. Moonlight bloomed.

Dewayne jolted, snapped fully into wolf. The howl that came out of him shook the walls—an injured bear with a bullhorn.

"Now what?" Wilson said, near hysterical.

Pérez grabbed the lantern and smashed it against the tile, over and over. "Whatever you're doing, do it now!"

Grits shrugged, drew the silver-loaded revolver from his waistband, and put three in the chest, two in the head. He held one back.

Dewayne looked perfectly human again—except for the seven fresh holes.

Wilson started to panic. "What are we going to do? You just shot a guy chained to a hospital bed! We're all going to prison—we're accessories to murder—"

Grits and Gravy were calmer. They'd seen worse.

"Don't get your panties in a bunch," Gravy said. "Earl said we just need to cut his head off."

"We're in a hospital—you can't just cut off someone's head!" Wilson shrieked.

"Sure we can," Grits said. "I already shot him in the face. Earl said we had to finish the job."

"Gentlemen, gentlemen—I'm so glad you listened about finishing the job."

Earl Mayfield stepped in, beaming like a proud papa. "Given the circumstances," he said, "let me handle this."

He produced a silver machete and took Dewayne's head off in one clean stroke.

Blood geysered.

Grits and Gravy high-fived. Wilson and Pérez made the noise normal men make when they see an old swamp man decapitate someone in a hospital bed.

"What do we do now?" Wilson wheezed.

"Now we get rid of the evidence," Earl said with utter calm.

He rolled out a big olive-drab duffel lined with plastic. Then he went to work: chop, toss, chop, toss. Dewayne's last burst of werewolf strength had helpfully snapped the shackles, so there was no hardware to fight. Torso and head went in. Earl balled the sheets, swabbed the worst of the spray off the walls, stuffed the linens in, kicked the zipper home.

Forty seconds, tops.

"Mind carrying the bag?" he asked Gravy.

"Not at all." Gravy slung it over a shoulder like a gym sack.

"And now what?" Wilson asked.

Earl smiled. "Now we get the hell out of here."

They stepped into the hall and ran into a stern older Cuban.

"Arturo Santos," Grits and Gravy said together.

"You know Arturo too? Very good—he's my ride," Earl said, breezing past.

"We need to talk," Arturo said, falling in with the fast walk.

"No shit," Gravy said.

Arturo said, "Meet us in ten minutes at the S&S Diner."

At the Charger, Gravy popped the trunk and dropped the duffel. He climbed in. Grits fired the engine.

"If Wilson was part of the setup, he hid it well. Plus, our portable moon didn't affect him," said Grits.

"Yeah," said Gravy, "but he's still up to something. I can feel in my gut."

Grits nodded in agreement but then quickly changed to the subject to S&S Diner.

"I don't know much," Grits said, "but this feels like a two-two-two-two morning."

"You got that right," said Gravy.

24

THE ENEMY OF MY
ENEMY IS A WEREWOLF

Friday, 8:41 AM
S&S Diner
1757 NE 2nd Avenue, Miami

IT WASN'T BURGER KING, but the S&S Diner's 2-2-2-2 special—two eggs, two pancakes, two strips of bacon, two sausage links—had Grits and Gravy in rare spirits as they slid into the booth across from Earl Mayfield and Arturo Santos.

Detective Pérez and Agent Wilson had a booth to themselves. Two untouched coffees. Two thousand-yard stares. Their brains were still circling the felonies they'd just assisted.

After Grits and Gravy finished ordering their second 2-2-2-2, it was time to get down to business.

"All right, Arturo," Grits said, "let's start with Earl."

"Yeah, Arturo," Gravy added, then, in his best Ricky Ricardo: "You gots some 'splaining to do."

Arturo didn't blink.

Grits persisted. "C'mon—that was pretty good. Give the man some credit."

"That was actually pretty good," Earl murmured.

"I've heard worse," Arturo allowed, a thin smile cracking his face.

Ice broken, Grits leaned in. "How'd you meet up with Earl?"

Arturo's face went back to stone. "Last evening I received a call from an underworld contact. Two pieces of news. First, our werewolf friend in your trunk wasn't only a killer—Karanovo used him to take a Colombian stash house and steal ten million in cocaine."

Grits and Gravy hadn't heard that one. Across the room, Pérez and Wilson stopped pretending not to listen.

"Second," Arturo continued, "he told me Earl Mayfield was in imminent danger. He gave me Earl's address and explained Earl's connection to you. I went and removed him—willingly—from his home."

"And the contact?" Gravy asked.

"I know him by another name," Arturo said, "but you know him as Prince Wym Blutmesser."

He pronounced it like a Wehrmacht colonel. Grits and Gravy flinched.

"You can just stick with 'Prince Wym,'" Gravy said.

Arturo went on. "My role requires relationships with many groups, criminal or otherwise. Since you arrived, those relationships have expanded into... stranger circles. The Soviet arms dealer arriving in Miami was of great interest to me. Though I'm fond of you both, my conversations with this vampire increased. From his questions, it was clear he saw Karanovo as a tool to use against you—to weaken or distract. From those talks I've learned something else: your feud with him must be resolved in a very specific way."

"The Laws of the Shadows," Grits said. "We've read them. Like instructions in Martian to build a submarine."

Earl added, "Convoluted but thorough. Nothing about tomatoes, however."

"In short," Gravy said, "they can't Pearl Harbor us—but they want us to die screaming."

Arturo nodded. "That sounds correct. But something changed in the last twenty-four hours. The fact that Prince Wym went out of his way to save Earl's life is important. Not benevolence—calculation. He believes you need Earl to succeed. Which means he's changing his approach to you and to Karanovo.

Before, he saw Karanovo as his tool against you. No longer. Now he thinks you're going to lose to Karanovo."

The table dimmed. As much as they hated Wym, they respected his tactics. If he'd moved his bet, they'd misjudged something.

Earl tried to buoy them. "Gentlemen, gentlemen, don't be so glum. This doesn't mean you're finished. You recovered that moonlight device. Any Egyptian symbols?"

"They're hot for Wepwawet," Gravy said. "Nina wore him, and Grits found a box in Karanovo's office with the same dog-in-a-pharaoh-hat."

Earl winced. "The Neuri. Oldest documented werewolf clan."

"If they're so old, how come there aren't more of them?" Gravy asked.

"You said there's a father and daughter—no mother?" Earl said. They nodded. "Maybe the mother was the true root. Her loss would gut the clan. Might be why they came here to rebuild."

Grits shook his head. "They're not building an army. Everybody they bite winds up in the morgue."

"Who says you have to be bitten?" Earl let it hang. "What's in the bite—saliva, venom? What if there's another way? They open a nightclub, pour thousands through every month. Dose the drinks with a werewolf tincture, wait for the full moon. Your Maniac could've been the guinea pig."

"New country, new start—fastest way to rebuild," Gravy said.

Grits' eyes sharpened. "They don't even need the real moon. They've got canned moonlight. Lock the doors, spike the drinks, hit the switch, spin the mirror ball—instant wolf pack. Nina said they want to expand. If they run out of stored moonlight, open a new club, dose a crowd, wait a month—boom."

He glanced at Pérez. "We checked another box, too. Deborah-Dawn Teats said a German handed her a Midnight Miami matchbook before her last date. I bet her German is really an Austrian. Wym's framing Karanovo."

Gravy added, "We found Daffodil Phil. He confirmed Karanovo hired the girls through the bodyguard, Golyam. Big man grumbled they're really here to marry off his sister—and she has to marry someone specific. 'The King of Light.'"

Earl brightened. "Exactly. The Neuri run on myth. They believe they'll rule when they unite light and shadow under a single crown: a King of Light and a Queen of Shadows. You, as a legendary vampire slayer, are 'light.' If Victor Karanovo is royal, marrying his daughter would realign the dark realm. Not to free it from vampires—to replace them. In Bulgarian, the prophecy goes—"

He launched into Bulgarian. Grits and Gravy stared.

"So why me?" Grits said. "What about Gravy? He looks like Hercules."

Earl laughed. "Oh, no. They hate blacks. Incredibly racist. In fact, they have a word—"

"We get it," Grits cut in. He looked at Gravy. "I'd marry you."

"Thank you, brother," Gravy said.

Arturo steered them back. "From my talks with Wym, there's a great... sum at stake at the center of your feud."

They nodded. They didn't like discussing it, but yes—their vampire haul was enormous, and Wym wanted it back.

"You were athletes," Arturo said. "I'm sure you encountered... gold diggers?"

Gravy laughed. "Encountered is an understatement."

Wilson finally chimed in, voice a little rough, hand rubbing his throat. "They don't want to team up. Daddy wants Grits to marry his girl with the big cans so they can take your money."

For a second, the magic drained out. Myth and prophecy gave way to a gold-digging pit lizard and her trashy family.

Earl reeled them in. "Victor wants to meet them at six. What should they be ready to do?"

"The enemy of my enemy is my friend," Pérez said.

All eyes turned.

"You share an enemy," he continued. "String Karanovo along on the marriage talk but make him prove loyalty first. If he's got a new wolf clan, have them fight the vampires. Let them bleed each other. You aren't bound by any ancient law. Put them in the ring and clean up what's left."

He stood. "By now the word's out that Dewayne Shelby vanished from the hospital. Since this place isn't surrounded, I'm assuming we're not suspects. It's Miami. Everyone will blame the Colombians."

Wilson stood too.

"What about Earl?" Gravy asked.

"We'll keep him underground," Arturo said. "I'll hide him until this shakes out."

Outside, as they headed for their cars, Earl had one more item. "Do you know what pheromones are?"

Grits shook his head.

"In animals," Earl said, "they're chemicals that trigger mating behavior. With werewolves, they can do more—enchant, cloud judgment, even slip inside your thoughts. Based on your stories about Nina, I believe she's been using them. It may sound silly, but you must find a way to block your sense of smell when you see her again."

Grits thought about the pool, about the way his body reacted despite her mouth and manners. Maybe she hadn't gotten into his head yet—but pheromones gave him an excuse for being a hound.

He thanked Earl. Goodbyes were said. Grits and Gravy headed for the Charger.

"Did you know 'Pheromones' is the name of Gus DeBarge's new group?" Gravy said.

Grits ignored him. "What's next?"

"I'll call Eleanor with the update. Then we probably oughta deal with the chopped-up werewolf in the trunk," Gravy said.

"Huh. Almost forgot." Grits grimaced. "He's gonna start stinking. Maybe we keep an arm and a leg. You up for a quick Everglades run?"

Gravy answered with a flurry of high-fives.

Neither man knew this would be the last time they spoke before the death of Gravy Watkins.

25

THE BRAZILIAN

F riday, 9:22 AM
    Midnight Miami
    1555 Collins Avenue, South Beach

AFTER THURSDAY NIGHT at the Midnight Miami, Ricardo "Sweetpea" Castilla felt recharged. Gravy's faith had knocked the rust off his confidence and, for the first time in months, cleared his head.

That clarity also showed him a way he might never have to wear a dress on the job again.

The Brazilian.

During the showcase, Sweetpea had locked eyes—just for a second—with a man he couldn't forget. Handsome in a way even the straightest, toughest guy would admit. Brown eyes like cold marbles. Tailored black suit, black shirt, an emerald scarf the exact green of the Brazilian flag. Then it hit him. Sweetpea knew the face from the FBI Top Ten posters that glared from the squad room wall.

Then the man vanished.

"The Brazilian" was Jose Gonzaga—enforcer, hitter, cleaner—on call for a few different Colombian crews. He wasn't the type you brought in for a nickel beef. If The Brazilian were a rock band, he'd be the Rolling Stones. He only played arenas at worst. And ten million in missing Colombian *yeyo*? That was a stadium date.

Law-enforcement chatter floating around the room last night confirmed it—ten million in powder had gone missing earlier in the week. Sweetpea's gut said The Brazilian had come to deliver a message to Victor Karanovo. Which meant the daughter was the likeliest pressure point.

There was no other reason for a ghost like him to risk being seen in a room full of Miami's big shots.

On a bright Friday morning, Sweetpea leaned on the tail of his forest-green '68 Mustang GT 390 fastback, parked a half block from Midnight Miami, and lit a Marlboro. He'd been on and off smokes for six months; three hours' sleep shoved him back on. *I'll quit next week,* he lied to himself.

He dressed to disappear: a beaten Big Daddy's Imperial Lounge tee, old Levi's, aviators. He didn't know how often Nina left the club, only that lately she'd been seen out with Grits—making Grits high on the Colombians' radar too.

Still, vampire hunters or ninjas or whatever the hell those two were, they'd be fine for a few hours.

Sweetpea picked the front as his post. Something about Nina said she wasn't a back-door type. She'd walk out the front to prove she wasn't scared.

Upstairs, Nina Karanovo stormed out of her father's office, breezed by the receptionist—who studied her shoes—and hit the elevator. Golyam, posted like a statue by the door, stepped in with her.

Before he could ask, Nina snapped, "All last night that Gravy Watkins blabbed about Burger King—Whopper this, Whopper with Cheese that. I thought that I had a Whopper the other night. But what is a Whopper with Cheese? And now all I can think about is a Whopper. Or a Whopper with Cheese? Whatever that is. Uggh!"

The elevator opened to the lobby. Nina led, the big man trailed. At the doors he touched her shoulder. She whirled, eyes hot—just what he expected.

"I don't care what my father says. I can go out whenever I want —by myself. You've got plenty to do for tonight and tomorrow. You do that. I'm going to see if this Whopper with Cheese is any good."

She strode out.

Sweetpea was finishing his smoke when she hit the steps—a white pussy-bow blouse, black jacket and skirt. On the sidewalk she yanked off her heels, jammed them into her purse, and kept moving, jaw set.

A green Oldsmobile Delta 88 Town Sedan nosed up to the curb. Two Latin men spilled from the back doors. In classic Colombian subtlety, they didn't bother to hide their pistols; carried low at their waists, pointed at her.

Sweetpea's instincts screamed *move*. He strangled them. If he wanted the bigger fish, he had to ride this out and follow. Pray they didn't settle it in the street.

Nina didn't look scared. She looked... inconvenienced.

They guided her behind the Olds toward the open rear door. At the sill she stopped. The one on her right said something. Nina widened her eyes in a cartoon gasp, then turned to the other guy. Sweetpea could read her lips: "How about this guy?"—jerking her thumb at Mr. Right.

She hit Mr. Right with a wicked left cross—bounced him off the car—then cracked Mr. Left with a right and sat him on his ass.

Nina sprang back, drew a pistol from her purse, and covered both men like she'd trained for it.

Then the driver's door opened. The Brazilian stepped out in an immaculate white linen suit. He didn't posture. He just looked at her.

Nina kept the muzzle swinging between the two on the pavement and the man in white, spitting a string of words that would've ended your network TV career immediately.

And then she surprised Sweetpea. Backing up, still covering, she could have slipped inside the club. Instead, she holstered the piece in her purse, set the purse down, and raised both hands.

The Brazilian watched. The two gunmen traded a look. Nina flicked her head—*come on then.* They eased in, took an arm each. One peeled off to scoop up her purse. The Brazilian slid back into the Olds. They walked her to the car and seated her in the center of the back seat.

Before she ducked in, Nina dropped a small white square to the pavement.

The Olds rolled right past Sweetpea. He popped his trunk, stared into nothing like he was digging for a jack.

As soon as the green boat turned the corner, he hustled to the spot.

A matchbook. The Mutiny at Sailboat Bay.

On NE 27th, a pay phone outside S&S, Gravy Watkins dialed the office. Before the swamp run, he and Grits had agreed to check in with Eleanor. Gravy hopped out of the Charger and made the call.

At Stone Detective Agency, Eleanor Stone felt startlingly human. She took advantage of the secret bedroom hidden in the office, allowing her a full night's sleep without worrying about a werewolf waiting at her condo.

She started her morning sweep. The service had nothing urgent; one message from PD: the black Cadillac she'd flagged Wednesday had disappeared. Still no word from Aaron Spelling.

9:29 AM: Gravy called with a quick update.

9:33: Gravy again—did she know where Grits was? He'd come back to the car and both Grits and the Charger keys were gone. So were the trunk's contents. She took the pay-phone number and said she'd call back. She tried not to picture an olive drab duffel in that trunk.

9:35: Sweetpea called. Where were the boys? She said Gravy was stranded at S&S and Grits was MIA. Sweetpea wasn't shocked. He'd scoop Gravy and meet at the office.

9:38: Eleanor rang Gravy—Sweetpea was *en route*.

9:39: Gravy called back to ask about Aaron Spelling. Eleanor hung up.

9:39: Eleanor started a pot of the green-topped coffee and hunted for the vodka her father used to stash.

Just after ten, Eleanor, Sweetpea, and Gravy stood by the coffee machine and compared notes. Sweetpea ran through what he'd seen outside Midnight Miami and gave them the short course on The Brazilian.

"I don't think it was staged," he said, pre-empting Eleanor. "She wasn't pulling punches. Something made her stop and stand down. Whatever The Brazilian said, she probably knows where Grits is."

Eleanor wasn't sold. "Or it's bait to get you. She knows your instinct is to charge in. This smells like a trap."

Gravy made a noise in his throat. Much as it pained him, she was right.

"If they're chasing their missing coke, they'll hit Grits's house sooner or later," Sweetpea said. "We stake it out first. Even if Grits is at the Mutiny, we need more intel."

They started for the door, but Eleanor stopped Gravy with a hand on his shoulder.

"Listen, Ernest," she said quietly. She rarely used what she believed was his real name, and it landed.

"I know you want to go crack heads, but we have to be smart. You stay here until Sweetpea and I check the house. Frankly, it's probably safer for me out there than here alone. If they come looking for you, you'll get your turn to do your thing."

Appeal to his chivalry—irresistible.

Gravy nodded. "All right," he said, resigned. "On one condition."

"Yes…?"

"If you see any Eye-Talians, you call me right away."

————

GRITS MCCOY SWAM UP from the dark.

The last thing he remembered was checking the trunk while Gravy hit the pay phone. Grits had a realization that Agent Wilson had been exposed to the moonlight lantern, but nothing happened to him. So if Wilson wasn't a werewolf, then what was he? No way he was a vampire. Could he be an Easter Bunny? Ecch! But suddenly—he saw stars.

He blinked at his surroundings. A hotel room… with an African savannah theme? Grassland wallpaper. Taxidermy—lions, rhinos, hippos. Tribal masks and spears that looked more cartoon than real. Paintings of "natives" so offensively stereotyped even a Klan Wizard would wince.

He was in a chair, arms wrenched behind the back, wrists and ankles tied tight.

"Well, Scooby Boo Boo, about time you woke up," a voice said to his left.

Nina Karanovo. Same chair, same bindings. Left eye ballooned shut, nose bleeding. Smiling like she was happy to see him.

"Where are we?" he asked, thick-tongued.

"At The Mutiny at Sailboat Bay," she chirped. "I think this is the Doctor J. Luther King Suite. These chairs probably have chlamydia. Speaking of chlamydia—"

She snorted like a pig—loud. A portly Colombian shuffled into their slice of the suite.

"—this is Gordo. Do you know what 'gordo' means in beaner? It means fat. Like Gordo. And his mom. She has chlamydia, too."

She snorted again. Gordo glared.

"So why are we here?" Grits asked.

"Because these bean-sniffing queers think we have their cocaine," Nina sneered.

"I don't have their cocaine. You got their cocaine?" Grits said.

"Certainly not," Nina answered in a bad British accent.

"Gordo, what about you?" Grits called. "You got the cocaine?"

Gordo looked offended—and a little scared. Cocaine jokes weren't big in Colombian circles.

"Oooh," Nina cooed. "Maybe Gordo does have it. Maybe he ate it. Thought it was powdered sugar and put it on a donut."

"No," Grits said. "Then he'd be running around. Gordo hasn't ran for anything in a while."

"Except his own mother," Nina said.

They both fake-laughed as obnoxiously as possible.

Gordo bore holes into Nina, then stomped off. A door slammed somewhere deeper in the suite.

Grits eyed her. Even with the beat-up face she looked like she was having fun. Hell, this was kind of fun.

But business was business.

"Nina, why don't you turn into a werewolf and get us out of here?" he asked.

Even swollen, her expression was pure disbelief. "Are you serious? Didn't you wear a helmet when you were driving? I'm not a werewolf. If I were, you think I'd let these beaners tie me up and punch me in the face?"

He let it go—either she was lying, or Daddy kept her in the dark.

"One more thing," Grits said. "Why does your father really want to meet me tonight?"

She smiled sly. "Uh-oh."

"What do you mean 'uh-oh'?"

"I mean Golyam's a tattletale. He probably told my father you were trying to play torpedo with me in your pool."

Grits had heard "torpedo" more in the last twenty-four hours than in his whole life. He'd be fine never hearing it again.

Nina leaned toward him, voice suddenly solemn. "All right, my turn. I need to ask you something important. Something I've wanted to know since I met you. I need you to level with me."

He waited.

"What the f#%k is a Whopper with Cheese?"

26

ELEANOR FROM TALLAHASSEE

F riday, 12:12 PM
Mutiny at Sailboat Bay
2951 South Bayshore Drive, Coconut Grove

GRITS MCCOY WAS RIGHT: Barry the Leprechaun kept his house spotless—and better than any cleaning service in Miami-Dade.

What Grits didn't know was why the place sparkled. Whenever Barry was sure Grits wasn't coming home—which was often—the little Irishman threw parties that became South Florida lore. The blowouts were so epic Barry had to use his magic not only to clean, but to rebuild and refurbish parts of the house afterward.

When Eleanor Stone and Sweetpea Castilla stepped through the empty frame where the glass front door had been the night before, they heard an Irish tenor crooning "Danny Boy" in a way that somehow made the song sound indecent.

Picking through broken furniture and chunks of plaster

toward the living room, they heard a male voice bark something in Gaelic.

Sweetpea and Eleanor stepped in. "I'm Officer Ricardo Castilla, and this is Detective Eleanor Stone."

Barry the Leprechaun and Patti from Daytona Beach were on the couch. Barry wore a Bob Griese #12 Dolphins jersey that looked like it had recently been on fire. Patti wore one of Grits' white linen shirts and not much else.

"Hi, I'm Patti from Daytona Beach," she said. "And this is Barry. This is Barry's house."

Eleanor locked eyes with Barry. He stared back in pretend panic, gaze ping-ponging between Eleanor and Patti before landing on Eleanor. He covered his mouth—naughty boy—and wiggled his eyebrows at her.

Sweetpea ignored him and held up a black-and-white photo of The Brazilian. "You know this man? We believe he's holding Grits McCoy against his will."

"Yeah, I've seen him," Patti said, casual as a weather report. "He's got a whole floor at the Mutiny. Maybe that Grits guy is there. I'm supposed to go up for my afternoon shift."

"Oh really," Eleanor said.

———

THE RUMORS and legends made the Mutiny Hotel and Club almost mythological: hot tubs filled with Dom Pérignon, Playboy center-folds as waitresses, hotel rooms built around ridiculous themes—Brazilian Rainforest, Moroccan Palace, African Savannah Fantasy Suite. Newspaper-headline drug lords sat in plain sight. And cocaine, cocaine, cocaine.

Eleanor and Sweetpea pulled up behind the Coconut Grove

hotspot a few minutes past noon with Barry and Patti crammed together in the Mustang's back seat. On the ride over they fine-tuned the plan. Patti would bring Eleanor in the back and steer her to the dressing area. Mutiny waitresses—Mutiny Girls—were attractive, often actual models. They didn't wear uniforms; per owner Burton Goldberg, they dressed "elegantly," big sun hats and high-end dresses provided by the hotel.

"There'll be plenty you can use," Patti told Eleanor. "You'll blend right in." Eleanor would never admit it, but the compliment from Patti felt good.

Once inside, Eleanor—and Barry—would work their way to the suite Patti thought belonged to The Brazilian. Worst case, they had a list of the crew's room numbers. For reasons she couldn't explain, Eleanor trusted the little man would be enough—though he unnerved her. The sporadic giggles and kissing from the back seat didn't help.

Because The Brazilian might recognize him, Sweetpea would stay posted by the car out back, ready to catch anyone trying to rabbit. Unlike Nina Karanovo, who strutted out the front door that morning, most folks fled by the rear.

Climbing out at the Grove, Sweetpea glanced at Eleanor. "So... Barry. Is he actually...?"

"Yep," she said. That was the last word about Barry.

On the sixth floor, in the African Savannah Fantasy Suite, The Brazilian finished his setup. He'd arranged tables like a trade-show booth—except these weren't new products and keychains. These were exhibits of his work.

Six Colombian minions milled about like judges at a science fair.

One display read *Mentirosos*—Liars. The photos focused on the mouths and tongues of the unfortunate subjects.

Grits' favorite—if *favorite* applied—was *Facas, Bisturi e Pinos* (Knives, Scalpels, and Pins). The black-and-white shots somehow made the carnage worse.

"Hey, bean sniffer," Nina called, "I've got an idea for you. How about *Os feijões e os peidos da minha mãe*?"

Grits looked for a translation. A small perk of captivity: free Portuguese lessons.

"That's 'his mother's beans and farts,'" Nina said, delighted.

He doubted the vocabulary would prove useful.

Both captives were quietly impressed with the other. Grits was accustomed to Gravy bailing him out—along with the perspective that came from already having died once. Whatever happened in the next few minutes, he'd get through it.

Nina didn't seem rattled either. Whenever the room quieted, she'd spit a filthy insult in Portuguese, then translate it for Grits— beans, flatulence, and the unusual sexual preferences of Brazilian and Colombian mothers. Don Rickles had nothing on her.

Still, Grits felt the strings. Somebody had engineered this to tilt him toward Nina. He didn't think she'd staged the kidnapping, but she'd seized it as an opportunity—for what, he couldn't say.

The door opened. A man Grits didn't recognize stepped in: Carlos Vazquez, leader of the crew that had lost ten million in cocaine.

Carlos had been productive. Yesterday, he found a videotape of a man in a wolf getup and sport coat wrecking his crew at the stash house. This morning he snagged the gringo race-car driver—and in the trunk of the gringo's Charger, an olive-drab duffel containing the head of the man in the sport coat. The gringo had already butchered him, saving Carlos time. He'd hoped to learn a few cutting tricks from Grits McCoy; experience with The Brazilian told him there wouldn't be much left of the man in an hour.

Carlos greeted The Brazilian warmly. Nina punctuated his steps with fart noises.

He toured the displays, lingering over *Facas, Bisturi e Pinos.*

"I must say," he told The Brazilian in heavy English, "I like the black-and-white. It gives the work a different quality."

For the first time, The Brazilian's face changed. He looked almost… doubtful.

"No, really," Carlos said. "It elevates your work."

The Brazilian nodded, satisfied.

Carlos stopped at a table with only a frame face-down. "And this?"

The Brazilian set the frame upright. No photos—just a title: *Animais da Amazônia.*

No translation required. Nina shouted that one of the *animais* would be a close-up of The Brazilian's mother. Carlos barely strangled a laugh.

Downstairs, Eleanor checked herself one last time. She'd found a slim black gown that fit like it was made for her and a white sun hat with a black band. She preferred a white sundress, but the dress didn't hide the .38 strapped to her thigh.

She thought about calling Gravy again. She'd tried three times while dressing. No answer. Enough stalling.

At the helm of a drink cart sat three silver ice buckets with Dom Pérignon and the proper flutes. Beneath the skirted shelf: Barry the Leprechaun, quiet—for now.

Patti from Daytona Beach breezed in. "Great to meet you. Good luck with your friend. Swing by before you leave so I can say bye to you and Barry—I wanna hear everything."

Like it was just another day at the office. At the Mutiny, it probably was.

Eleanor crouched and peeked under the cart. Barry lay on his side like Burt Reynolds on the cover of *Cosmo*, still in bow tie and green briefs.

"Listen," she whispered, "this is serious. I don't want Grits hurt. Wait for my cue. Also... you sure that's the outfit?"

Barry eyed his ensemble, then shot her a *are you kidding?* look.

Eleanor straightened—tap-tap-tap on her shin. She lifted the cart's skirt again.

Barry wiggled his eyebrows.

Upstairs, The Brazilian tugged on elbow-length black gloves—welder's gloves, thicker and longer. He had Carlos cinch the straps, then check them again.

From a closet he fetched a 3-by-3-foot metal case, carried like it held nitro, and set it near the *Animais* table.

He moved before the two chairs.

"I'll keep it simple," he said, baritone pleasant despite the circumstances. "Tell me where the cocaine is."

"I don't know," Grits said. Nina suggested a location inside The Brazilian's mother.

The Brazilian retrieved the olive-drab duffel from Grits' trunk and pulled out a severed head.

"Is this the man who murdered our crew and stole our cocaine?"

"I don't know," Grits said. Nina wondered aloud if the man had been decapitated by standing too close to The Brazilian's mother during a bout of gas.

Unamused, The Brazilian opened the case and slowly lifted a glass object.

He set it before them.

A glass boot with a metal screw top. Inside, hundreds of ants.

The opening was just right for a human foot. He let the idea sit, then spoke.

"These are bullet ants. The sting is the most painful of all insects. One sting hurts for more than twenty-four hours. In this boot, I have over two hundred."

"Oooh," Nina mocked, then offered an alternate origin for the ants involving his mother's lower geography.

The Brazilian placed the boot equidistant between them.

"Let me go first," Grits shouted. "I'm already wearing boots— lemme try another pair!"

"No, no, no!" Nina shouted louder, explaining how it would let her share the experience of being near his mother's private parts.

The Brazilian punched her in the stomach, then jabbed her right eye.

Grits' gut flipped. He didn't like torture, period. Seeing a woman take it lit him up.

"Booooo!" he jeered. "She gets enough attention already. What about me!"

The Brazilian ignored him. He tapped under Nina's chin with a gloved knuckle. She opened her eyes as much as the swelling allowed.

"Young woman," he said, "regardless of what you tell me, no matter what you say, you will die a horrible death in the next few hours. Everyone here will share in your pain. That I promise."

Nina grinned. "Works for me. Your mother probably needs a rest."

Muffled laughs.

She turned to Grits, regret in her swollen eyes. "Whatever you do, don't meet my father tonight."

The Brazilian backhanded her so hard her chair toppled. Two lackeys righted it.

Grits started bouncing his chair, shouting. Rage white-hot. With each bounce he felt give in the frame. If he could distract them, he could break free.

Carlos walked over and put a gun to Grits' head. The click of the safety was crisp.

Grits froze, then used the silence. "Before today's over, I'm shoving that boot up your ass."

In Nina's honor he added, in detail, what he'd do to The Brazilian's mother afterward.

In the hall, Eleanor—now a Mutiny Girl—pushed the cart past the numbers Patti from Daytona Beach had given her. As they reached the first, Barry under the cart began to sniff like a hound. At each door: a sniff, then a precise "Nope."

At 650 he stopped. "Yes. Yes. Yes."

Eleanor breathed deep. When she got up this morning, storming a Colombian cartel suite in disguise with a mythical Irishman hadn't been on the list.

"You're sure?" she whispered.

Barry, for once serious, bobbed his head like a piston.

She squared her hat and checked the .38 on her thigh. "Here goes nothing."

The Brazilian bent to lift the glass boot. A loud knock hit the suite door.

"Room service," a woman called.

Carlos, pistol up, moved to the door. "We didn't order anything. Go away."

The voice ignored him. "Three bottles of Dom Pérignon for you. Courtesy of Patti from Daytona Beach."

Patti's name drew a pleased murmur from Carlos' crew.

"Who are you?" Carlos asked.

She hadn't planned a cover name beyond the outfit. "Eleanor... Eleanor from Tallahassee."

Another murmur.

Grits' heart jumped at her voice, but he kept his face flat, feet planted.

Carlos didn't want to insult Patti from Daytona Beach—or turn down free champagne—but nobody could see what was happening inside.

"Leave it outside," he said. "We'll get it later."

As he spoke, the door turned from wood to a brown mist—and vanished.

Eleanor stood in the opening behind the cart. For a beat she was as baffled as the rest—then remembered the leprechaun under the skirt and rolled in like nothing was odd.

Carlos frowned. She looked the part, but he didn't know her. He raised his gun.

Eleanor lifted her hands. "I'm just here with champagne." Panic scratched at her throat; she swallowed it.

Standoff. Eleanor frozen, hands high. Carlos unsure. The others hesitant to disrespect a gift from Patti from Daytona Beach. Grits noticed The Brazilian reach into his coat and come up empty —gloves too thick for a fast draw.

Something tickled Eleanor's calf. Something crawled beneath her skirt onto her thigh. Bushy eyebrows wriggled against her skin.

A faint "Danny Boy" hummed from under her dress.

She kept her face neutral while her skirt rippled like a toddler was crawling between her legs.

Carlos' gun tracked from her face to the moving dress—and he didn't notice the pistol turning to brown cloud just like the door.

"What the hell is that!" he shouted.

Eleanor needed a cue she'd never given. The words flashed up.

"Say hello to my little friend!"

Barry launched from beneath her skirt and landed on Carlos' chest, feet planted, tiny hands gripping his shoulders. Face to face, he wiggled his eyebrows, then his mouth stretched impossibly wide and he bit off Carlos' head in one gulp.

Carlos' spurting corpse staggered and fell. Panic detonated. Crewmen clawed for guns that no longer existed.

Grits rocked forward, somersaulted, and slammed the chair to pieces, coming up with a jagged slat in his fist. He wanted blood.

He drove the splinter through the nearest man's windpipe.

Another charged with a machete. Grits spin-kicked his shin just below the knee. The leg snapped, bone slicing free; the now-discarded machete hung in the air. Grits caught it and took the man's head clean.

Barry zipped around the room like a hummingbird, doling out throat-sized bites with each pass. The living dwindled to zero fast.

Eleanor drew her .38 and sighted on The Brazilian. She hesitated; she didn't want him dead—she wanted him caught. A voice said, "He's mine."

Grits and The Brazilian faced each other ten feet apart. Grits held the machete, both of them lacquered in blood. The Brazilian still wore the gloves—and terror.

He moved first. He grabbed the metal ant case and hurled it through the window. Glass blew outward. He dove after it.

Grits reached the window in time to see The Brazilian bounce off an awning three floors down onto the big deck—the Gangplank Tiki Bar over the pool. A planned escape route, no question.

Grits yanked a spear from the wall. Maybe those years of spring track would finally pay off.

He backed to the door, ran, and launched the spear.

Grits and Eleanor watched it arc out over the courtyard. Barry popped his head from beneath Eleanor's skirt to watch too.

The Brazilian sprinted toward the deck rail, aiming for a second awning two stories below. Safe first floor, then his safe house before his pursuers even cleared the Mutiny.

As this thought passed through his mind, a giant African spear passed through his left shoulder and pinned The Brazilian face-down to the wooden deck of the Gangplank.

Grits surveyed the suite. The Colombians were down. The door had reappeared. So had the guns, scattered around their owners.

Nina was gone.

"What's our exit?" Grits asked.

"Sweetpea's waiting out back with the Mustang," Eleanor said.

Grits grabbed a leather jacket from a chair and wrapped the glass boot. "You two hit the fire stairs. I'll be right behind."

He climbed out the window.

It took a full minute for The Brazilian to comprehend he was stapled to a deck by a spear, due to the way his skull met the wood now underneath him. He realized that was not going anywhere, so he thought about the decisions that brought him to this moment.

When he reserved his rooms, he'd considered the "Amazon Erotic Rainforest" suite but decided debuting the bullet ants was overkill enough.

The Brazilian regretted that decision.

Hands grabbed his belt and slit his pants open.

"I hate to break my word," Grits said, "but I'm not gonna be able to shove this up your ass."

Cold glass slid against his bare cheeks.

"However, this is the next best thing."

Grits jumped and drove both steel-toed boots into the glass.

The glass container shattered. Two hundred bullet ants spilled into his pants. The Brazilian made sounds no human throat had produced until that moment.

Grits, Eleanor, and Barry reached the Mustang together. Grits high-fived Sweetpea and thanked him. Sirens were close now.

"In 650 you've got enough evidence to make your career," Grits said. "Including the Magic City Maniac's body. You'll find The Brazilian on the third floor."

Sweetpea handed over the keys. As he turned for the hotel he called, "How will I know where The Brazilian is?"

"Follow the screaming," Grits said, and peeled off.

As they rounded the corner, Grits asked, "Where's Gravy? Is he okay?"

Eleanor didn't answer—because she didn't know. Gravy not returning her calls was completely unlike him. A cold weight settled in her stomach. Something was wrong.

27

BAD INTENTIONS

F riday, 2:23 PM
     Burger King
     1309 NW 20th Street, Miami

ELEANOR HAD long since grown tired of Burger King, but it's hard to tell a man "no" when he's spent the morning held hostage by a Colombian cartel. They hit the drive-thru on the way back to the S&S Diner, where they'd left the Dodge Charger earlier. In the spirit of unity, Eleanor ordered a chocolate milkshake.

Barry the Leprechaun got a Fun School Meal. His prize was a ruler, which he used to fluff his eyebrows.

On the ride, Eleanor went out of her way to mention—several times—that Grits would be heading straight home, and how important it was that there be no surprises waiting for him. Grits wondered why she was laying it on so thick; Barry always kept the place spotless.

She just wanted to be sure the hint landed. It did.

At the S&S, Barry climbed into the front seat, pantomimed driving, then pointed at the Charger and waggled his eyebrows at Grits.

Grits handed over the keys. Barry drew a few stares crossing the lot—man in a leprechaun get-up tends to do that—but downtown Miami had seen stranger things by far in the last year.

Before he got in, Grits rolled down his window. "Thanks again, Barry."

Barry did a little dance, then held up one finger. He reached under his hat and produced a tiny scroll, unfurled it, and showed them:

Where is my gold?

Give it to me now!

Then he bared his teeth and growled.

"I don't have your gold, Barry," Grits said.

Barry stopped, tipped his hat, did another jig that ended with him touching a finger to his backside and acting like he'd burned himself, then wiggled his eyebrows at Eleanor.

Grits and Eleanor pulled away.

"Don't you want to see if he can actually drive?" Eleanor asked.

"I watched him bite a man's head off today," Grits said. "If he can do that, I figure he can reach the pedals."

Hard to argue.

On the way back to 80 West Flagler, Eleanor figured this was as good a time as any to recap what she'd learned over the last twenty-four hours.

"So, leprechauns and werewolves are definitely real?"

"Yep," said Grits.

"And vampires are real, including one named Prince Wym, who is Austrian and also owns a blood-storage company?"

"Yes, yes, and yes. You just told us about the blood company, but that all sounds about right."

"What else am I missing?"

Grits hesitated. There was still a lot. He thought about the Maiden, but that would be too much. So, he decided to give her something light.

"Easter Bunnies."

"Really? Easter Bunnies. Plural?"

"Unfortunately."

"But aren't they good guys?"

"I guess. I heard vampires are allergic to them, or something. But in my experience, all they do is get in the way and leave jellybeans everywhere. Take my word for it. Finding jellybeans in your underwear sounds hilarious until it happens to you."

———

ON THE SIXTH floor of the Mutiny at Sailboat Bay, a steady stream of officers congratulated Vice Detective Sweetpea Castilla. He hadn't just captured the elusive Brazilian alive; he'd nabbed him with a treasure-trove of photographs documenting his crimes.

Detective Rafael Pérez stood at the window of Room 650, watching paramedics and cops debate how to free the screaming man pinned to the deck by a spear while avoiding a swarm of bullet ants—pouring, from this angle, out of The Brazilian's pants.

Behind him an officer marveled, "I can't believe this idiot documented everything. Look—he's in the picture next to the body and giving a thumbs-up. What a stupid asshole. Sweetpea, you just won the lottery."

Pérez heard FBI Agent Ronald Wilson scoff and mutter under his breath. Wilson had vanished the night before, then turned up this morning at the hospital. He was back in the standard Bureau blues, rumpled like he'd slept in them.

Pérez steered Wilson to the far side of the suite for a little privacy and got in his face.

"What is it with you?" Pérez said through his teeth. "We just grabbed one of your Most Wanted, and you're acting like a fat kid who didn't get enough cake. What's your problem?"

"I'll tell you," Wilson said—also doing the gritted-teeth thing. "I was sent here to grab a Soviet arms dealer who waltzed into the country through our own channels. And I've got nothing. Zip. Just stories about werewolves running a disco."

Pérez knew Wilson was petty and selfish, but he also knew the feeling—big bosses breathing down your neck, results or else.

"Listen," Pérez said, softer. "This is far from over. There's ten million in coke out there, and these guys don't have it."

"Little Angelo," Wilson spat. "That fat bastard. Maybe he's got it, but is he capable of this much damage?"

Before Pérez could answer, a female cop gasped. "Sweetpea, come look at this—look at the shoe. It's the Magic City Maniac! He's in this duffel! They chopped him up!"

Relief at not being an accessory to murder gave Pérez a fresh charge. "Once we lock this down," he told Wilson, "you and I hit every spot Little Angelo uses. He'll surface. You'll be there."

Wilson looked grateful. "Thanks for looking out for me. Means a lot."

While Wilson drifted toward the crowd around the green bag of Dewayne Shelby, Pérez took the long route back to the window. A paramedic on the deck below raised the spear in triumph to applause—then yelped, clutching his hand, and dropped it. The butt of the spear smacked The Brazilian on the back of the head.

Agent Wilson glanced at Pérez by the glass. They had all fallen for his clueless-Fed routine earlier in the week. Now Pérez even thought he cared about a big arrest.

The full moon was tomorrow. On Saturday they'd all learn the truth about Agent Ronald Wilson.

———

BACK AT THE Stone Detective Agency, Grits and Eleanor made a quick sweep. No note from Gravy. Nothing looked disturbed.

Eleanor called the service. No messages from Gravy—and none from Aaron Spelling. She cursed herself for thinking about *The Love Boat* at a time like this.

Grits was rattled. So was she. In their line of work, the boys had a habit of disappearing, but usually together. Alone, each of them was more vulnerable, and someone might be trying to exploit that.

Belaboring it wouldn't help. Six o'clock with Victor Karanovo was coming fast.

"The service has nothing on Gravy," she said. "I don't like it either, but if anyone can handle himself in broad daylight, it's him."

"It's not just that," Grits said—though he didn't realize how much the absence gnawed at him. "It's something Nina said when we were tied up—right before the Colombians started the rough stuff. The last thing she said was not to see her father tonight."

Eleanor sat beside him. The jealousy she resented pricked anyway. She ignored it.

"At best, you're dealing with a Soviet arms dealer and his daughter. At worst, they're both werewolves. Either way, assume bad intentions. They haven't earned the benefit of the doubt."

Grits nodded, unconvinced. He felt like the answer to all of this was right in front of him and he still couldn't see it.

Eleanor checked her watch, sprang up. "Geez—it's after three. Go home and get ready for your big night. Take Sweetpea's car.

Catnap. Long hot shower. Twenty bucks says Gravy's already at the Midnight Miami turning it into a *Love Boat* roller disco for you."

Grits snorted, the weight on his shoulders easing a notch. He hugged her.

"Thanks for coming to get me," he said. "We know we can always count on you. We just don't say it enough."

They held a beat too long. Grits broke it. "I'll call when we're done. I'll call your place. It's Friday in Miami—go home, sit by the pool, have a drink. Maybe catch some rest."

He pocketed Sweetpea's keys and headed out.

To make him feel better, Eleanor had shoved her worries down. To make herself feel better, she decided to keep them down a little longer.

She snapped her fingers—the closed-circuit security system. They'd installed it months ago. She still hadn't made checking it a habit.

In the supply closet, the stacked CCTV monitors rolled black-and-white views of the office and the street. She tapped her temple, trying to recall the rewind routine, then ran back the last few hours. She started with the office camera.

Relief washed through her at the sight of Gravy. The time-stamp showed the ten-o'clock hour. She was in the right spot.

Her hand flew to her mouth. "No, no, no!" she cried.

28

THE MAIDEN

F riday, 4:07 PM
Gesù Catholic Church
118 NE 2nd Street, Miami

DURING HER YEAR with Grits and Gravy, Eleanor Stone overheard plenty—things she chose not to let stick. The constant vampire talk. The Laws of the Shadows. The never-ending *Love Boat* chatter. But some things wouldn't be ignored, mostly because they always came as a set:

Gesù Church. Father Johnson. The Maiden.

Those words tended to show up when the boys were in over their heads—and then they'd head to Gesù.

After learning the reality about leprechauns, vampires, and werewolves, and then watching the CCTV footage and learning why Gravy was missing, Eleanor knew she was over her head, too.

She took West Flagler east and covered the half mile to Miami's oldest Catholic church in ten minutes. Before climbing the front steps, she stopped to collect herself. Church wasn't a problem—she was baptized and confirmed, a "High Holiday Catholic" (more generous than true). She was more nervous about what she'd have to say to a priest—words that would either bring help or get her an evening visit from Social Services.

Inside, muscle memory served: holy water, Sign of the Cross, the first two genuflections at the right spots. Now to find Father Ed Johnson before late-afternoon confessions.

She'd attended Mass here, so she might have seen him. She scanned the priests, trying to match a face to the name. When she saw him, she knew.

"Father Johnson?" she asked.

"Yes, my child," said Father Ed Johnson, a kindly man pushing sixty, hair thinning and whitening at the same time.

"My friends recommended I talk to you," Eleanor said. "My friends Gr—my friends Francis McCoy and Ernest Watkins."

A priest hears enough in confession to keep a straight face through an earthquake. Father Johnson's "Yes?" carried just the hint of a question mark.

Eleanor puffed her chest for confidence—pure Gravy. "My friends Grits and Gravy—do you know them?" For a second she worried he'd think those were the names she'd given her breasts.

The poker face slipped; concern crept in—not for himself or the men, but for the young woman in front of him.

"Do you want to light a candle for them?" he asked gently.

Did he dodge the question? She wasn't sure, but time was wasting. She went for it.

"I need to see the Maiden," Eleanor said, standing as tall as she could—which, mercifully, returned her bosom to a more appropriate posture.

His expression shifted to the one reserved for parishioners in mid-nervous breakdown. His eyes flicked left, then right, as if hunting a rescue. Eleanor sensed it was reflex, not refusal.

"Father Johnson," she pressed, "Grits and Gravy are in grave danger. I don't know where else to turn. I have to see the Maiden." She met his eyes and tried to pour every ounce of urgency into the look.

This time his small glances seemed to make sure no one was watching.

"Come with me," he whispered, turning toward a door by the confessionals.

He moved quickly; Eleanor had to jog twice to keep up. A few turns later he opened an unmarked door and started down a tight corkscrew stair—straight out of an old castle.

Two stories below, he stopped at another unmarked door and caught his breath. "When you open the door, follow the hallway. When you're where you're meant to be, you'll know."

"Father, thank you," she said.

"Peace be with you," said Father Johnson.

"And also with you," Eleanor answered. Confirmation class finally paying off.

The door was old wood with a metal pull—older than any door had a right to be in twentieth-century Miami, yet not out of place.

She pulled it open and stepped through.

Candles lined the walls at eye level in iron brackets, one about every ten feet. The last landing had been stone; here the floor was dirt—well kept and impossibly dry for a tunnel not far from a large body of water.

She walked. Ten yards—left turn. Twenty yards—left again. Then again. And again.

The pattern made no sense. She should have caught a glimpse

of the first door, but it never reappeared. The candles never dwindled; each one looked freshly lit, hardly any wax spilled.

Every turn felt like the first; the corridor refused to exist behind her. She stopped counting turns. She kept moving, ignored the knot in her stomach and the impulse to go back. She tried not to think about passing dozens—no, hundreds—of brand-new candles.

Time slipped its leash. Minutes or days; she couldn't tell.

She turned left and nearly hit a wall. Finally—a right turn.

Down this stretch, the floor stayed the same, but the candles were gone. Faint, bobbing white light glowed from a room about twenty yards ahead—like light from a single giant candle.

Eleanor stepped into the room.

"Eleanor Stone," said a woman's voice in a heavy French accent. "I am glad to finally meet you in person."

At the center of the room stood a woman on fire.

Not singed—burning. A bonfire at its peak. The flames roared; the woman did not burn up. Moses' burning bush had a sister.

Through the fire, Eleanor could make out a small figure—five-five, maybe, on tiptoe. The heat blurred everything but the eyes: white, steady, burning right through the flames. The rest of the face was blackened and charred.

The Maiden spoke again. "*Ma fille*, I know my appearance is shocking, but you came to see me for a reason, *non*?"

Eleanor's mouth worked; her mind blanked. The Maiden didn't need the prompt.

"You are here because of your friends, Grits McCoy and..." She finished the sentence in a language Eleanor did not recognize.

Seeing her confusion, the Maiden corrected herself. "*Pardon*. I believe you know him as Gravy Watkins."

Eleanor managed a nod. The Maiden gave her more.

"Grits McCoy and the man you call Gravy Watkins were

chosen by me. I needed righteous warriors, men of pure heart, to help battle the darkest forces—evils so great they would either drive mankind mad with knowledge of them or, worse, pull the world deeper into corruption."

Eleanor steadied. The logic landed.

"Grits and Gravy are being tested," the Maiden went on. "Their iniquitous enemies believe they've found a weakness—their bond as friends, and their instinct to protect the ones they love."

The word *tested* stuck and made Eleanor angry. "After all they've done for you, you're still testing them?"

The Maiden was quiet, then laughed softly. "*Non, ma fille.* You misunderstand. Their enemies test them—and their enemies will fail."

She stepped closer. The heat didn't touch Eleanor.

"However, I am using this moment as a test—for you."

That surprised her. It must have shown.

"Did you think it an accident you are with Grits and Gravy? That it was happenstance for them to meet your father? Coincidence they bought your family business?" the Maiden asked.

She let it settle before continuing.

"They need you. You are their balance. Without you, they see the world only through friendship. You can give them the perspective they cannot have.

Both of them chose to fight the world of shadows. They had a choice and took it. Now it is your turn. Until now, I have clouded your mind so you would not comprehend all you heard. No longer. I have selected you for this opportunity, but I cannot force your path. Very soon you will face a choice. They will need you to make a decision they could not bear to make."

Questions avalanched—*Why me? What choice? How will I know?* The Maiden smiled as if she'd heard them anyway.

"*Ma fille,*" she said, voice soft as a lullaby, "you will know when you will know. And I believe you will do what is right. That is why I chose you. For now, return to your office and wait. Stay, and wait. They will come to you. I look forward to seeing you again soon."

Dismissed.

The sensation was like waking up.

Eleanor Stone sat at her desk at the Stone Detective Agency, the main lights off, the green banker's lamp the only glow. Outside, the sounds said Friday night.

She checked her wristwatch, then the wall clock, then back—both read the same: 11:43.

Six o'clock had come and gone. Whatever had happened to Grits and Gravy—whatever trap had been sprung—had already happened.

The Maiden was certain their enemies would fail.

Eleanor couldn't say she shared that confidence.

29

THE LIFE AND DEATHS
OF GRAVY WATKINS

Friday, 11:24 AM
Stone Detective Agency
80 West Flagler, Miami

SITTING STILL WASN'T GRAVY WATKINS' style—especially with his best friend Grits McCoy missing.

Gravy never allowed himself to sit still. He was always on the move. Riding his motorcycle. Trying out his newest roller skates. Lifting weights. Handling the correspondence for the Vicki Lawrence Fan Club. Creating new weapons to fight monsters. Lifting more weights.

If he kept moving, he wouldn't have the chance to go to sleep.

And if he didn't sleep, he wouldn't dream of Her.

But for the moment he had to wait. To keep from climbing the walls, or resting his eyes, he went back to important business: finalizing his preferred romantic co-stars for when he and Grits finally got the call to appear on *The Love Boat*.

A month earlier they'd even taken Grits' boat out to sea to work on the list without distractions. By sunset they'd agreed Lynda Carter was off-limits—no sense risking the friendship—and each had trimmed his personal roster down to a Top 30.

When Eleanor heard, she congratulated them on their "hard work." It took two days for the sarcasm to land.

Properly chastised, they'd promised to cut to a Top Five.

Now, alone at Eleanor's desk so he could catch any calls, Gravy exhaled and studied the legal pad.

1. Vicki Lawrence
2. Pam Grier
3. Jayne Kennedy
4. Charo
5. The Pointer Sisters

He was still trying to figure how to fit Vicki Lawrence as her *Mama* character onto the list when he shut his eyes to concentrate. A big mistake.

The dream always started the same.

A crisp November night. A modest estate outside of Rome. The mighty warrior watched the sun go down until disappeared behind the sea.

After a lifetime of battle, the mighty warrior wanted quiet and simple. And he had earned it. Paid for it with his blood and his lancea. His valor and spear helped Constantine I vanquish his rivals to become the sole emperor of Rome. Constantine the Great.

His life was simple. He tended livestock —he had grown very fond of beef —and kept up his property. He had not beaten his swords into plowshares, but he could have. Behind the home he built a smithy and worked iron for those who sought his skill.

The extra coins were welcome, but unnecessary. He mostly loved how the trade kept him strong.

Muscles, broader than most men's, rippled under brown skin, that maintained an even hue as the mighty warrior left his chest and arms unbridled by clothing, even on this cool autumn evening.

His mind wandered to the talk he'd heard in the city.

Rumors of attacks in the black of night. Creatures from nightmares. Bodies found drained of blood. Graves cracked open and emptied. A cabal assembled to stop Constantine and his new religion—the same faith of the warrior. A coven that had sold their souls to the Devil, now cursed to seek the blood of the living.

Yesterday in the market, men whispered that veterans famed for service under Constantine were being targeted.

If anyone—or anything—came for him, they'd best come ready. His name carried weight. Even those who didn't know it would learn quickly by the Cross fixed above his door on one of his shields. Beneath the Chi-Rho he had carved: In hoc signo vinces.

"In this sign, conquer."

He didn't realize how much he credited the rumors until his wife's voice startled him.

Gravy Watkins' eyes popped open when the voice of Dee Wheatley came over the intercom.

"Uh, hi—it's Dee Wheatley. Gravy, are you there? I want to talk."

"Yes—hey, baby," he said, finding the right button and buzzing her in. "C'mon up."

He waited a very long two minutes before he heard a knock at the door.

Dee's hair was still braided with neon beads from the night before, now pulled into a ponytail. She wore a cutoff Miami MetroZoo T-shirt, hot-pink dolphin shorts, and pink-and-coral tube socks over white tennis shoes.

"Listen," she began. "I want to apologize for the way that I behaved last night. My emotions were really high and seeing that jerk Wilson really got me going. And I took it out on you of all people! Especially after you've done so much for me in the last few days. I'm really sorry."

"No need to apologize," said Gravy. "That was a crazy night. Let's just put it past us."

Gravy put out his right hand for a handshake like he was getting her to agree to a new insurance policy. She jumped past his hand, gave him a hug, and placed a gentle kiss on the cheek. Dee bounced back to where was standing previously, so she was out of range from any additional embracing when she said, "How about lunch? My treat."

His heart did that thing only a woman could make it do—then the thought of Grits hit. "Thank you, but I'm stuck here waiting on a call."

She eyed him. Sounded like the detective's version of "I'm washing my hair." She pushed.

"How about I go get lunch and bring it back? We can wait together."

He ran the math. He might have to bolt at any moment. But sending her away could be a bridge too far later. And it gave him a shot to talk her out of going near Midnight Miami for a few days.

"Sure, baby. That'd be great."

Her grin was pure sunshine. "Yes! I know you like to eat healthy—there's this new raw macrobiotic vegetarian place I've been dying to try."

"A what-what?" he said, a little too sharply. Several of those words didn't sound real. But she was already out the door when it slammed.

The November wind pushed the door close behind him as the

mighty warrior walked into his house and took in the beauty of his bride.

He had given up war; he had also given up bachelorhood. The modest estate near the mouth of the Tiber had come with a bride.

He scooped his wife easily into his arms and kissed her. He found his hand instinctively going to her stomach, which had just started to show the fruits of her womb. Those hands—callused by war and iron—would soon hold something more delicate when winter's cold passed.

He carried her toward their bed. Knowing he'd keep her there the rest of the night, she reminded him the servants were off for Dominica—the Lord's Day—and she needed to finish the kitchen.

He set her down—then froze. He might have laid down the sword, but his instincts hadn't dulled. As the sun slipped under the horizon and autumn night swallowed the sky, something was wrong.

She felt it, too. The silence of the fields turned loud—no insects, no birds, no rustle of grass. Nothing.

Then a sound. Faint, growing. A steady squeak—the wheels of a cart.

Gravy Watkins heard an automobile slamming on its brakes. Not an uncommon sound in a town like Miami, but the sound was off. Not right.

He cranked open the casement window and leaned out and looked down to Flagler. A moment later he spotted Dee on the sidewalk below—and the blue van with its side door open.

Before he could say a word, Doctor Fun and Cheryl grabbed her, hustled her inside, and slammed the door. Tires squealed.

Gravy tore out of the office and flew down seven flights of stairs in bounds. Somewhere in the back of his mind he registered that the pair had dropped something on the sidewalk.

On the concrete lay a sealed white security envelope. He teased up the flap and unfolded a sheet of paper.

At the top, an address in blue ink. Under it:

.   .   .

**ANSWER this pay phone at noon
If we see you before then
SHE DIES**

UPSTAIRS AT THE OFFICE, he went to the large Miami street map on the wall. The address was in Liberty City—right where he'd tangled with Doctor Fun and Cheryl earlier in the week.

Gravy Watkins was a walking atomic clock. It was 11:37 AM. Time, for once, wasn't on his side.

He assessed his options. Grits had picked him up this morning —no car. The Charger was at the S&S. Eleanor had left with Sweetpea, so her Gran Fury should be in the garage. A quick check of her desk turned up the keys.

At the door he hesitated. He was supposed to wait for Eleanor's call. This was almost certainly bait. He knew he wasn't thinking straight.

What would Grits do? As he weighed it, he saw again the hungry way Little Angelo had looked at Dee at Midnight Miami.

Decision made. He'd trust Eleanor and Sweetpea to find Grits. He'd walk into the trap.

The mighty warrior drew on a cloak and took his spear—his lancea — from the wall, feeling the iron head's weight balance against the staff. The weapon had been a decoration for a year, but it hadn't forgotten what it was.

He hid the spear beneath his cloak. His wife's eyes widened. He gave her his best smile and told her he was only checking the noise and not to worry; then, more firmly, he told her to stay inside.

He stepped out and let his eyes learn the dark. Soon he saw the source of the sound. On the road a woman pushed a two-wheeled cart—

a carrus— that should have had a donkey in front. An oil lamp swung from its frame. Bundles moved in the bed. Children, it seemed.

He stood still and watched her move. Ambushes had come before in women's clothing—men in disguise before their gait gave them away. This one moved like a woman—hips and shoulders telling the truth. He watched the push and the huff, the wobble of the load, the cart's squeak.

A woman, yes. But no one—especially not a woman with children —had reason to be on this road at this hour.

She called to him—feminine, frightened. He knew fear's sound. He'd heard it on battlefields. If she was acting, she was the best he'd seen.

His chivalry pulled him forward.

At 11:59, Gravy Watkins stood by a pay phone in Liberty City. At 12:00, it rang. He answered.

A new address in Hialeah. A time. Be there. Answer. Click.

He hopscotched north all afternoon—Hialeah. Pembroke Pines. Hollywood. Dania. Fort Lauderdale. Farther still. Each stop pulled him farther from Miami—and from the six o'clock meeting with Victor Karanovo. Farther from Grits.

At 7:15 he answered a pay phone outside the Palm Beach Zoo. Different voice, different tone.

A warehouse address in West Palm. Dee would be inside. This time the line didn't click. Gravy asked, "Is she okay?"

Heavy breathing. "Yeah. For now."

He swallowed what he wanted to say about Little Angelo. "You gonna be there?"

More breathing. "Yeah. I'll be there." A beat. Then, low and ugly: "I'm going to kill you—and make that black bitch watch."

Click.

Back at the Gran Fury he checked the map. Industrial strip. Friday night. Deserted.

It was 7:20. Even if he turned around now he'd be lucky to hit

Miami by nine. Whatever the meeting with Karanovo had set in motion was already rolling.

He turned into the park just after 7:40. He'd stopped for a full tank for the ride home. The place felt abandoned.

As he crept closer, he eased his speed, head on a swivel. He rolled down his windows to listen.

He turned onto the court. The warehouse sat ahead—small-hangar size—its big doors open.

The approach was naked. Buildings on either side set back far. No cover.

Something sat inside—three-quarters of the way back.

A woman in a chair. Bound. Gagged.

Dee.

He stopped the Gran Fury sideways at the door and left it running. Inside, rows of shelving and boxed freight lined both sides—perfect for an ambush.

Dee was alive, crying, fighting her bonds.

"Angelo!" Gravy called, voice booming. "I'm here. Let her go."

His shout echoed back. No reply. He moved forward.

"Angelo! You got what you wanted. You have me. I'll surrender. Let her go."

Nothing.

The threshold was the point of no return. He said it once more and got only his own echo back.

He crossed inside and lengthened his stride.

Dee wrenched the gag free. "Get out! It's a trap!"

The mighty warrior approached slowly. The woman at the cart talked—troubles and woes of the day—while he listened and kept his eyes on the flanks. The road and fields lay open. Nowhere to hide. If there was danger, it sat in the cart or wore the skirt.

He studied the bundles. Five small figures in oversized clothes. The lamp's sway muddied their faces.

The clouds parted and allowed a beam of moonlight to shine on the face of one of the children.

He saw the face and teeth of a jackal.

The warrior leapt back as the thing sprang, a hooked hand swiping. The claw tore away the warrior's cloak but gave his spear freedom.

He struck. At first he thought he'd missed, but then he realized his strikes had no effect. On the next thrust the creature caught the iron head in its hand— and snapped it off. The abomination grew as he watched, stretching to seven feet, preening, laughing, waiting for the warrior to gape.

He didn't. He drove the jagged butt of the shaft forward, through its chest.

The monster burst into flame.

No human book would record it, but the mighty warrior had just become the first man to kill a vampire.

He felt another behind him. Without turning he rammed the blunt end back, punching through belly into gut. No fire—wrong spot. He ripped the shaft free and slammed the jagged tip into its sternum.

Flame. Number two.

Wings beat his face and hands. Two more came from the air. He swatted one to the ground, but the second tore the spear from his grip. The grounded one sprang; he slid aside, caught it by throat and wings— an unholy marriage of man and bat—and spun, once, twice, and hurled it toward the Cross over his door. It froze at the sight, sailed, and exploded before it struck.

Number three.

He pivoted and sprinted for the smithy and its iron. The Cross would guard his wife if she stayed inside.

On cue her scream split the night. He glanced—and saw his wife had stepped outside. Before he could speak the ox cart hurtled at him.

Then nothing.

Pain dragged him up from dark. His home burned bright—roof timbers buckling, smoke choking the night air. Heat pressed on his skin.

Three spears impaled his body—one for each kill— and held him upright, wood through his flesh, wood through ribs, wood wedged cruel in bone.

He heard his wife's cries. Two others held her up like a broken doll. She lived, but barely—mechanical sobs, eyes wide and empty—like the emptiness torn in her belly.

The woman from the cart stood before him in her true shape—a foul concoction of woman, wolf, and bat, eyes like wet coal, mouth rimmed in red.

He blacked out, returned, and heard her say, "No, you can't die yet."

Her left hand flicked and held him in life, dark magic pinning his soul so she could finish her sport. She licked her bloody mouth and right hand like a cat after cream.

"Before you leave us," she said, "I wanted you to know that you were going to have a baby girl. You could have named after me ..."

Gravy Watkins had nowhere to hide as Little Angelo stepped from the shadows to his right. The wannabe gangster raked the air with a Thompson submachine gun. The burst chewed through Gravy as he emptied the magazine.

Gravy hit the concrete.

Not like this.

Not again.

Somehow, he made his way back onto his feet.

Doctor Fun and Cheryl walked up and sprayed him with their own tommy guns.

The last thing Gravy Watkins heard was Dee Wheatley's screaming, braided into the laughter of the two little demons.

And the last thing that he thought of was the name of the mother of all vampires.

Lilith.

Then he didn't hear or remember anything at all.

30

THE RISE AND FALL OF
THE KING OF LIGHT

Friday, 6:04 PM
Midnight Miami
1555 Collins Avenue, South Beach

GRITS McCOY ROLLED BACK into Key Biscayne just before four on Friday and walked through the front door like a normal person. He didn't know the door hadn't existed a few hours earlier—Barry had literally worked his magic in the interim.

Barry didn't know his repairs had cooked the phone line. Incoming calls got a busy signal; outgoing calls got the same dead buzz.

A little after five, Grits headed for the Midnight Miami. He hadn't accounted for drive-time traffic and slid in a shade past six. He and Gravy prided themselves on punctuality; left alone with one job, he'd already blown the schedule. Off his game.

Stepping out of the car, he admitted he had no real plan. His partner—his best friend—was missing.

One clear thought cut through: he'd always been fearless. That's how you win races—you dive without worrying about the wall. But without Gravy's balance—and, more and more, Eleanor's —those same instincts could get him killed. Again.

Worst time for soul-searching. He shoved it away. Race mode.

He checked himself in the glass: navy Giorgio Armani sport coat, white linen shirt, light-brown trousers. Rattlesnake steel-toed boots. Revolver in the back waistband, loaded with his last silver bullet.

He rapped the glass and muttered, "Gentlemen, start your engines."

Golyam lumbered to the door, scanned the sidewalk, and swung it open.

They crossed the humming lobby unnoticed—staff moving with Friday-night purpose.

"Where's your black friend?" Golyam asked.

"Good evening to you, too," Grits said. "Honestly? Don't know."

Off the elevator on four, he saw the lobby from the proper side this time—the receptionist's desk empty. As they passed, he glanced at Nina's door and shoved her out of his mind. He'd watched Colombians pound her face a few hours ago and heard her last words—don't meet my father. Think about her later. Race mode.

Golyam held open Victor Karanovo's door. Grits stepped in. The door closed with a thick *chunk*—the kind of final sound a prison makes.

Victor stood behind his desk, drink in his left hand, dark suit as always. The expression wasn't quite menacing—more leer than glare. Not an improvement.

He gestured Grits to a chair and sat; Golyam took the adjacent seat to Grits' left. Victor propped on his elbows like a man about to pose a philosophy question.

"My daughter Nina has told me many things about you," he said. "But there is one question she could not answer."

Grits side-eyed the big man. "Hope it's not about us playing torpedo in the pool," he stage-whispered. Golyam didn't blink.

Victor ignored him. "I know of your wealth. You could live with comfort and pleasure that few men could imagine. Yet you risk your life—and your friends'—for nothing. For strangers. For enemies. This very day you faced unimaginable torture."

"What's your question?" Grits said.

Victor held his gaze. "With all that you have, why do you fight against the shadows?"

Reasonable question. Grits didn't have a complicated answer.

"Because it's the right thing to do."

Victor slid to a new subject like he hadn't heard. "Where is your friend—the black?"

The idiocy gave Grits a jolt of anger and sarcasm. "I don't know. And this guy doesn't seem to know either."

He slapped Golyam's thigh. The big man jolted like a dozing dog.

Victor looked faintly amused. "You really don't know, do you?"

"I already told you I don't," Grits said, real frustration slipping in. "Is that why I'm here? You want to play hide-and-seek with Gravy?"

"Hide and...?" Victor frowned and set his glass down. It clinked oddly against something on his hand.

Grits' eyes went to the sound. Victor jerked his hand away, lowering it out of sight, but not fast enough. On his pinky: a black onyx ring inlaid with Wepwawet.

The same ring Nina had worn the first night they met—and

last night. The same wolf god etched on the onyx box behind Victor's head.

Facts snapped together. Two offices connected by a secret passage. One a decoy—racks of men's and women's clothes. An extra black dress like the one Nina wore when Victor was downstairs without her. No photos of father and daughter together. Never seeing them in the same room.

The fact that Victor Karanovo was wearing the same ring Nina had worn the night before.

"Son of a bitch," Grits murmured.

Victor lifted the glass again—minus the ring now—and smiled a strange, rubbery smile.

"Where's Nina?" Grits asked. "She joining us?"

"No," Victor said, smile still wrong. "She is busy with other matters."

Beside him, the big man shifted. That line wasn't in his script.

Grits stared at the box. Held closed by a simple hook. Almost inviting you to open it.

"Victor," Grits said, "something's been bugging me since I broke into your office last night. By the way, in case you didn't know, I broke into your office last night. Anyway, I can't stop thinking about it."

Victor waited.

"What's in the box?" Grits pointed.

"This box?" Victor tapped it.

"Yes."

"This one?"

"Yes, asshole. That box."

The smile widened. "Do you really want to know?"

Grits wheeled to the big man. "Do you know what's in it?" Golyam jumped and looked confused.

"Does he know?" Grits asked Victor.

Victor slowly shook his head. The smile kept growing.

Grits turned back. "You really don't know?"

"No," Golyam said, voice gone small. Grits figured the big man knew on some level and didn't want to.

Grits slid his chair back to see them both. "Nina, I want you to open that box."

Victor Karanovo flicked the hook and swung it open. Inside: the preserved head of the real Victor Karanovo.

Golyam shot up like a startled mastiff, the burst of air knocking Grits backward.

By the time he stood, "Victor" had become Nina—her true form—swimming out of her father's suit. The jacket and trousers now hung off her like a kid playing dress-up.

"Took you long enough, Scooby Boo Boo," she said.

The big man made a sound like a scared child trying to growl. He finally managed, "Nina... why—how?"

She went to him, pulled his head to her chest, and stroked his hair, whispering in Bulgarian.

"So the big guy's your brother?" Grits asked.

She kept stroking. "He is my brother. My son. My lover."

Grits' face twisted. His torpedo did too. "Nina, I gotta tell you. That's just gross. That's some nasty West Virginia shit."

She looked back at him and continued as if answering a different question. "Last year my father made a deal with your government to bring us here. In exchange for secrets about the Soviets, we got protection. They knew nothing of our clan, our nature."

She left the still-whimpering Golyam and glided to the bar, her father's pants shushing across the carpet. She poured a heavy Scotch.

"Of course his ideas for the clan were Old World—same old failures. So I killed him."

She pantomimed a sword swing, stuck her tongue out, crossed her eyes.

Still in Victor's oversized suit, she hopped onto the desk's edge, close to Grits. "You already know my plan. Open Midnight clubs in every major city—"

"And use the moonlight tech you stole from Prince Wym," Grits said.

She reached into a drawer and produced a large metal syringe. "Yes—paired with my greatest innovation. Science to beat the Old Country's dead ways. I used different dishwashers as guinea pigs until I got the formula right this week. Soviet truth serum and my blood. We'll grow our clan without the old theatrics. They won't even know until it's too late."

"That's what I was missing," Grits said. "How you were turning people without anyone noticing."

He heard how eager he sounded. What the hell was wrong with him? And why was she starting to say *our*?

She began sliding out of the suit. "My love, my king," she purred, naked now, sliding into his lap. "Miami is a toy. I only kept this place to occupy myself until I was sure of you—to know you were the man of the prophecy. A king from the world of light to take a queen from the shadows. Together we rule the Kingdoms of the Shadows—and then the world."

Her mouth brushed his ear. "Today I became sure. Even suspecting me, you couldn't stand to see me hurt by the Colombians. Despite your wealth, you still risk your life for others—even enemies. You are my King of Light. Think of what we could do with the power I give you."

Grits remembered Earl Mayfield's warning about pheromones —and then the dream took him.

He saw himself leading an army of man-wolves against Prince

Wym's vampires, the undead burning by the thousands. King of Light. Victorious.

Then Miami—wolves sniffing out the coke, smashing dealers, the city cheering.

Cuba—wolves devouring Communists. Fidel cornered; his head torn free; Nina mounting it on a stake in Havana as the crowd roared.

Moscow—blood flooding the Moskva; the Soviet Union erased in an afternoon.

Washington—The Holy Emperor of Light making the President crawl and beg; no mercy; his children tearing him apart.

Miami crowned as the Empire's capital, a fortress city. On the throne beside him: the Goddess Empress of Shadows. Peace through terror.

A young woman in white approached with her head bowed. She lifted her face—three claw marks raked across it and through the place her throat should be. She tore open her dress; from sternum to knees there was nothing left—devoured.

The face of Eleanor Stone looked up. "Grits, why did you do this to me?"

The spell broke. Grits shoved Nina off, scraped his chair back, and went for the revolver. He aimed for her face and fired—right as Golyam smacked his arm up.

"Big mistake," the big man said.

He grabbed Grits by the head and slammed his face into the desk. Again. Again. Blackness.

Consciousness returned as a tearing pain ripped his groin. Blood pumped from the inside of his right thigh. Two canine punctures stared up before they drowned in red.

He was sprawled across Victor's desk. Beside him stood Golyam and Nina; she was finishing her shift back to human, nude, wiping her mouth with her wrist, lips stained a pretty rouge.

"I'm sorry it had to be this way," she said. "But you gave me no choice. However, I will give you one."

Grits stared at the wound, then at her.

"Tomorrow night, around 10:40, the full moon rises—and you will be mine," she said. "With my bite, you belong to me whether you accept the privilege or not."

"I thought you were going to tell me about a choice," he said through clenched teeth.

"Option one: come to me before moonrise. Surrender. We will be bound in marriage. Your fortune becomes ours. You will reign beside me, and I will spare your friends."

He blew a raspberry. "Nope. Option two?"

"If you don't come—if you run, or worse, try something stupid —when the moon rises you will still be mine. I will force the marriage, take everything, and make your friends suffer. I will make you skin Eleanor Stone alive and I will wear her like a pelt— so you never forget that you did this to her."

"Let me talk to Gravy and get back to you," he said.

She softened, reached to stroke his hair; he flinched. She drew closer anyway. "You really don't know, do you? You can't feel it?" she whispered. "Your friend Gravy Watkins is dead. First he abandoned you for a woman, and then I had him killed."

For the first time since she'd met him, Nina saw fear and pain in Grits' eyes. He looked like a man holding back tears.

She touched his hair again; this time he didn't stop her. She climbed onto the desk beside him. "I am sorry for your pain," she said. "But it was the only way we could be together."

Tears welled. He shook his head no, then nodded yes like he understood.

She held the back of his head and searched his eyes. A single tear slid down his cheek.

"Nina," he said, voice wavering, "let's make it easy. There's been enough pain and fighting. Especially between Isaac and Gopher. I'm ready. I can tell you now." His eyes filled again; he smiled weakly.

She didn't know who Isaac and Gopher were, but she smiled back. "Yes, my love."

He sat up slightly, mouth opening like he was searching for the words—but really just setting himself for the highlight of his performance. A perfect headbutt.

He smashed his forehead into her face.

Nina reeled, blood pouring from her broken nose.

"Pretty good acting, huh?" Grits shouted. "I've been practicing for *The Love Boat.* I'm not just good looks and a tight ass—I've got range!"

Golyam moved to her, waiting for orders. She snapped her nose back into place.

"Not bad," she said. "But I'm still giving you until tomorrow."

She glanced at the big man. "Do what you want with him—don't overdo it. He's got a big night tomorrow, and I want all his plumbing in working order."

"Good-bye, honey!" Grits called. "See you tomorrow! Don't forget to check for fleas!" He really needed to workshop his werewolf insults.

Golyam loomed over the desk.

"You actually good with all this?" Grits asked as the big man reached for him. "Your sister-mom murdering your brother—dad—whatever Victor is. Uh, was." He was stalling, but he also wanted to hear it.

"She is the leader of the clan," Golyam said. "She is family. When the full moon arrives, you will be family, too."

"Not really an answer," Grits said. "But it's a lot to take in."

The big man grabbed his shirt collar and hauled him upright, drew back a ham-sized fist.

"Wait," Grits said. "I thought we were family."

"Not until the full moon."

Oh well, Grits thought.

He fluttered his lashes. "Be gentle," he said demurely. "Tomorrow's my wedding day."

Golyam went to work, raining blows down on Grits McCoy's head and face.

31

WEEKENDS WITH WYM

S aturday, 1:43 AM
Midnight Miami
1555 Collins Avenue, South Beach

As FRIDAY BLED INTO SATURDAY, the Midnight Miami still throbbed at capacity—bodies dancing, noses powdering, egos preening. Prince Wym drifted through the second-floor crush, content in the anonymity these places afforded. He blended. Or so he believed.

In truth, plenty noticed him—black on black, silk and leather, sunglasses indoors at night. A new fashion scene called "gothic" had been birthed off his wardrobe choices alone. But the attention never pierced who he was: not just a vampire, but a High Prince of the Shadows. Or so he believed.

"Heyyyy, Wym," a voice called. "How about that? Just when I thought this night couldn't get any better."

A human ear couldn't have heard it over the pulse of the

music. Wym's hearing was not human. He focused on the familiar drawl—the worst kind of familiar. Grits McCoy.

Wym knew Grits had entered just after six. He hadn't seen him leave.

On a black leather couch lay a wreck in a blood-splattered sport coat and shirt. Aviators failed to hide the swollen, purpled eyes. A bandage, poorly duct-taped to the inside of the man's right thigh, seeped. Grits had taken a methodical beating from Golyam. The bodyguard had started hauling him out, then abandoned the errand when Nina summoned him. Someone had slipped Grits a pill out of sympathy; it dulled the pain and left him high as a kite.

Wym slid off his sunglasses to be sure of the prize in front of him.

"It's you?" Grits grinned through split lips. "Thought so. Have a seat! Take a load off."

He patted the cushion, then chanted "Wym" to the beat of Rick James's "Super Freak." "Wym wym wym-wym. Wym-wym, wym-wym—" He paused to spit blood on the floor.

Wym sat and stared with open disgust. "What happened to you? What are you on?"

"Nothing. High on life." Grits fluttered his lashes. "I'm in love, dontcha know? Getting married tomorrow."

He tried to sit up, slumped back, and sang in a shaky falsetto:
I'm the King of the Light / She's my Lady of the Night.
She'll rip off Eleanor's face / If I don't take my place.
He groped for the next line and came up empty.
She's so bold / Gonna take all my gold / And then we—
Frown. Nothing.

Wym drew a long, serrated silver blade from his silk coat. One slash and the insect that occupied his time would be no more.

Grits wagged a finger. "No. No. Nope. If you do that, you don't get your gold back."

While Grits repeated "that... back... that... back," Wym slid the knife away. If he wanted his fortune returned under the Laws of the Shadows, he had to defeat Grits in proper duel—not murder him on a couch.

He considered what Grits had just blurted. Wym despised the filthy werewolf clans, but he'd studied them. The Neuri—the Karanovos—clung to an old prophecy: a Queen of Shadows would wed a King of Light. He'd known for months Nina had killed her father and stood in his place. Wym had been waiting for the right time to use it against her, but his arrogance had kept him from seeing the move the moment she chose Miami.

Grits sagged, drifting toward unconsciousness. Wym weighed the angles. The Karanovos had outmaneuvered the duo. He'd heard about their play on Gravy yesterday and hadn't believed anyone could take that black warrior down—certainly not this second-rate clan. But they had Grits. The bite on his thigh said he'd be fully turned by this time tomorrow unless he killed Nina first.

Wym's forces could crush the Neuri, even with Grits among them, but it would be long and costly. Worse, once Nina married the King of Light, the Karanovos would have lawful claim to the fortune Grits and Gravy seized when they killed Dracula. And Wym couldn't engage Nina directly now; her bite had claimed Grits under the Laws of the Shadows. Any direct move on the soon-to-be Queen would be forbidden.

There was only one play: help Grits and Gravy beat the Karanovos.

The enemy of my enemy is my friend, he thought, and felt his stomach turn.

He produced a small glass vial—a clotting draught humans didn't know existed. He usually used it to keep victims' blood off his carpet. On Grits it would clot and, as a side effect, speed recovery.

He tipped the liquid between Grits's lips. A weak protest, then acceptance.

Wym scanned for the cleanest way to extract him. As always, he impressed himself. He'd entered their club entirely undetected. Or so he believed.

When Nina called to Golyam's mind, he left Grits on the couch and hurried to the office where she had worn Victor's face.

He found her in back, bathed in the glow of CCTV screens, in human form and nothing but her dead father's dress shirt. He was still staring lustfully at his sister-mother when she snapped her fingers.

"Come here, you dog. Look at this."

On one monitor, Prince Wym sat beside Grits. The knife flashed and vanished.

Nina understood instantly. Wym needed Grits alive to reclaim his treasure. Which meant he had every incentive to help the race car driver kill her before moonrise. If she was going to take a shot at the prince, it had to be now.

"The three whores we used on the last dishwasher—have they all had the new injection?" she asked.

Before Wym could lift Grits and spirit him toward the second-floor exit, three impossibly beautiful women materialized—icy blonde, flawless dark-skinned beauty, and an exquisite Korean dolled up as a geisha, the loveliest of the lot.

He recognized them from the security footage Nina/Victor had shown Little Angelo. And he smelled them. These three carried Karanovo blood, likely via syringe like Dewayne Shelby. They were werewolves already and didn't know it.

They fawned over him, whispering filthy promises as they herded him to a side room.

The sign read WHITE ROOM. Dewayne's artificial-moonlight chamber. A trap.

Wym Blutmesser's pride colored everything. A lone vampire killing two werewolves was a feat. Three? That made you a legend.

Inside, the woman with the long black hair eased him onto a couch. A synthesizer throbbed. A beat dropped. The room blinked to black, then lit with pulsing disco strobes—red, yellow, pink, blue—on the rhythm. Any moment now the stored white moonlight would join the rotation.

Behind Miss Faux Geisha, the other two began undressing each other, mouths and hands everywhere. Misdirection. The third fondled Wym with her left hand while palming a loaded syringe in her right.

He met her eyes and broke the fingers holding the syringe. Her squeal cut out when he drove the needle into her chest. It would have killed a human. With the moonlight about to flood the room, he knew he hadn't seen the last of her.

The other two were so wrapped up in their act they didn't notice their partner drop. But Nina did. Watching the feed, she barked Bulgarian curses and sprinted to the master light panel. A button. The White Room detonated in moonlight.

The blast of white stunned Wym. The fallen Asian yanked the syringe from her chest and jammed it into his foot. He kicked her in the face with the same foot—too late. Enough tranquilizer remained to wobble him. He staggered like a sailor on a rolling deck.

He hit the floor, measuring the fog sliding through his body. Seconds, he judged. Unfortunately, seconds were enough for the other two to complete their change.

He played possum. When the pair pounced, he exploded between them and landed on the far side of the room, opening both their throats with silver daggers on his journey.

As they clutched at their windpipes, he targeted the closer beast—slash the knee, cut the Achilles, drop it, bury the dagger in the heart. He left the dagger and sawed the neck with his serrated blade. The head came free. By the time he ripped the heart-knife back out, the severed head had softened to human—the black woman first to fall. One down. Two to go.

The moonlight kept pulsing, feeding the other two, knitting their wounds. The Asian was still down, but not for long. The blonde roared; the sound rattled inside the soundproof room.

She charged. He slipped the first two swipes, then sprang wall-to-wall horizontally, never touching the floor. Gravity baffled her. When she paused to find him, he landed on her back and dragged the serrated blade for her throat—she raked his back with both hands, ripped him forward, and hurled him into the wall.

The wall lost. He did better. Best of all, he hit the side away from the Asian; if he'd landed near her, she would have chewed him from the ground.

He saw the blonde coil to lunge, jaws wide. He flicked his left wrist and produced a cloud of silver dust. She inhaled and collapsed, gagging. He gave her the kindness of a quick cut. Two down. One to go.

He was already composing the legend in his head when the fully recovered Korean werewolf launched a heel into his face.

In her office, Nina's curses didn't fix cameras. The blaze of moonlight had fried most lenses. The last working eye showed the blonde's death, then went black as the third wolf's kick carried Wym's body through it. Nina could hear the fight, not see it.

She couldn't let Wym leave Midnight Miami alive. She'd finish it herself.

A secret panel hissed open to reveal a crossbow loaded with a giant wooden stake. Bare legs under a white dress shirt, she grabbed the crossbow, slipped into a hidden passage, and reached the White Room entrance in moments. She kicked in the door and leveled the bow.

Prince Wym Blutmesser was gone.

On the floor lay three severed heads. And Nina knew Grits McCoy was no longer in the building.

———

Wym slid the unconscious Grits into the trunk, climbed into his limousine, and snapped, "Eighty West Flagler." The car rolled.

He popped a panel, jabbed a needle into his thigh, and hooked himself to an IV—modified blood that kicked recovery into overdrive. The aches from three beasts began to fade.

Across from him sat his sister—and lover— cradling an unconscious Cuban teenager and drinking delicately from her neck. As Wym changed from nightclub chic to black princely robes, he excitedly recounted the evening—finding Grits and, more importantly, slaughtering three werewolves.

The limo stopped at 80 West Flagler—the Stone Detective Agency. Outside, metal creaked; the trunk opened; glass shattered. Seconds later Wym ducked back inside, flustered, and rattled off new instructions to the driver.

"What urgency, my brother?" the princess asked, then returned to her meal.

"I have much to accomplish before sunrise," he said. "Much work."

He laid out the plan in detail. When he finished, she frowned.

"I do not wish to seem doubtful," his sister said carefully.

"Go on, my dear," he purred.

"I do not see why we go to such lengths for Grits McCoy and Gravy Watkins. These low creatures are our enemies, and their existence stains our house."

"That is simple, my dark flower," Wym said. "Tomorrow night they must fight a mighty clan of werewolves. The battle will tax them; if they win, it will be narrow. They must win so we may defeat them ourselves and reclaim our treasure. I can give them the tools. And I will have our forces ready to strike the instant their battle ends."

She hesitated. The rules of engagement dictated by the Laws of the Shadows were very convoluted, but an ambush sounded disqualifying.

Wym read it on her pale face. "On the night of a full moon, we have full right to engage without notice. The usual rules do not apply. When they are at their weakest, I will strike—and I will have my vengeance on Grits and Gravy."

32

LITTLE ANGELO GOES TO HELL, OR ROCKY II PART 2

Friday, 7:57 PM
Warehouse, West Palm Beach

GRAVY WATKINS REALIZED he was having that dream again.

Forced to relive the last moments of his life. Listening to the cries of his dying wife. The worst pain wasn't the spears—it was not remembering her name, while the name of the woman who killed them both stayed bright.

Lilith.

The second time he heard that name was when a burning woman, engulfed in flame but not consumed, came to him. She told him he was dead, and then she gave him a choice.

Head to his eternal reward and see his wife again. Or return to this world on a mission.

Destroy Lilith, the mother of vampires.

Dee Wheatley's cries brought Gravy back to the moment. Little Angelo was trying to mash her down across a big wooden crate, fighting to trap her wrists. She was twisting, kicking, still screaming—but running out of gas.

Gravy Watkins remembered why he was on this Earth and who he really was.

He remembered the reason the Maiden teamed him with Grits McCoy and sent them after Dracula: to grab the attention of the world of shadows in a way that could not be ignored.

To draw out Lilith, the mother of the vampires. And to send her to Hell.

But first, he wanted to add some kindling to keep Hell's flames hungry.

Doctor Fun and Cheryl stood ten feet away, pointing their tommy guns at each other and going *rat-a-tat-tat* with their mouths like a couple of dumb kids.

Doctor Fun never felt the thrown silver dagger that pierced his skull and severed his brain stem. Cheryl momentarily felt the pain from the dagger running west to east through his throat, but felt nothing more after Gravy removed his head from his body. The corpse of the good doctor received the same treatment after Gravy retrieved the dagger.

Dee's noise was thinning out. Little Angelo finally pinned her arms. He crawled onto the box and loomed over her, puffing, sweat pouring, and croaked, "Oh yeah."

Those two words made Gravy angrier than he'd ever been in his long life.

"Angelo Michael Frusciante," Gravy said, voice level and loud, "Hell from beneath is moved for thee to meet thee at thy coming: it stirreth up the dead for thee." He didn't realize he was speaking Latin.

Little Angelo turned his fat head. Those coal-black eyes found Gravy. He slid off Dee and off the crate. Dee scrambled behind it, eyes fixed on Gravy and nothing else.

If it was a miracle Gravy wasn't full of holes, it was an equal miracle his clothes still hung on him. The red suspenders were attached; the jeans barely scuffed.

Little Angelo shrugged out of his jacket and came on.

He didn't blink at going mano a mano with a man who'd been dead a few minutes ago. He kept that dead-eyed stare—until he saw something few ever did.

Gravy Watkins popped off his suspenders.

Dee said, "Oh, shit."

They charged. Haymakers, hooks, crosses—no feeling-out, no defense—just two freight trains colliding and echoing around the cavernous space.

Gravy relished the hurt; pain meant living. He let Little Angelo land a couple. A left broke his nose and watered his eyes. A right cross buzzed his feet.

Give the pig a sliver of hope. Let him think there's a chance. But Gravy already knew the ending. Hell was waiting, and Gravy Watkins was the ride.

He picked up speed. Jabs turned into fingertip shots to joints. Body blows slid into the kidneys. Little Angelo swung a right; his shoulder popped out of the socket.

Time to end it.

Gravy drove the four fingers of his left hand into Little Angelo's windpipe. As the fat hands flew to his throat, Gravy stamped his left boot through the right knee. The leg folded into a crooked V.

Gravy hooked him under the arms—hands still clutching at his own neck—and dragged him to a steel reel, one of those giant spools used for transporting telephone line. He heaved Little

Angelo onto the flat surface so his meatball head and neck hung over the lip.

He smashed Little Angelo's face twice. A few more would send him below.

A machine whirred to life. A blinding white light flooded the room from a belt-mounted moonlight lantern clipped under Angelo's jacket, searing the air—then Little Angelo flung Gravy off him.

Little Angelo Frusciante transformed into a full werewolf. He opened his arms wide and howled.

If the night beast expected Gravy to be fearful or impressed, disappointment came quick—and would soon be the least of his problems.

Gravy snatched a silver dagger from his boot and charged the exposed werewolf. He caught him in the groin and hauled the blade up to Angelo's throat, like he was field-dressing a deer. Gravy was face to face when the howl flipped to a high squeal.

"Miss Wheatley," Gravy called, clean and authoritative, "I recommend you avert your eyes for the next few moments."

Dee clapped both hands over her ears, turned her head, and stared hard at the concrete.

Gravy pushed Little Angelo onto the steel reel a second time. As he had done with Doctor Fun and Cheryl, he would heed Earl Mayfield's command to "finish the job."

Before he did, Gravy paused, searching for the meanest thing he could say.

"*Rocky II* was bullshit."

The hurt in Little Angelo's eyes was sweet. Two silver slashes later, Little Angelo's head bounced to the floor, and Sheol widened its mouth to receive Angelo Michael Frusciante.

Gravy climbed off the reel and snapped his red suspenders

back into place. He stepped into the open so Dee could see him—and so he didn't have to see her up close. He knew that look. He'd seen it plenty: fear at the sight of what he was.

"You okay?" he asked.

Dee laughed. "Me? Am I okay? I think I should be asking you."

She surprised him by running over, checking him like a mechanic—fingers brushing the nicked suspenders, palms across his chest to make sure he was real—then burying her face against him and squeezing with everything she had.

"Thank you for coming for me," she sobbed.

"All in a day's work, baby."

He eased her back by the shoulders and crouched to meet her eyes. "I know everybody's running hot, but I've got to get back to Miami. My brother Grits needs me. Car's full of gas and still running. Let's go."

Dee dabbed her eyes and nodded.

She headed for the car. Gravy took one last look around. He meant to lock the place before hitting the road—then something snagged his attention.

Dee slid into the passenger seat and watched him through the windshield, his head moving between the Gran Fury and the shadowed aisles.

She hopped back out just as he walked to the trunk and popped it.

"What are you doing?" she asked.

"Figuring how much cocaine I can fit in this car," he said.

Ten million dollars in coke later—trunk and back seat packed, a tight column of smoke already fingering the sky from the warehouse fire—Gravy and Dee headed south on I-95, following the speed limit like saints. Somewhere behind them, sirens began to stitch the night together.

"This might sound crazy," Dee said, "but I'm more scared driving around with these drugs than anything else today."

"I'm not worried," Gravy said, easy. "I'm a licensed private detective, and Miami-Dade will back our story. Plus this looks just like a police car—folks'll steer clear."

"Gravy," she said, flat, "you're a giant black man and a celebrity wearing nothing but red suspenders. Everybody who passes us slows down to stare."

Gravy shook her off with a smile.

"Sooo," she said, "you might not believe this, but I've got a few questions."

There were few things Gravy hated more than *these* questions, but he didn't have much choice.

"Shoot, baby," he said—then winced. "Uh, no pun intended."

She giggled. "First—when they shot you... were you dead?"

"Hm." He hunted for the words. "Not really."

"Not really? How is 'not really' even an option?"

"A long time ago, I died, but I got a chance to come back to finish some business. Since then, I've got a tolerance for death. Like chicken pox—you get it once, and you don't get it again."

"Did that hurt?"

"When I got shot?"

"Yeah!"

"Hurt like hell. I might not die, but I still feel it. I don't heal so much as snap back to how I'm supposed to be. The pain still comes with the trip."

Dee still couldn't believe it. "What if you got your head cut off?"

Gravy looked thoughtful. "That's a good question. Decapitation is the big loophole. Lose your head, and it's bye-bye—probably even for me."

She saw from his face she needed to switch topics. "So how old are you?"

"I'm pretty old."

"Like Aunt Esther from *Sanford and Son* old, or Miss Jane Pittman old?"

That got him laughing. "You know the Twelve Apostles?"

"Yes?"

"They all signed my yearbook," he said, cracking himself up. The joke was off by three hundred years or so, but worth it in his mind.

She snorted. "Come on—that joke is sooo bad. That's so terrible it's funny." She laughed and yawned at once, then brightened. "So you've gotta be the smartest man who ever lived. You must know everything."

That one landed hardest.

"The human brain's a sponge. Only holds so much. Mine's a sponge thrown into an ocean. Some things stick, some wash away. I meet folks I knew twenty years ago and don't recognize 'em. Hell, I think I taught my boy Earl about werewolves in World War II, but I don't remember a lick. I don't get to choose what stays."

"What's the oldest thing you do remember?"

"My wife. Our last day together. Every time I sleep, I go back to that day."

Dee had many questions she knew not to ask. So she said, "Your wife—what was her name?"

He couldn't hide the pain. "I… I don't remember anymore. Like I said, I don't control what fades. I just call her *Her*. But I know I'll see Her again. When I finish my mission."

Despite her youth, Dee felt the weight of it—the victories and the ache underneath. Everyone he loved, lost again and again, even their names washed away.

She yawned. Gravy saw his escape from more questions.

"Listen, you've had a long day. As you can tell, I'm not going anywhere. You can grill me later. Close your eyes. Get some rest."

She looked like she wanted to argue, but his words gave her body permission. She kissed his right bicep, tucked her cheek against it, and drifted off.

Miss Jane Pittman, Gravy thought. That's pretty good. Might have to put that one in the rotation.

33

REUNITED

S aturday, 2:27 AM
Stone Detective Agency
80 West Flagler Street, Miami

DETECTIVE RAFAEL PÉREZ was impressed by the coffee from the green pot. Eleanor said her old man got the recipe from the Dodgers during spring training. Pérez made a note to figure out how to duplicate it for Homicide.

To keep his mind off everything else, he wondered where Agent Wilson had disappeared to. Pérez hadn't seen or heard from him since they left the Mutiny that afternoon.

He watched Eleanor pace the office, waiting for anything to happen.

Without thinking, Pérez dove to the floor when the sound of shattering glass exploded beside him. For a second he figured a coffee pot had blown. It also sounded like something had come through the seventh-floor window. He kept his eyes squeezed shut and brushed his face for glass.

When he looked, he was staring at the night sky through a jagged hole where the window had been—and at what had been thrown through it by an Austrian vampire.

"Grits!" Eleanor cried, dropping to the crumpled man on the floor and cradling his head.

"Do I know how to make an entrance, or what?" Grits said through swollen lips.

Following Eleanor's lead, Pérez helped haul him to the big sofa.

Pérez didn't know where to start, but Eleanor did.

"So the meeting went even better than you expected?" she said.

Grits laughed, then winced—his ribs didn't care for the joke. "You could say that. Short version: Nina's been Victor the whole time. Then she bit me. Then her wolfman beat me for a few hours. Then somebody threw me through your window. If I don't marry her and fulfill a prophecy, she kills everybody I know. Either way I turn into a werewolf at the full moon."

Pérez stepped out to check the hall and make sure nothing else was flying in. Eleanor pulled the first-aid kit off the wall.

She sat on the couch and leaned into his face. "Where's Gravy?" Grits asked.

"We still don't know," she said, too dry for comfort. "Last word, somebody saw him in Liberty City this afternoon. That's it."

"Nina told me he was dead."

Eleanor tore an alcohol swab and dabbed above his eye.

"Ow! Did you hear what I said?"

She paused and met his eyes. "Yes. And I'm pretty sure he'll be back here soon. Now hold still—this cut is nasty."

He didn't realize it yet, but her certainty settled him.

"What makes you so sure?"

"Because," she said, opening another swab, "I spoke to the Maiden about you two today."

She gave him the short of it—the flaming woman who didn't burn, the warning, the test. Then she rooted in the kit again. "How'd you meet the Maiden?"

Grits realized he'd never told her. "Back when I was running Winston Cup. Day of my last race—the big wreck."

"The one where four guys died?" she said.

"You mean five."

Eleanor was puzzled as she spoke back to him the names of the dead drivers. She wasn't a Winston Cup fan, but the names of the dead drivers were honored in the South like they were Confederate heroes.

"You forgot one," Grits said.

"Who?"

"Me," he said, smiling as best he could.

Eleanor stopped working. Her look said *Explain*. He did.

"When I hit that wall, I was dead. Like dead dead. While my body was pinned in the car, the Maiden came. Said I had a choice. One: go back to life, keep racing, become the richest, most famous driver in the world—even that forget we ever talked. Two: be a hero and fight the darkness. Save a lot of people. I took door number two."

She thought of the Maiden's line about pure hearts, but an old question finally forced its way out.

"If you gave up fame and fortune, how do you two have so much money?"

Grits clutched imaginary pearls. "You don't have to—," she started to say, but he stopped her.

"By this time tomorrow I might be on a leash in somebody's

backyard," he said. "So why not. You've heard how Gravy and I started together, right?"

"You met at a roller disco and got in a fight?"

"Close. Celebrity roller disco… then we killed Dracula."

Eleanor remembered the Maiden saying she'd clouded Eleanor's mind about the craziness she'd overheard this past year. This one would've been near the top.

"*The* Dracula? 'Blah, I vant to suck your blood' Dracula?"

"Yep. The real one. Per the Laws of the Shadows, when we killed him, we inherited all his gold."

Impossible—but it explained a lot she'd chosen not to think about.

"So that's why you built a vault that looks like a church?"

"Yep."

"And why Prince Wym is after you?"

"You got it."

"How much money are we talking?"

"You know the federal budget?"

"Yes…"

"Like that, but with more zeroes."

"You gave up fame and fortune and ended up with fortune and fortune?" she said.

He put his hands up—then winced. "I don't make the rules. Apparently, this was all part of the Maiden's plan."

Eleanor's face made clear that Grits needed to share more detail.

"A long time ago, Gravy went toe-to-toe with the mother of all vampires. She killed him—but the Maiden gave Gravy a do-over. Come back, she said, and finish what you started. He's spent hundreds of years hunting her, but the monsters hid their queen. So the Maiden wrote a new play to really get their attention and draw every bloodsucker out of hiding. Pair Gravy up with me, take down Dracula, claim his fortune, and wait. We moved to Miami—sunshine, home-field advantage while hiding in plain sight, and now they all come after us."

"And that's why you want to go on *The Love Boat*? So they'll come after you?"

"No, we just want to go on *The Love Boat* because it's the greatest TV show of all time."

The door opened. Gravy Watkins filled the frame.

Eleanor wanted nothing more than to hug the giant, but she held back. The two brothers needed the moment.

Gravy stooped to Grits' level. "Pérez caught me up. I'm sorry I wasn't there."

"What happened?" Grits asked, and there was pain in it.

"Little Angelo grabbed Dee. I went and got her. She's out front with Pérez. Safe."

"No apology needed. You did right," Grits said. "You okay?"

"Got shot up with a tommy gun. Like James Caan in *The Godfather*, only with less back hair. Then I killed those two little shits and cut Little Angelo's head off."

"Awesome," Grits said, and they high-fived.

Eleanor knew it was past tense now. Somehow, they never lingered. It drove her nuts, but she finally understood: two best friends with pure hearts couldn't afford to dwell on the impossible or they'd go crazy. And she also knew one of them would say something dumb in five minutes to make her regret thinking nice thoughts.

But before her prediction came true, a solemn Rafael Pérez came in with Dee Wheatley. "You guys need to see something," Dee said.

They stepped into the wrecked main office, glass everywhere. On the floor lay a small shivering bundle, quietly warbling an Irish tune.

Grits knelt and lifted it. Inside was Barry the Leprechaun—bloodied, mangled, like a chewed dog toy.

Gravy and Eleanor crouched beside him. Grits stroked the red hair. Barry's eyes found him and brightened.

"My gold?" he whispered.

Grits looked up at Gravy. Gravy hurried to his desk, rifled drawers, came up with a quarter.

"Here's your gold, little man," he said, setting it on Barry's torn chest.

"Oooh... my gold," Barry breathed. He clutched the coin like a lost child found. "Thank you. Thank you so much," he said.

Then he closed his eyes and breathed his last.

The little bundle that Grits was holding got smaller and smaller.

Then Barry was no longer there.

Grits and Gravy stood. They spoke low so the others couldn't hear, then Grits turned to the room.

"Everybody go home and get some sleep. We'll be in touch in a few hours. One way or another, this ends today."

34

THE LAST SUPPER

Saturday, 3:47 PM
Gesù Catholic Church
118 NE 2nd Street, Miami

WHEN THE MAIDEN met Eleanor Stone she spoke like a loving mother to a cherished daughter. With Grits and Gravy, gentle hands wouldn't do.

The moment the men stood before her, the Maiden lit into them—furious, rapid-fire, a full broadside over their conduct these last few days and the desperate spot it had landed them in. She was so angry she delivered the whole monologue in French—a language Grits McCoy didn't know, and Gravy Watkins did know but pretended he didn't.

When she finished, Gravy offered the counterproposal.

"Well, thanks for the feedback, but here's our plan. With Arturo Santos' help—and Detective Pérez—we've put together a small army of Cuban exiles to hit Midnight Miami tonight.

Once they heard a Commie was involved, Arturo had to turn guys away. We figure the place will be jammed with werewolves, so the exiles come in hard and lay down lead. They'll hurt 'em bad, even if they can't finish 'em. Then Grits and I take off Nina's head. That breaks her line, frees anyone she turned, and Grits won't have to marry her and live in a doghouse like Snoopy."

They did their usual hand-slap routine, minus the pelvic thrust—out of respect to her—and looked to the Maiden expectantly.

After a silence, and maybe a groan, The Maiden said, "If the club is already full of werewolves, won't Grits be a werewolf?"

The duo glanced at each other. Grits said, "We've got that covered. An... ally gave us a way to keep moonlight off me long enough to get to Nina."

"And who is this ally?" the Maiden asked.

"Uh," Grits began, "Prince Wym."

The Maiden screamed.

Gravy jumped in. Wym—wanting the pair available for his own ends—had delivered a package to Grits' house with instructions. First, a suit cut like a vampire sun-suit but tuned to block moonlight so Grits could move without turning. Second, a special car to lead the assault, loaded with weapons. Finally, Wym had set a fire in the Everglades to blanket Miami in smoke and delay moonrise for a few hours—forcing the Karanovos to rely on their canned moonlight inside Midnight Miami. Keep the war in one box.

The Maiden folded her arms. "And why is your mortal enemy, Prince Wym, doing all this for you?"

"So he gets to kill us himself," Gravy said.

"Or in their words," Grits added, "'feast on our flesh.'"

"Oy vey," the Maiden said.

———

AFTER SHE RETURNED TO MIAMI, Dee Wheatley spent most of her time with Eleanor. The men thought nobody should be alone, so they paired off. Since Eleanor's Plymouth was stuffed with the missing cocaine—a secret the four agreed to keep—the women cabbed to Eleanor's Surfside condo for showers and a few hours of real sleep.

Around four, the phone rang.

Grits said, "We'd be honored if you'd join us for dinner. We've got something special to discuss, and it'd give us an excuse to take you out."

Listening, Dee looked charmed. Eleanor didn't fall for it.

"I told you two to stop taking women to Burger King," she said.

In the background Gravy made wounded noises. Grits said, "I'm hurt you'd think that."

Dee chirped, "You know, I never did get to take you to that new raw macrobiotic vegetarian place—"

Angry noises erupted down the line. "What did you just say?" Grits barked. "Are you speaking Dutch?"

"I don't think those are real words," Gravy said. "Is she having a stroke?"

"Guys," Eleanor cut in, "cool it. I know where we're going."

At 6:30 Eleanor leaned toward Dee and whispered, "Sorry about this. But we were always going to end up here."

"What are you ladies talking about?" Gravy arrived with a tray of milkshakes. Dinner at the Biscayne Boulevard Burger King was already done; dessert had started.

The second Eleanor heard the "v-word," she knew there was only way to avoid a food fight: steer to the nearest Home of the Whopper.

"Just girl talk," Eleanor said, then pivoted. "Didn't you two have something special to share? Isn't that why we're here?"

Gravy sat beside Grits. The men exchanged a look. Grits took point, sketching the attack plan—and their role in it.

"If this goes sideways tonight, you're both in real danger," he said. "Nina will send me after you. We're not letting that happen."

Gravy slid two thick envelopes across the table.

"New IDs and passports courtesy of Uncle Arturo," he said. "A hundred grand in cash each courtesy of us. When we roll out for Midnight Miami, Earl Mayfield takes you to the airport. Pick a flight far away. They'll be busy with us—you'll travel clean."

Dee bristled at the fatalism. "What if everything goes right?"

"Then you get a free vacation," Gravy said.

Eleanor thought of the Maiden's warning—the decision the men couldn't bear to make. Ever since she'd learned Grits would turn at moonrise she'd suspected what that choice would be. She hated saying it out loud, but she did anyway.

"What happens if you can't beat her—and she turns your best friend into one of those monsters?"

Grits looked to Gravy and nodded.

For the first time since Eleanor had met him, Gravy dropped the Gravy Watkins act. The radiant grin and easy charisma fell away. What remained was a weary warrior carrying the burden of keeping the world—and the people he loved—safe from great evil.

"I know what I'm taking on," he said. "And I know what he means to you. Though it would break my heart—though I'd rather die myself a thousand times..."

He stopped, gathered himself, and finished.

"If it comes to that, I'll take him out myself."

35

NO COVER CHARGE

S aturday, 9:17 PM
Midnight Miami
1555 Collins Avenue, South Beach

"IT'S A VITAMIN SUPPLEMENT. You want to take it," the big man said.

"I'm a waiter. Why do I need a vitamin supplement shot?" the smaller man whined.

Golyam spun him around and jammed the syringe into his shoulder.

As the waiter yelped, Golyam rumbled, "See? Don't you feel better?"

All day long, Nina and Golyam had been jabbing anyone who crossed the threshold of Midnight Miami—employees, hangers-on, every warm body they could catch—with a mix of Soviet-grade truth serum and Nina Karanovo's own werewolf blood. Once it hit, they all took orders like champs.

"Look how clean this place is," Nina said, watching the newly dosed janitors scrub the bathrooms like their lives depended on it. "We should've done this months ago—just for the toilets."

She'd been preparing for this night for months, giving of herself in the most literal way. Every day she drew her own blood and banked it. Once she nailed the ratio—how much of her blood to truth serum—she mixed batch after batch and stacked it in one of the walk-ins.

Bartenders were jabbed the second they clocked in. The serum loosened their gears, then came the order of the night: *anyone who takes an injection drinks free.* Doormen and bouncers got stuck too —then told to forget IDs, forget cover, and definitely forget the fire code. Pack the place.

While Golyam prowled for stragglers, Nina stood on the roof and cursed the night sky.

Prince Wym's smoke from his forest fire did its job, laying a hazy dome over South Beach. She cursed herself for sending the three whores after Wym instead of letting Golyam tear the leech's throat out. His time would come soon enough.

She was ready. She'd already changed into her sacred war gear —black leather armor cut for her lupine form, protection without losing speed. Her fingers brushed the Wepwawet sigil on her chest: opener of ways, leader of armies, usher of the dead. Tonight Nina Karanovo, Queen of Shadows, would do all three.

Behind the smoke she could feel the moon coming—feel it in her blood. And with it, she felt her lover. Her King of Light. He'd be here soon. He would be hers.

She'd hoped Grits McCoy would come willingly, see reason. She was literally offering him the world. Since he wouldn't take it, she'd bend him to her will and start by making him tear Gravy Watkins to pieces.

As for Eleanor Stone, Nina had revised her plans. Instead of skinning her and wearing her like a pelt, she'd make her new husband eat Eleanor alive—one bite a day, every day—for as long as it amused her.

———

HAVING PROVIDED the wheels for Grits and Gravy, Prince Wym's minions would signal him the moment they rolled. His legion would move right after—bound for Midnight Miami and the reclamation of what was his.

The dark prince paced his lair and took questions from the Law Priest. Mostly boilerplate questions about the presence of religious icons: crosses, crucifixes, the Chi-Rho, a living symbol of the Resurrection, etc.; relics and such that would not allow Wym to engage in battle. The dark prince assured him that Midnight Miami would be free of such items.

Then, Wym peppered the Law Priest with questions. No surprises, not tonight. Wym recited, in exacting detail, everything he'd done in the last twenty-four hours to "assist" his enemies. Check. Composition of the suit and the weapons he'd sent. Check. His presence inside the battlefield earlier today. Check. The killing of the three she-wolves. Check. Was the Law Priest properly impressed? (Reluctant) check.

And on it went. Check. Check. Check.

Finally, Wym presented an ancient blade—a broad dagger, an unholy marriage of stone, steel, and silver. Its red hue wasn't patina; it was history. He described how he meant to use it—to skin his foes alive, to feast on their flesh—and asked the only question that mattered: could this be the weapon that restored his family's honor and fortune?

Check.

———

Outside Arturo's in Little Havana, Grits McCoy and Gravy Watkins gave each other the once-over. Grits wore the suit Wym provided, the love child of a vampire's sun suit and a Winston Cup fire suit, with a small helmet and smoked visor he'd snap down when they rolled.

Gravy wore thick blue jeans and black combat boots. His red suspenders were wider than usual, reinforced to cradle the blades strapped across his bare back. A revolver loaded with six silver rounds rode his belt—the contingency plan if they failed and Grits turned.

Detective Pérez's call confirmed the Cuban exiles were set and waiting. Goodbyes were said to Eleanor and Dee. Everybody tried to thread the needle between hopeful and final. The hugs—Gravy with Dee, Grits with Eleanor—lasted a beat too long, and no one minded.

Earl Mayfield rolled up in a retired taxicab, camouflage for the airport run. His arrival started the clock.

Eleanor refused to leave on a down note. She asked about the car Wym had supplied. The boys lit up like kids. Grits trotted to a shape under a black nylon cover and whipped it off.

The car took a second to process. Under the armor and paint it was the black '75 Eldorado that had vanished from the impound; above that, it was something else entirely. Tank-like plating. A battering ram welded to the nose. Wheel wells flared to swallow off-road truck tires. Paint was midnight, dressed with Grits's old 13 on the doors and a Duke's Mayo logo on the hood—just like the Charger from his Winston Cup days.

"I hope Duke's doesn't have a lot of werewolf customers," Eleanor said with a weary smile.

"Shh," Grits said, finger to lips. "Our secret."

Then came the real goodbye. Grits stepped to Eleanor, kissed her long and hard; she kissed him back.

"I'll see you real soon," he whispered, then joined Gravy. Eleanor crossed to the cab with Dee. Earl pulled away into the night.

Something moved in Grits's chest—fear. Not of pain; that never bothered him. Fear of losing someone he cared about. He let it wash over him, just for a breath, then tucked it away for later. Race mode.

Gravy watched the change come over his friend—feel, then focus. The two men shared a look, then grinned.

"Gentlemen, start your engines," Gravy said.

They turned toward their war wagon—and stopped.

Agent Ronald Wilson stood in the street.

Given how illegal the evening was about to be, everyone had agreed Pérez and Sweetpea would sit this one out. Wilson, though, had fallen off the grid completely. After Nina's reveal, they'd stopped thinking about him at all.

But the way he looked now—well, that was new.

He stood there in the same FBI suit from the first day, only it looked like he'd slept in a mud puddle. His face was pale and slick with sweat. Hair once combed neat was now a wild, wet halo around his bald spot. His eyes were the eyes of a frightened man.

Wilson was holding something in his right hand. It was purple.

"Is that a...," Grits whispered.

"I hope not," Gravy said, quieter still.

Grits searched for gentle words to cool him down, but Gravy got there first.

"Wilson, what are you doing, you honky bitch?" he barked.

Agent Wilson's mouth tugged into a sick smile. He spoke slowly, like a feverish kid unsure if he was awake.

"The full moon draws near. My time hiding in plain sight is over. You boys thought you had it all figured out, but you missed what was right in front of you."

He opened his hand wider. Grits and Gravy saw what he held. They fought not to panic. Their faces lost the fight.

"Wilson," Grits said softly, "let's talk about this."

"C'mon, man," Gravy added, voice trembling a hair.

Agent Ronald Wilson lifted his right hand high—and smashed the egg against the pavement.

36
———

HIGH NOON AT THE
MIDNIGHT MIAMI

S aturday, 9:34 PM
Midnight Miami
1555 Collins Avenue, South Beach

Nina Karanovo still stood on the roof, staring at the smoke ceiling that kept the full moon from her. No amount of cursing would punch a hole in it.

When Grits McCoy kissed Eleanor Stone in Little Havana, the Queen of Shadows felt a jolt rip through her. For a heartbeat she rode the wire of his emotions—fear, loss, anger, resolve, love.

Two things snapped into focus. First: Grits McCoy would never be hers completely. She could bend him, break him, drive him mad, but some spark of the true man would always live. Second: Grits and Gravy were on their way—and they weren't coming to surrender.

Nina sprinted inside toward the second-floor control booth, calling to Golyam through the cord between their minds.

The big man shouldered past doormen and latecomers, slammed the front doors, and threw the locks. He yanked down the metal grating and chained that, too, ignoring the protests.

From her perch in the control room, Nina looked out over the club. She'd never seen Midnight Miami so jammed. She palmed the light board, breathed in the moment—the end of years of planning and blood—and pressed the button.

Red.

Yellow.

Pink.

Blue.

Red. Yellow. Pink. Blue.

White.

Red. White. Yellow. White. Pink. White. Blue. White.

White. White. White. White. White. White. WHITE. WHITE. WHITE.

WHHHHHHHHHHHHHIIIIIIIIIITTTTTTTTTTEEEEEEEE.

The charge of a thousand new souls ran through her. The building shuddered with the collective cry of her newborn clan.

In Little Havana, Grits and Gravy coughed through the pastel-purple smoke that had exploded from the egg thrown by Agent Ronald Wilson. As the cloud thinned in the summer air, they saw what stood where the man had been.

"Oh hell no," Gravy said.

"Not this. Not now," Grits groaned.

They'd always known something was sideways with Wilson. They should've dug harder. Too late.

Ronald Wilson was an Easter Bunny.

Of everything that slithered and crept through their world, none irritated Grits and Gravy more. Easter Bunnies were useless —a nuisance with legs. No prey hunted them, they hunted nothing, and all they could do was hop and make jellybeans. There were rumors vampires were allergic to them or something, but they'd never seen proof. In every melee Grits had seen, the bunnies died first, messily, and the only legacy was six months of finding jellybeans in your shoes, ashtrays, and underwear drawer.

Wilson looked exactly like a department-store bunny—same proportions, same grin—except it was all real. Real fur, a sick sherbet blend of pink and purple. Real buck teeth. Real eyes, wet and veined and bulging, enough to make you queasy.

He also wore underwear—enormous white Jockey briefs. Now that the smoke was gone, they could see why.

"Man," Gravy said, "what the hell is wrong with your balls?"

"There's nothing wrong with my balls," Wilson whistled through his choppers.

"Come on," Grits said. "There is obviously something very wrong with your balls."

Wilson looked like a Jockey ad gone to hell. His disgusting bunny penis was smashed against the cotton; the right testicle was bad enough, but the left was the show—swollen and laced with veins like a nest of snakes trying to climb out.

"I have a varicocele. It's just varicose veins. Lots of guys have it. Perfectly normal," he huffed.

"If Jim Palmer was here," Gravy said, "he'd punch you in the mouth."

"The time has come for us to fight," Wilson declared. "The full moon nears. Now we can battle the shadows together!"

"So you knew all along about Karanovo, you son of—" Grits started, then staggered. He felt the surge—moonlight flooding the bodies inside Midnight Miami. Those were his fellow werewolves unless he and Gravy stopped Nina.

"It's time," he said. "We have to go."

Easter Bunny Wilson bounded into the Eldorado before they

could stop him. Grits and Gravy climbed in. Grits snapped down helmet and visor.

"Look at the bright side," he said. "It can only get better from here."

The armored black Cadillac roared. Headlights—and the glowing Duke's Mayo logo—flared, and they tore into the smoky dusk.

———

Inside Midnight Miami, Nina stood in full wolf, battle armor gleaming. The DJ booth was gone; she would speak to her army from center stage.

She surveyed the newborn Neuri. The dance floor was a sea of fur and neon. Wolves leaned over balcony rails, eyes on their queen. Clothes had mostly shredded in the change—jean jackets reborn as vests—but the hair dye and New Romantic paint jobs had come along for the ride. Fur ran pink, green, purple; some wore mohawk stripes from crown to tail.

A circus, she thought. A freak show. Maybe the Old Country had been right about some things. Later. Tonight was the prophecy: the coronation and marriage of the King of Light and the Queen of Shadows.

She rose to full height atop the platform.

"My children! My clan! Your king—the King of Light—comes to us tonight. He is coming now!"

Howls answered her.

"But know this," she said, voice dropping. "Your king has gone mad with desire for me. When you see him, bring him to me!"

The howls climbed.

She punched the board again, flooding the club with only

white moonlight, then bared her fangs and roared, "And if anyone keeps you from your king—devour their flesh to the bone!"

Her last word was drowned by an explosion of brick, glass, plaster, and steel. The #13 Black Cadillac smashed the grating, plowed the lobby, and fishtailed onto the jammed floor. It spun to center stage, launching wolves like bowling pins.

As it rotated, Grits and Gravy popped their doors and fired shotgun blasts into the incoming throng. At the same time, waves of jellybeans flung from the car—Wilson's unsolicited contribution—adding an unexpected visual to their already dramatic entrance.

The plan was simple: hold the throng until the Cuban battalions poured in. Seconds later, machine guns rattled from the gaping entrance. The Cuban cavalry had arrived.

Phase I was a success. Phase II would be harder.

The partners hustled to the trunk, loaded with weapons for this evening's festivities, emptying the last shells into anything with teeth on the way. Grits's suit—Wym's handiwork—flared white, drinking the pulsing moonlight. He felt it working...and wondered how long it would.

Easter Bunny Wilson pinwheeled into a three-wolf pack. They snatched him out of the air and spiked him to the floor. Clouds of pink-purple fur puffed up. New record, Gravy thought. Damn Easter Bunnies.

Grits and Gravy shrugged into preloaded tactical vests—black pistols with ball ammo for the unwilling turned, silver pistols for Nina and Golyam—and Gravy strapped on enough silver steel to stock a museum.

Grits was still admiring the shine when something heavy dropped on him from above. He rolled, fired twice into the face of the first beast, then double-fisted pistols upward and stitched the air. Wolves were coming off the second-floor rail like paratroopers. Gravy saw it too and started harvesting them mid-fall.

The rain became a storm. Pistols clicked dry; fresh ones came up; the stack dwindled. Around them the Cubans were getting swamped. The fight was ending before it started.

Then a voice boomed over the chaos.

"Torpedoes—away!"

Word of the coming assault had run up Washington Avenue all day. When Tom Torpedo heard that Grits and Gravy were in danger, he raised his own cavalry.

Tom stood on a camo-painted Ford Bronco with tractor tires and stadium speakers. He wore matching camo bikini trunks and a neon-pink sombrero even bigger than Thursday's. An outsized machete rode his right hand like a conductor's baton.

He pointed. Fifty homosexual men—dressed like Tom and carrying identical machetes—charged the wolves, screaming.

From the Bronco, the guitar lick of Petey Maymoore's "Freak for the Cheeks" ripped. Tom's two muses danced beside him as the hook hit:

Oh, smack smack

Yeah, clap clap

No need for you to speak

I don't think I'm unique

But you gots to know, baby,

I-i-i-i am a freak—

A freak for the cheeks

The gays carved a path with cheerful savagery. With their help, the Cubans cleared the floor and shifted fire upward, knocking leapers out of the air and driving the rest to cover.

"Good job, vegetarians," Gravy said.

"When this is over, we gotta start eating more okra," Grits answered.

On the second level, Nina and Golyam waited. The partners traded a look. Phase II.

They sprinted, used the Cadillac as a launch ramp—hood to roof to rail—and landed on the balcony, moving toward the platform.

Face-to-face at last.

Time was bleeding out. The white pulses kept healing anything still breathing; the machine-gun rhythm was breaking up with more screams in the mix.

Nina, all wolf and battle leather, looked like a Frank Frazetta painting come to life—plates and straps giving protection without stealing speed. Even this monstrous, she was beautiful.

"I must admit, my King of Light," she said, "you and your mighty friend have proved your worth."

"Nina," Grits said, "surrender now. We can stop this. We can figure it out."

She looked at him with a sad kind of pride. "My Scooby Boo Boo, I have gone too far. There is no redemption for me. What is started must be finished. Only victory or death."

Gravy felt it—Grits softening when the moment required steel. Not now.

Nina felt it too—and refused to exploit it. If she was to die, it would be an honorable death. She reached into what she'd learned when Grits kissed Eleanor. She found the words that would permanently sever whatever tied them together.

"I know where you've hidden Eleanor Stone. She's at the airport. I'll go now. I'll find her and peel her like a grape."

Grits's hand flashed. A silver hatchet spun for her face. She slipped just enough; it chewed leather and nicked her neck. The silver burned; she staggered. Grits bounded off a speaker and kicked her under the chin, knocking her off the platform.

People thought they had Grits and Gravy pegged—two goofs

who loved cheeseburgers, boobies, and *The Love Boat*. Dumb jocks with fast cars and faster women. There was truth in that, especially the Burger King part.

But what people never understood about both of them was the real bond—a coin with two sides. On one side: pure hearts. They saw the best in everyone and protected the ones who couldn't protect themselves—especially the people they loved.

On the other: an incredible anger. Fury at a world where they lost friends and parents. Where women and children were abused and discarded. Where evil men—and creatures in the shadows—preyed on the frail and the weak.

The distractions kept them from being consumed by that anger. But when it came down to it, Gravy Watkins was the only person Grits McCoy ever met who was as angry as he was. And like Gravy, he knew how to use it.

Grits let his rage sharpen. Silver axes in both hands, he climbed to claim the high ground—and caught a dropkick that sent him skidding.

He rolled with it, tucked, hit, and sprang. Nina met him with a blur of clawed strikes; he caught and answered them with his axes, the rhythm quickening until she was defending, not dictating. Her paw armor saved her hands from being lopped clean off.

Time for the last lesson the Maiden taught him. Grits began to spin—controlled frenzy, axes coming from everywhere, no openings to counter. She leaned away from a throat cut at the last instant; the blade missed flesh but sliced the straps holding her Wepwawet plate. It flopped forward. Her chest and heart now vulnerable.

Across the platform, Gravy and Golyam circled. The confined space took away some of the big man's advantages; that was Wym's gift, whether he knew it or not. Golyam's armor—leather and metal plates laced by straps—had gaps at the flanks and under the arms. Getting to them meant risking Golyam's jaws around his throat.

They drew steel. Golyam's broadsword was a slab. Gravy's blade was elegant and double-edged—and silver. He had more, but silver wouldn't last long against that anvil.

No time. The broadsword hissed past his nose. Gravy pivoted and flurried. The wolfman read every beat; sparks showered.

Steel rang. Golyam's broadsword shattered Gravy's silver, the continuing arc cleaving through Gravy's right kneecap.

Gravy went to the ground, leaning forward, neck exposed, no sword to guard it. Golyam was already pivoting, in motion to deliver the *coup de grâce.*

Gravy had cheated death a hundred ways, but one rule held even in the shadows: take the head, end the man. He braced for it. He thought of Her.

Nina had to adjust for her exposed chest. She crossed her armored forearms and bulldozed Grits, shoving him backward across the stage. He juked left, pirouetted, chopped for her back; she backhanded; his axe bit leather; her claws snagged fabric.

Time slowed. Grits watched the world the way he watched a racetrack at speed. Nina stumbled over a downed speaker— enough to show him a target. He could bury an axe in her chest or—

Behind her, he saw Gravy on one knee. Golyam pivoting to end it.

Grits had to choose where to take his one shot. What would Gravy do? Grits knew. He threw the axe.

Nina stumbled, recovered, and prepared to pounce, but dropped to her haunches to dodge the silver blade.

And she saw it: the suit. Where her claws had caught, the glowing white flickered and died to black. Other damaged patches were already black. She had an idea.

Before Golyam's blade found Gravy's neck, the sword was met by flying silver axe. Sparks flew as the big man could not finish his stroke.

Gravy retrieved the silver six-shooter meant for Nina–or Grits–and fired two rounds at Golyam's face. The first missed, but the second caught the side of his neck.

The wolfman's hands went to his wound and provided Gravy the opening he needed. He surged off his good knee and rammed his broken silver blade up under Golyam's flank where the straps crossed—through leather, through flesh. He pushed upward, cutting the straps loose, and drove the blade into the big man's heart.

Howling, Golyam stumbled back, pinned by the wall. Outside he might have escaped; in here he was cornered.

It would've finished a man, but Golyam was not a man. Gravy had to finish the job.

The wolf slipped into his human face, a scared, enormous child. Pity tugged at Gravy. He'd been nothing but a dog to his father and his mother-sister. Who knew what else they'd done to him?

Gravy chose to give him the dignity of an honorable death. From far back in his mind a song rose. He sang, in Bulgarian:

Maritza rushes,
stained with blood,
A widow wails,
fiercely wounded.

Golyam's dimming eyes brightened. He answered, voice rough, the old anthem *Shumi Maritsa:*

O Bulgarians,
the whole world's watching.
Into a victorious battle,
let's gloriously go.

Together they sang the chorus:
March, march,
with our general,
Let's fly into battle
and crush the foe!

Golyam nodded. He closed his eyes, leaned forward to show his neck, and began the chorus again. Quietly, Gravy drew another silver sword from his back and, in a single clean motion, gave the Bulgarian warrior the peace he'd earned.

Nina and Grits circled each other. She made the first move. She attacked and repeated the bulldozer. Grits let her close, spun as she passed, and tried to mount her back—exactly what she wanted. Her claws sank into the moonlight suit. She thrashed, shook him loose—and came away with a big chunk of fabric.

Grits bounced back to his feet. Nina stood with her arms wide. Grits knew this was too easy, but he would worry about that after he sunk the axe into her heart.

Time slowed down again. But not like before. His arm began the motion to throw and then. Nothing.

Then felt the pain begin on his right leg, At first, it felt cold. Then hot. Very hot.

Grits saw the large tear in suit's leg. The oddness of the sight compounded by the material flickering from white to black.

Nina charged. He stood frozen. Two swipes tore the rest of the suit away; a backhand smashed his helmet. He sprawled on his back, naked to the pulsing moonlight.

He was back in the race car the night he died—the first moment he saw the fire, then the long moment as it breached the fire suit and worked its way over him.

But that was nothing. He felt the light run through him. He felt his humanity pushed out of his body.

Agony.

Something ancient unrolled—prophecy reaching its hour. Gunfire and howling stopped. Faces turned to the stage.

Gravy walked from the other side of the platform, dragging this right leg, which had yet to recover, six-shooter revolver in hand, four silver bullets remaining. Nina saw the gun and ducked behind speakers. Her voice slid into Grits's mind.

Kill Gravy Watkins now.

Grits shoved himself upright, mouth open in a soundless cry. Hair crawled across his skin. His mouth and nose pushed into a snout. He saw his friend. He saw the last hope for humanity.

"Gravy—do it," he forced out—the last of his human face falling away.

Gravy threw the pistol down and shook his head. "No."

Nina rose and walked to dead center. Her time had come—her coronation in red. She moved closer. She wanted to feel the spray when Gravy's blood hit.

"Kill him now," she commanded.

The werewolf that had been Grits McCoy roared and launched —claws out, arcing for Gravy.

Four gunshots cracked through Midnight Miami.

37

ELEANOR'S CHOICE

S aturday, 9:37 PM
    Intersection of NW 27th Avenue and NW 11th Street, Miami

THE MOOD in the fake cab was dour, which made sense. Eleanor Stone and Dee Wheatley had just said their teary goodbyes to Gravy Watkins and Grits McCoy. Even Earl Mayfield—grizzled Florida swamp rat that he was—had a little extra moisture in his eyes.

One more light and the yellow "taxi" would hit the Dolphin Expressway straight to Miami International, where the ladies could pick any destination on the board. That was the plan: keep Eleanor and Dee safe if Grits and Gravy failed.

Which is why it surprised the hell out of Earl when Eleanor leaned up and murmured, "Earl, change of plans. Take a right at the light."

He started to protest. Eleanor produced her .38. "Right at the light. Then pull over."

He took the right.

Dee's eyes went wide. Whatever this was, she wasn't in on it. Her confusion doubled when she saw Sweetpea Castilla and Detective Pérez idling on motorcycles at the curb.

Eleanor asked Earl for his silver-bullet six-shooter, which he quickly handed over. As she hopped out, Sweetpea passed her a bundle of black clothing—police body armor—which she pulled over her outfit.

Earl and Dee climbed out in time to hear Eleanor say, "I have to get down there. Grits and Gravy need me."

Dee blinked. "But what about what Gravy said? I thought he was real clear—he'd handle it if—"

"That was his *Love Boat* act," Eleanor said.

"What?" Dee and Earl asked together.

"Gravy's been rehearsing a big dramatic monologue for when he gets on *The Love Boat*," Eleanor said, buckling straps. "He wrote it himself. He's adopting a dog that might have rabies from Doc Bricker and promising he'll put the dog down if he has to. I've heard him practice it a hundred times."

Earl frowned. "Doc Bricker has rabies?"

Eleanor ignored him and continued. The instant Gravy started doing his *Love Boat* voice, She knew he'd never kill Grits. And then a bigger thought clicked: nobody had considered a sneak attack on Nina Karanovo.

Since yesterday, she'd chewed on the Maiden's line about "a decision they could not bear to make." At first she figured it meant killing Grits if the full moon beat them. A few hours later Eleanor had the real epiphany: the decision they couldn't bear was risking her life.

At Burger King, she'd excused herself, hit a pay phone, and

looped in Sweetpea—who'd been itching for action—and Pérez, who'd been itching even worse. Since no one expected them, they'd run a side job: assassinate Nina Karanovo.

Sweetpea kick-started his Kawasaki KZ1000J. Eleanor swung on behind him.

"You're going to kill Grits?" Dee blurted.

Eleanor took a helmet. "Only if Option One fails."

"What's Option One?"

"Put that bitch Nina Karanovo down like the dog she is."

She snapped the helmet's visor down.

Eleanor, Sweetpea, and Pérez roared into the twilight.

Well, that was unexpected, Dee thought. She looked at Earl.

The werewolf expert grinned. "Have you decided where you're going'? I hear Detroit is beautiful this time of year."

Sweetpea bobbed and weaved through traffic, earning honks and rude hand signals. He knew the fight at Midnight Miami would be quick and ugly; every second counted.

Eleanor clutched him tight, letting loose a small involuntary yip every time they hit a bump. She shut her eyes and ran the plan again.

Pérez muscled his bike to keep up. Adrenaline had him locked in. For years he'd dreamed of returning to Cuba to liberate his people. This wasn't that—but a shot at a Communist werewolf queen would do.

Earlier, waiting for Grits and Gravy, Eleanor had studied the Midnight Miami plans from the Pérez/Wilson file—especially the secret passage Grits used.

The plan she pitched to Sweetpea and Pérez was simple: sneak in the secret way; find Nina; fill her with silver.

They slid into the alley behind the club. Gunfire echoed. Eleanor led them to the hidden door—exactly where she expected it.

Pérez checked his M16—a birthday present from *Tío* Arturo—and made sure Sweetpea did the same. "I'll clear the way," Sweetpea said. "You follow. Where first?"

"Second floor," Eleanor said. Nina would be up there, using the platform to run the show. If she was on the floor, they'd have the high ground.

The door was locked. Sweetpea put a round through the handle. The door swung.

"Time to make the donuts," Pérez said, stepping into the stairwell.

They cleared the first turn clean. At the second, two wolfmen charged. Pérez dropped them with two crisp double-taps.

A third came out of nowhere and tackled Sweetpea. They tumbled toward Eleanor. She braced on the rail; the pair rolled past. She fired twice into the wolf's skull. It howled and stayed down. She hauled Sweetpea up.

"Thanks," he said, and they pushed on.

At the second-floor passage, a door with two-way mirror glass gave a perfect view of the platform.

A growl rumbled behind them. Sweetpea and Pérez stepped off and opened up fire.

Eleanor looked through the glass. Nina was crouched behind stage gear. Eleanor had her shot.

She turned the knob. It turned—but the door didn't open.

She shoved. The frame had been torqued in the fight. Jammed.

More howls. More shots from Sweetpea and Pérez.

Through the glass she saw Grits McCoy bare-chested at center stage—his body changing shape.

Eleanor yanked the door. Nothing.

She saw Gravy draw the silver-bullet revolver—then throw it down.

"No. No, no," she said.

Nina slipped from behind the equipment, chest and back exposed, and started toward the center.

Eleanor kicked the door. Nothing.

On the stage, Grits became all wolf and launched.

The door finally screeched open. Nina turned at the sound.

Eleanor raised her revolver and fired—four silver rounds into Nina Karanovo's exposed chest.

38

———

THE REVENGE OF PRINCE WYM

S aturday, 10:21 PM
    Midnight Miami
    1555 Collins Avenue, South Beach

ELEANOR STONE MOVED across the platform, pistol trained on Nina Karanovo. Two rounds left.

From her perch she looked down to the floor: dazed club kids in shredded neon, hemmed in by Cubans with machine guns and what looked like a platoon of very fit male swimmers without a pool. In the middle, a black armored Cadillac idled, the Duke's Mayo logo glowing on its hood.

Beside the riser lay Nina—on her back, blowing pink foam. Four tight silver holes across her chest.

She'd reverted to her true human form—but it wasn't the sexy, radiant number that had spent a week trying to reel Grits in. This Nina had a lazy right eye, the mustache of a fourteen-year-old boy, deflated breasts, and a beer gut that could hang with the fattest guy at any Dolphins tailgate.

Eleanor had started the week debating which European city to visit first. Now she was deciding whether to end a werewolf queen's life.

She knew this choice would be the one that truly changed her life.

Nina began to speak, but Eleanor had already made her choice. "Nice mustache," she said, and put a silver round through Nina's forehead.

Grits McCoy came to shirtless and sprawled on a stage, not entirely sure where "here" was.

A big black arm reached down and hauled him up. Gravy Watkins gave his friend a side-hug and steered him toward the far rail of the platform.

"How'd we do?" Grits asked, truly not sure.

His best friend smiled. "We did just fine."

Across the platform, Eleanor—riot gear, helmet off—appeared with Sweetpea Castilla and Detective Pérez. She hugged the brothers hard, lingering a beat longer with Gravy. "How'd you know I'd be there?"

Gravy let her go so he could look her in the eye. "The Maiden and I knew you'd make the right call."

Through the gaping hole out front, Tom Torpedo's Bronco fishtailed into the night. Sirens grew. Eleanor nodded toward Nina's corpse. "Save the chit-chat. Let's take her head and go."

"Hey, uh, guys?" Sweetpea squeaked, pointing down to the floor.

Eleanor turned. A dozen death-white men in head-to-toe black leather stood in formation, each toting steel. Anybody not on the stage made a very fast decision to get out of the building.

Two figures stepped out front. First, a fussy cross between a vampire priest and an attorney: the Law Priest, in collar and bifocals, clutching a leather tome the size of three phone books, a dozen ribbons bristling from its edges.

Second, a pale slender man with neon-red eyes full of fury and hatred.

"Hey, Wym!" Gravy called. "Thanks for the car. We're done with it. We left the keys in it."

However, Eleanor knew by the changing posture of Grits and Gravy that this was not a joke.

Prince Wym sneered. "Tonight, I claim my vengeance."

Grits cupped both hands to his mouth, blew a long raspberry, then said, "Ambush? Nah. That's definitely against your stupid rules."

Wym slanted a look at the Law Priest—*Am I good?*—and got a brisk nod.

Without another word, Prince Wym strode toward the stage. The rest of the warriors were side-by-side to him with only the Law Priest staying behind.

Then they all stopped like they'd hit a wall.

The group pushed forward again and were seemingly stopped by the air. A third attempt resulted with several vampire warriors knocked to the floor.

The Law Priest flipped pages, stabbed a finger at a ribboned clause, then shouted over the din, "No blood may be spilled, nor harm inflicted, in the presence of the living sign of the Resurrection!"

The Law Priest moved his finger from his book and stabbed it toward stage right.

Everyone looked.

Easter Bunny Wilson stood on the platform. His purple-and-pink fur was matted with blood, one giant tooth snapped in half, his left eye gone, a few wet cords of nerve dangling where it used to be.

Eleanor and Sweetpea retched and fought it down. Pérez did not.

On the floor, Wym and the Law Priest bickered viciously. The Priest kept pointing to the book, then at Wilson—whose sacred role as an Easter Bunny was stopping Wym's battalion from advancing.

Overhead, something popped. Flames licked the walls. A speaker tore loose and smashed down a few feet from Grits and Gravy.

Gravy called out, "Forget Nina. We gotta get out of here!"

The crew bailed off the riser—by the time they hit the floor and looked up, every vampire, including Wym's custom battlewagon, was gone. The crew sprinted for the hole the Caddy had made when they arrived.

Out on Collins, the night exploded behind them. Firemen and cops who'd rolled on the machine-gun calls dove behind trucks, clearing a lovely lane for escape. Easter Bunny Wilson jumped, snatched Pérez like a sack of laundry, and bounded into the dark.

Eleanor grabbed both men by the arms and pointed toward Earl's cab idling beyond the tape with Dee Wheatley waving from the curb. Grits, Gravy, Eleanor, Dee, and Sweetpea piled in. Earl stomped it. The decommissioned taxi shot south as Midnight Miami burned the sky behind them.

First stop: Grits's place in Key Biscayne. Eleanor waved the others off and helped the still-groggy, still-shirtless racer up the walk.

"I know I'm a little punchy," Grits said as she steered him up the stairs, "but I feel pretty good."

"Uh-huh," Eleanor said.

"I was only a werewolf for, what, thirty seconds? Don't remember much, but it felt like a hell of a nap."

"Uh-huh."

She guided him through the bedroom into the big master bath, settled him on the toilet lid, and turned on the shower.

"Did you see me with the axes? That was fun."

"Uh-huh."

Steam began to fog the mirrors.

"You're welcome to crash in one of the guest suites," he said.

"Uh-huh." She closed the bathroom door.

"Sheets are clean. Pillowcases too."

"Uh-huh," Eleanor said, unbuttoning her blouse.

"Uh-huh," Grits echoed.

Downstairs, Barry the Leprechaun and Patti from Daytona Beach cuddled on the couch, waiting for *Elvira's Movie Macabre.* Tonight's feature: *The Killer Is in the Shower with You.*

"Barry," Patti asked, "who are those people who just went upstairs to your bedroom?"

Barry had used his leprechaun magic to fake his death that morning for two reasons. One, he didn't want anyone but Grits and Gravy getting hands on his gold. Two, if Grits lost the gold, he might lose his ocean view residence, which would force Barry to find a new party house. A staged demise would fire the boys up and, when he popped back, they'd be too happy to interrogate him.

He glanced left, glanced right, threw up a big "Who, me?" shrug. Then he fished out his Burger King ruler and waggled his eyebrows at the Mutiny Girl.

"Oh, Barry," Patti from Daytona Beach sighed.

Gravy insisted on walking Dee Wheatley to her third-floor door. Earl and Sweetpea waited at the curb.

"Gravy's one of my best friends," Sweetpea confided, "but I don't know a man worse at taking a hint."

On the ride over, Dee had offered a buffet of reasons for Gravy to come up—drink, snack, view, roller-skate laces, new house-plant. Gravy blew past every single one. Chivalry, though, meant he'd see her to the door.

"Hey, guys!" Gravy called from the balcony. Earl and Sweetpea leaned out. "Dee's got a Burger King milkshake machine, but it's busted. She wants me to take a look. You two go on—I'll get a ride home later."

Sweetpea shot a thumbs-up. Sliding back into the seat he murmured, "Well played, Dee. Well played."

Gravy was mildly disappointed to discover there was no milk-shake machine. He got over it fast.

And for the first time since 1967, Gravy Watkins slept the whole night through.

Around 3:30 AM Pacific, a private jet settled onto a nameless strip outside Los Angeles.

The lone passenger came down the stairs, popped the belly hatch, and hauled out two very odd bags. Prince Wym Blutmesser tossed both into the limo's cabin and slid in after them.

Waiting there, another sister—and another lover. She already knew he'd failed. She didn't blame him (who plans for an Easter Bunny?), but others—some in their own house—would be less forgiving.

She decided to get the business over with. "My dear brother, I'm aware of the evening's...unfortunate outcomes, and I see no reason to discuss them. However, the Baroness wishes to see you at sunset."

Wym gave the smallest nod.

Her curiosity drifted to the luggage. "May I ask about your... bags?"

Wym tapped the black body bag. "The charred body of Nina Karanovo of the Neuri. She's swimming in silver, but the head is attached. I believe she's still useful."

"And...?" the princess prompted, annoyed she had to drag it out.

Wym patted the olive drab duffel. Inside lay the decapitated head of Dewayne Shelby—along with the rest of him. Under the moon, the bag had wriggled the whole ride, as if the parts inside were alive.

Which they were.

"This," Wym said, smiling thin, "is how I end the story of Grits and Gravy."

EPILOGUE

Tuesday, 11:57 AM
Stone Detective Agency
80 West Flagler Street, Miami

"DOC BRICKER, I realize the responsibility I'm taking on. I also realize how much he means to you—especially since he was a gift from your third wife."

Gravy Watkins paused to switch off the smile. He thought about a new word he'd learned (tofu) to keep his grin in the "off" position.

"And I know you overheard Gopher and Isaac talking, but they weren't talking about me—they were talking about the kitten Julie's hiding in her bathroom."

"Yes, yes," Grits said softly, encouragingly. "You're nailing it. Bring it home."

Gravy dabbed artificial tears into his eyes. "But Doc, you have to know—if I find out this dog has the rabies..." he gulped, "...

though it would break my heart, though I'd rather die a thousand times over—if that happens, I'll take him out myself."

Grits rose giving a slow clap. "Honestly? That's some of the best acting I've seen. And I've watched *Cannonball Run* four times."

They sealed it with a ridiculous series of hand slaps and finished with wildly inappropriate pelvic thrust apiece.

A polite throat-clear cut through from the doorway. Eleanor Stone stood, arms crossed. "Hate to interrupt drama class, but the press conference is on."

In the days following the battle at Midnight Miami, Arturo Santos's network had worked overtime to paint the aftermath in his terms—ideally with Colombians taking the blame. The presser would show whether it stuck.

"Thank you, Eleanor," Gravy said, breezing past her toward the big TV.

"Thank you, ma'am," Grits added, catching her hand and then hurriedly releasing it with a mouthed *sorry*.

Since the weekend they'd agreed to forget what happened late Saturday (rolling into Sunday) and stay just friends. They were both fine with that. For now.

On screen, Detective Rafael Pérez and FBI Agent Ronald Wilson stood at a podium before a sea of microphones. Pérez was mid-answer.

"...so I am confident we did apprehend the perpetrator of the five murders the press labeled the Magic City Maniac. And that same man, Dewayne Shelby, was subsequently kidnapped from Parkway Hospital and killed by Colombian drug dealers for reasons yet to be determined."

A reporter yelled, "Any comment on rumors Shelby's remains were stolen from the morgue?"

"No comment," Pérez snapped, pointing to someone else. "Fire at Midnight Miami?"

"Prelim points to arson by the Colombians," Pérez said. "We've handed it to the Fire Marshal. As of now, Victor Karanovo and his daughter Nina are presumed to have perished in the blaze."

Grits and Gravy traded a look. Nina's body hadn't been found. Neither of them believed she was gone for good.

Another reporter called out to Agent Wilson. "You said the ten-million-dollar cocaine bust came from a concerned citizen. What can you tell us about this citizen?"

Wilson stepped up. Back in his cleaned FBI suit, an eye patch now covering the absent left eye—almost cool, if you ignored the busted teeth—and spoke.

The mics picked up a series of whistles.

Pérez gently moved him aside. "What Agent Wilson said is he can't discuss his informant—other than he's grateful for the help she provided."

"Is it true the Easter Bunny was seen at Midnight Miami the night of the fire?" another reporter blurted.

Pérez grabbed the mic and lit the guy up. As he did, Agent Wilson stared straight into the lens. Grits and Gravy both felt the look land on them.

"Ecch," Gravy said.

"That's enough of that," Grits muttered, clicking off the set.

Eleanor gave them the face. "Agent Wilson saved all of our lives and used the missing cocaine to spring Dee's brother. Doesn't he deserve a little respect?"

The partners looked at each other, then back to her. "Did you not see his balls?" Gravy said.

Eleanor winced. "He did have some really weird balls."

A pounding knock rattled the front door.

"I'll get it," Gravy said, bouncing out.

"I forgot to tell you," Grits said to Eleanor. "Talked to Sweetpea last night. After this week he's getting a promotion—

running a new vice squad just for narcotics. No more wigs and dresses."

Before Eleanor could answer, Dee Wheatley breezed in. "I wanted to say goodbye. I'm off to New York—meeting record execs. Found out where Petey Maymoore was, too. He wasn't at the Mutiny doing cocaine all week—he was in Calcutta helping orphans. I was completely wrong. Now he's the one taking me to New York!"

"What about Juicy and the band?" Eleanor asked.

Dee grinned. "Petey didn't forget them. He cut a deal with Berry Gordy. Shemp DeBarge needed players for a new group. Juicy and the boys are going to Motown."

Gravy cleared his throat and muttered "told you so" at Grits and Eleanor.

"We're heading up early so I can be there when my brother gets out," Dee said. "Leaving tomorrow morning. I wanted to say thanks."

After hugs all around, Gravy walked her down. A limo waited at the curb.

On the sidewalk they shared one last kiss. "Thank you," Dee said. "I wouldn't be here without you. I'll call when I'm back."

Gravy figured this was the last time he'd see her in person. He'd be hearing her on the radio soon enough. Maybe seeing her in the movies. Their roads were headed different ways. He was okay with that.

"Sure, baby," he said. "Have fun in New York. Say 'hi' to any DeBarges you run into."

When Gravy came back upstairs, he was surprised to see Eleanor waiting for him. She had a solemn look on her face.

"Gravy, I need to talk to you and Grits about something important."

She didn't waste time. After the events of the past week,

Eleanor had made another choice: she no longer wanted to move on from the agency her parents had founded. She wanted back in —with skin in the game. She wanted to forgo her final payment from the sale of Stone Detective Agency and buy back in as a partner.

The brothers exchanged a look. They'd hoped for this. "Yes," they said, fast—and privately agreed to pay her balance anyway.

But with one condition.

As Grits produced a captain's hat, Gravy said, "Eleanor, we're doing a new scene. Grits overhears Isaac and Gopher talking about Helen Keller, and now he thinks he's going blind. Will you play Captain Stubing?"

THE END

Grits and Gravy will return!
Coming soon to a theater near you...

Grits & Gravy in
SEX SAILS

ACKNOWLEDGMENTS

Thank you very much to Scott for serving as my unofficial editor and sounding board.

Special thanks to Roben Farzad, whose book *Hotel Scarface* helped me to capture the feel of Miami in 1981.

And finally, thank you to the wonderful "Mrs. Chase" for her support and feedback, including that the first draft was "too long" but also "better than I expected."

ABOUT THE AUTHOR

S. M. Chase is the author of *Midnight Miami*, the first book in **The Grits & Gravy Mysteries.**

For more on the next adventures of Grits & Gravy, go to smchase.com.

www.ingramcontent.com/pod-product-compliance
Lightning Source LLC
Chambersburg PA
CBHW031141160726
47991CB00004B/1519